Bleed for Me

Kitty Rose

Contents

PLEASE READ

Bleed for me is a **DARK** romance with many potential triggers within the pages. If you may have a difficult time with certain topics, please review the trigger warnings below before proceeding.

While I want everyone to read and fall in love with Mick & Paige just as I have, your mental well-being is so much more important. If you have any questions regarding the triggers, please reach out to me! I'm more than happy to elaborate to ensure you are safe to continue.

Murder (graphic & creative), drug use reference, child abuse, domestic violence (note: this is NOT between the main characters), attempted child kidnapping, degradation, cheating/other woman drama (note: this is NOT between the main characters. It is, however, a large plot point), touch her & die, stalking, non-con/dub-con between main characters, rape (not by main male character but please note the previous warning), sexual assault (not by main male character), mention of sex trafficking/forced prostitution (adult & minor), blood play, knife play, kidnapping, rope play, sensory deprivation, torture.

*Please note, some phrasing is due to the author's dialect.

This one's for all my fellow little book whores who love their book boyfriends obsessed, possessive, and full of red flags.

Mom, if you read this - just remember I warned you.
I take no responsibility for the awkward family dinners.

Prologue

Mick

I always knew that I was different than other people. Something in me just didn't connect with others. A darkness filled my soul. It wasn't until I stumbled upon my little obsession that I began to feel. To really *feel* something. Like a blacklight being dragged over the expansive dark and showing the hidden stains tucked away from view.

Blood.

That was what I craved.

It wasn't intentional, my first kill. But I suppose most aren't. It really was just a slip of the hand, perhaps a poor choice of wording.

I had been walking toward the market downtown when some idiot bumped into me, obviously intoxicated on a several years long bender. There, inside his eyes, reflected the same emptiness in mine. Yet, it was artificial. A dulling of the senses by opioids and alcohol.

I had turned my nose up at him and tried not to inhale so as to avoid the reek of body odor and piss. Turning away, I made my way further down the street. My mind full as I ran over the list in my head again.

Bread, tomatoes, cereal, milk...

I am abruptly interrupted again by the same asshole. This time, rather than shuffling to the side, he looked me up and down in his drunken stupor.

"Hey man," He hiccuped. "You look like yous got some extra cash. I needs s-some money." He slurred, eyes drooping and popping back open with each word. Struggling against the effects on his body, he swayed on his feet.

Rolling my eyes, I shoved past him. "Piss off junkie." I growled, starting toward my destination once more.

"Hey!" Ignoring the shout, I picked up my pace. "Motherfucker! I said give me your m-mo-money."

I felt the tip of a blade poke into my spine. Halting my steps, I slowly turned around, the blade gliding along my side. The sharp metal resting on my stomach once I was fully facing the man. Apparently he was still able to hold a weapon steady, even while barely keeping himself upright.

Maybe he's ex-military or something. Fucking VA, you'd think they would take better care of their members.

With a sigh, I lifted one arm into the air and reached around for my wallet with the other. Keeping my eyes level with his glassy ones, I pulled my wallet around and opened it.

"I think I might have a few dollars but I really don't carry cash on me."

Honestly, who does anymore? We live in a paperless world, all our transactions traceable. Financial ruin just a few clicks on a keyboard away.

"You can have what I've got in here but you have to put away the fucking knife first. I don't respond well to threats, especially not from strung out assholes." I gritted out, awkwardly rifling through my wallet one-handed.

He glared at me and shuffled his feet, clearly debating my demand. His eyes darted back and forth between my hands and face. Finally, shaking his head, he slurred, "Naw. Money first. Hurry up or Imma have to stab you & take it anyway."

A fuzzy haze began to cloud the corners of my vision.

This degenerate is really pushing his luck.

I made to reach for the cash nestled in my wallet but at the last second twisted my wrist and grabbed onto the hand holding the knife against me. "I said. Drop. The. Knife." I hissed, rage overwhelming my thoughts.

The motherfucker laughed. It was a grating, slightly hysterical, sound. The movement caused his arm to shake, pushing the knife further into my clothes. Twisting my wrist while shoving him back with my other arm, I attempted to break his hold on the blade. Instead, I only succeeded in making him stumble further. I quickly released my hold and watched as he tumbled. Tripping over his feet he fell forward, letting out a soft groan that turned into a loud screech as he landed on his hand holding the weapon. Red liquid seeped out from under his body as he sobbed.

I stared, motionless, at the blood forming a small puddle.

It's...beautiful.

Something clicked in me. An instantaneous shift. I felt my world tilt as it found a new center point to rotate. A new purpose. This is what I needed, I suddenly needed it like I needed air.

Finally snapping from my stupor, I quickly dropped to my knees next to the man. I shoved harshly on his shoulder, eliciting a pained groan as he rolled onto his back, the blade sticking out of his chest. It looked to have missed his heart but had sunken deep into his flesh. No doubt a result of his hindered reaction time due to the drugs pumping through his system.

I raised my eyes to meet his, relishing in the pain I saw there. And, like the moment I saw his blood pooling underneath him, this moment felt just as monumental. A small grin started to form as I watched him try to shrink away in fear. Something on my face must have shown the desire in me. Perhaps the darkness had finally taken over my form and I was now just as much the monster on the outside as within. "Well, this has certainly taken a turn, has it not?" My grin grew as I watched the horror fill his glassy eyes. "If only you had put away that damn knife." I tsked, slowly shaking my head. "Suppose there isn't much else to do about that now though."

"P-please" He whispered, pain laced through his stuttered word.

"Please what?"

"Help me."

I couldn't help the laugh that bubbled out of my chest. "Oh, I can help. Of course. Who wouldn't help someone in your situation? Just a sad, pathetic, idiotic drug addict." I bit out the last words, the rage returning in full force. "You are nothing. A waste of space. A drain on society. Completely and utterly *worthless*." The familiar words flowed out of my mouth, memory and reality blending together.

Suddenly, I wasn't seeing the man in front of me anymore. His face began to morph. Scraggly beard bled into rough scruff surrounding a stern jaw. The soft green in his eyes changed to a muddied blue, still hazy with drug use. Hair shifted from brown to dirty blonde. Greasy locks hung around his face and lightly rested against his shoulders. I watched as this nameless person changed into the man who haunted my dreams. The man who called out the darkness in me as I tried to hide away. The man who stole my mother from me. The man who fucked up my life every day growing up.

Agony filled me as I let out a sharp gasp and lunged forward. Gripping the hilt of the knife roughly, I ripped out the blade. "How? How are you here?" I screamed into his face. Emotionless orbs stared back, a hollow dark laugh leaving his lips. "No. You don't get to laugh at me." I seethed as I reached my arm back. Bringing it back down with as much force as I could, I stabbed. Again and again. Blood spraying from each harsh yank.

As I continued my brutal assault, he continuously shifted. Changing before me from the man of my past laughing and egging me on to the sad man begging for help, pleading for me to stop.

Back and forth, reality no longer clear.

When I was too exhausted to continue, I fell back onto my heels, panting and staring at the body before me.

It was never him.

I violently shook my head, trying to clear my vision and mind.

Fuck.

Quickly glancing around, I was grateful to see no one.

On shaky limbs, I pushed myself up and started to cautiously wander around. Looking for something, anything, to help hide what I'd done. A few steps out, I saw an alleyway with an overflowing dumpster.

Well, it's better than leaving the body in the middle of the sidewalk.

Making my way over to the dumpster, I rummaged around, finding a large bag, only partially full, and dumping the contents out. Another quick search revealed a few towels that I snatched up as well.

I made my way back and bent over. Carefully working the bag around the lifeless corpse, using the towels as a barrier between my hands and his body. After a moment of hesitation, I yanked out the knife and roughly wiped the end onto his clothes. After cleaning off the blood the best I could without touching him, I slipped the knife into my jacket pocket.

With one more big breath, I bent and threw the now filled trash bag over my shoulder and stumbled my way back to the alley.

Dropping the body in front of the dumpster, I started to rummage around again, removing just enough trash to fit the corpse into the bin without it being obvious it was in there. Bending over again, I hefted up my victim and threw him over the lip and piled the trash back in. Arranging it the best I could while moving quickly, not sure when my luck would run out and someone may pass by. Huffing, I stepped back and dusted my hands off. I glanced back and saw the blood still pooled on the sidewalk, towels strewn carelessly around the mess. Taking a deep breath, I gazed at the crimson liquid darkening from prolonged exposure to the air.

Closing my eyes, I tried to feel remorse. I really did try, but instead, all I felt was...peace.

Exhaling slowly, I opened my eyes again and made my way over one last time to the spot of my awakening. Gazing down, wanting to prolong this moment as long as possible, I inhaled and relished in the coppery scent filling my nose. Finally, I knelt and grabbed the towels, mopping up the coagulating blood until there was only a stain remaining on the concrete.

There, that should be good enough. No one is going to notice another stain on the ground unless they're really looking. Right?

I let out a heavy sigh and jogged back over to the trash bin to shove the soiled towels as far down as I could.

Then, without another glance back, I turned and made my way home.

Chapter 1

Mick

8 years later

"Damn Mick, you really don't fuck around." Jesse laughs, punching my shoulder.

I smirk and shrug. "What can I say? I know what I like." Looking back down to my phone, I quickly type out a response then turn my attention to the annoying fucker in front of me. Okay, that's unfair. Jesse Rolland is, I suppose one could consider, my best friend. We've grown close the last seven years and know everything about each other. Well, almost everything. He may not know that I am the villain in the nightmares of the residents of Santa Fe, but other than that, there are no secrets between us.

"I can't believe she didn't kick you in the balls dude. Seriously, what were you thinking?" He takes a long pull of his beer, humor in his eyes as he stares me down.

I shrug again, taking another drink of my own before answering. "I like to be upfront. I'm into some kinky shit and don't like surprises. It's too easy for something to quickly change from mind blowing to assault if there aren't clear boundaries agreed beforehand." I wink at him, chuckling. "And there was definitely no lack of enjoyment this time, on either end. She may have the personality of a wet dog but damn can that girl fuck." Images of Veronica tied up and gagged flash in my mind. I have to subtly shift to adjust my growing hard on as more images flood in.

My hand around her throat, yanking her head back roughly by her hair. Ripping the gag from her mouth to shove in my dick in one hard thrust.

I can practically hear her gagging and moaning as she writhed beneath me, eyes filled with tears. The soft vibration of my phone pulls my thoughts back to the present.

Veronica

Hey babe, you busy tonight?

Me

Yeah, I got a work thing. I'm free on Thursday though.

Veronica

**sad face emoji* Ugh, you're always working when I'm horny. *cat emoji* will be waiting for you on Thursday*

I smirk down at my phone. The only thing better than a good fuck is satisfying my bloodlust. And I've let it go too long as is.

Me

You're always horny for my cock. Just play with that pretty pussy of yours until then. I'll text you when I'm heading over.

Veronica

*Yes sir *wink emoji**

I slide my phone back into my pocket and look back toward Jesse. He's absentmindedly fiddling with the label on his beer bottle. "What's up?"

This time it's his turn to shrug. "I dunno, man. I just wish I could get out of my head enough to do some of the shit you do. I'm just too worried about hurting her, ya know?" I nod, even though, no - I don't know. I really don't give a fuck if the girl gets hurt. In fact, it turns me on even more, if I'm being honest. But I have to be careful with that shit. One bad move and suddenly I'm being dragged before a judge and put on some list. "I just know that Rik would like it. She's told me as much and I can tell she's starting to lose her patience with me. But, if it went too far, I wouldn't be able to forgive myself." He looks up then, his eyes pleading with me, looking for answers. Needing validation.

I reach over and throw my arm around his shoulders. "Well, Jesse, if your girl wants it rough, you gotta give it to her rough. You guys have been together long enough you feel comfortable having the conversation, yeah?" One eyebrow quirks as I stare at him. He nods but doesn't say anything else. With a soft sigh, I continue, "How about this, I'll send you a list of all the resources I know of and you can look and see what interests you. There's also all kinds of sites that help to ensure you know what you're doing before you jump in. The most important thing to remember is to have a safe word and make sure you both use it and listen immediately if it's said." He nods again, some of the darkness clouding his eyes lifting.

One thing I've learned over the years of friendship with Jesse is that the man needs a push. He can get stuck and spiral in circles over the *what ifs* for all of his life until someone comes along and forces him to jump into action. That's why we work so well, I enjoy pushing others and he gets to actually live. I ruffle the mop on his head he calls hair and push myself up. "Well, I gotta head out, but I'll try to get all that stuff over as soon as I can."

"Thanks Mick. Seriously, I don't know what I'd do without you."

"Have a shitty ass sex life?" I chuckle. He tries to throw a punch my way but I dance out the way, my chuckle breaking into full blown laughter. "Hey, don't shoot the messenger. Before we met each other, you were as vanilla as they come dude." He opens his mouth and then closes it again, wanting to deny it but he can't. Can't deny the truth.

"Shut up asshole." He mutters instead, rolling his eyes. "Get the fuck outta here before I have to pummel that arrogance out of your ass."

"Oh you wish you could get this ass." I wink at him before turning and heading out the door, his laughter following me out.

Chapter 2

Paige

When will this day be over? Ugh!

Glancing up, I see the nasty old woman making her way toward me again.

Sure, it's my job to be nice to people, but can't I have just like one freebie for the really terrible customers? Because I would use that to tell this horrid woman where she can put her attitude.

"This is not what I ordered. How hard is it to get a simple drink right?" The woman sneers. "A latte, with skim milk, one-and-a-half pumps of sugar-free hazelnut, with extra foam. Simple." She shoves her drink at me and I have to forcibly bite the inside of my cheek to keep from slapping it out of my face.

"I'm sorry you're not happy with your drink. I can remake it for you?" That's not what she ordered, and she knows it. This bitch just wants to have an excuse for a free drink and, honestly, I'm past the point of caring. What difference does it make to me if my job loses out on a few bucks? Better than having assault charges on me for giving in and teaching her some fucking manners.

Scoffing, she starts to shake her head. "Why would I want someone so incompetent to make my drink again?"

Oh, I don't know, so you actually get something to drink?

I bite down harder on my cheek.

"Let me speak," *Oh no, here it comes.* "To your manager." She stares at me, daring me to argue. I won't, not now.

Instead I force a smile on my face and spit out between my teeth, "Of course, let me get her." Turning on my heel, I practically run to the back room.

Why can't this day end?

"Hey Brandi?" I call out, looking around the storage room briefly but not seeing my manager anywhere. Sighing, I turn and head toward the office in the corner. I already know she's going to be annoyed, there's at least one of these every week and the girl does not get paid enough to deal with this. "Brandi?" I call again as I softly knock on the door.

"Yeah? Come on in." Pushing the door open, I cautiously step inside. "What's up Paige?" Glancing up, she takes in my expression and hunched shoulders, letting out a dramatic sigh. "Seriously? Another one?"

"Sorry, B. The Karens just won't stay away." I try to smile at my weak attempt at a joke but I just don't have it in me anymore. Today has officially beat me. I must have had a bank of bad karma that all got shoved my way in the last twelve hours, that's the only explanation I can think of to describe the hell I've had to endure.

Releasing another loud sigh, Brandi pushes back from her desk and stands up. "I wish we could have one of those boards with mugshots and ban customers for life. I'm so sick of all these cunts thinking they're winning at life by harassing my employees." She looks over at me and I can see the side of her mouth lift up into a smirk. "Maybe one day they'll get what's coming to them. Can't be worth all the bad juju over a $6 cup of coffee." I snort which brings a full smile to her face. "Alright, let's go take care of this. What's the rundown?" Rolling my eyes, I fill her in as we make our way back to the front counter. Seeing the line forming again at the register I shoot Brandi another apologetic look and make my way over to take more orders.

I've made my way through about half the line before Brandi passes behind me to the other register and starts typing in the info to issue a refund. Resisting the urge to roll my eyes again, I look up and smile at the person stepping up to the counter. As my eyes lift up, I suck in a sharp breath.

Standing before me is the most beautiful man I have ever seen. Sure, men aren't usually described as beautiful but he is *gorgeous*. As if a Greek god statue came to life. His short blonde hair hangs in loose curls around his temple, striking steel blue eyes, a sharp jawline lined with stubble that's darker than his hair by a few shades. His gaze is intense, a darkness hidden behind his eyes that seems to bleed out around the corners.

Resisting the urge to look at the rest of him, I swallow and force my throat to work as I blurt out, "Hello, um, what do you want? I mean, do you know what you'd like to drink?"

Oh god, you sound like an idiot. Come on Paige, be professional.

I force another smile on my face, feeling the awkward tension in my cheeks.

Greek god man smirks down at me, a twinkle of humor in his eyes. "I know what I want."

Ohmygod, why did that sound so dirty? I hope it's me he wants. Stop it, Paige. No you don't.

My smile strains as I wait for him to continue, not trusting myself to say anything. He stares at me for a long heartbeat before leaning forward, glancing down then back up to meet my eyes. "An Americano please, Paige."

"How...how do you know my name?" I breathe, eyes widening.

He licks his lips before answering, eyes alight with some emotion I can't quite place. He nods toward my chest and I feel my cheeks heat instantly. "Your name tag." He replies in a hushed tone. My face flames even more.

Of course, my freaking name tag.

If I could, I would smack myself in the face.

Gah, why did this happen today of all days? I am so not on my game.

Not that I *have* game, but still, it's even worse today.

"Oh right, yeah. Um, one Americano coming right up!" I punch in the order a little more aggressively than necessary and am about to tell him the total when I see he's already holding out a $20 bill.

"You can keep the change." After I take the money from his hand, he turns to head off.

"Wait!" I call out. "What name for the order?"

Looking over his shoulder, his eyes rake over me slowly before landing on my face. Appearing to debate with himself for a moment before answering, he finally simply says, "Mick."

"Mick." I whisper, then louder reply, "Okay, thanks, we'll have it right up for you Mick."

And just like that, I've decided I need a vacation. And to get laid. Badly.

Finally.

I sigh heavily, my shoulders slumped in exhaustion, and lock the door. The last few hours of my shift were even more stressful. All I could think about was that mystery man.

Mick.

After getting his coffee, he left quickly without another word or glance my way. I don't know why I was surprised. I had taken the chance to look him over more through quick peeks while making orders. He was wearing faded jeans, black oxfords, and a simple dark button up with the sleeves rolled up. He wasn't wearing anything particularly fancy or expensive looking but he had this air about him. As if he was the most important person in the room, regardless of the room he was in.

And here I was, a frumpy mess in three-day-old hair tossed haphazardly in a bun on top of my head. Stains on my clothes from the spots our work aprons don't cover and smudged makeup.

Yeah, you're a real catch. I think while staring up at the ceiling, letting out a heavy breath.

I need to stop obsessing over a man I'm never going to see again. Even if something in him called to something deep down inside of me. He felt...dangerous. But in an intriguing way. Like going to a haunted house, or sitting down to watch a scary movie. The anticipation and butterflies building up as nervous excitement increases until I'm screaming, high on the adrenaline.

Shit. I really *need to get laid.*

I can't help but laugh at my pathetic self as I make my way back toward the coffee bar to start cleaning up for the evening. Brandi left for the day about an hour ago so it's just me closing up the shop tonight. Which is totally fine, not a problem. Really. Just a little scary. As I run the cleaner through the espresso machine my mind wanders to the news article I read this morning.

> ***23 confirmed deaths in the Santa Fe area estimated over the past 8 years. We are, again, urging residents to be cautious and not travel anywhere on their own, especially at night, as this seems to be the perpetrator's preferred time to attack. With new information coming to light that connects all of these murders, we are treating this serial killer as a high threat and have called in additional resources in our man-hunt to keep citizens safe.***

Shuddering, I pull my attention back and finish wiping up the counters before moving on to the floors. I moved here a few years ago after a rough break up. Really I just needed a fresh start, somewhere no one knew me as *Seth's girl* and the drama that went along with it. Of course, I had to choose somewhere that would be the home to a serial killer.

And not just any killer, one that appears to be a ghost. Never leaving enough evidence behind to find him, even with the large amount of murders in such a short amount of time. The Blood Shadow is the "unofficial" nickname for him.

I shudder again, remembering why the nickname stuck.

As much as he ghosts in and out of the scene, like a shadow, the thing that has connected all the murders is the sheer amount of blood found at the scene. From the reports, it's something out of a gorey horror film. Think Rob Zombie level gore. It's almost as if the murderer gets off on the blood splatter. Shaking my head, I try to pull my thoughts away from murder. Seeing how I am all alone downtown, in the middle of the night. It's not an ideal topic to ponder.

As I try to think of something else to distract myself from the menial tasks, my mind keeps wandering back to dark blue eyes and blonde curls.

Just great, all I can think of tonight is mysterious hot men & terrifying elusive murderers. Absolutely perfect.

Looking around, I see the only thing left to do is take out the trash. I debate leaving it for the opening crew but know I don't want to deal with the fall out of that. Instead, I quickly scoop all the trash from around the shop and make my way out back to the alley.

Propping open the door, I peek around the corner to make sure there's no murderers waiting to jump me. Softly laughing to myself to calm some of the hysteria growing inside, I rush toward the trash bin and toss in the bags. Facing the trash bin with my back to the alley, a tingling sensation starts to make its way up my spine. I swear I can feel someone staring at me.

Glancing over my shoulder, I don't immediately see anyone. I look around and peer into the dark shadows the best I can, resisting the urge to call out "hello" like some movie bimbo. Instead, once I see there is no one directly between me and the back door, I bolt. Running like my life depends on it, I make it back inside and pull the door closed hard behind me.

I know I'm just being paranoid, I worked myself up and now my mind is just fucking with me. Still, it doesn't hurt to be cautious.

Instincts are there for a reason, right?

After several minutes of panting and clinging to the door handle, I finally ease my grip and head to grab my things, ready to get home and finally end this godforsaken day.

Chapter 3

Mick

She's gorgeous. I've never seen anyone so effortlessly beautiful. Her pale skin contrasting with the inky black hair she had tied up on top of her head. The curves hidden underneath that atrocious apron. I relished in the brief glimpses I got whenever she would bend over to pull something out from under the counter, her ass on perfect display in the painted on jeans she was wearing. And her eyes. Large doe-like orbs the color of liquid caramel.

I haven't been able to stop thinking about her, picturing her face, reddened from her blush.

God, blood flow looks otherworldly on her. I bet she would bleed so beautifully. I could probably orgasm just from the sight of it.

I shake my head roughly. I already have a victim planned for tonight and I haven't lasted this long without getting caught by not sticking to my plans. Only the first time was unpredictable. After that, I've meticulously hunted, stalked, and planned out each of my kills.

The thing that really fucks over most serial killers is they have an M.O. Some pattern or preference in victims, which ends up with them getting caught. But that's not me. Anyone can be my target. Well, except for children, there's too much innocence in them for my bloodlust to be satisfied. But adults, we're all fucked up - all have reasons that we don't deserve to breathe anymore. Even the most seemingly pious person has their fair share of demons and skeletons in the closet. Perhaps not as many as me, but still enough to justify their sacrifice for my own needs.

I fiddle with the tip of my blade, pressing lightly into the pad of my thumb. Not enough to break the skin but to feel the slight prick of pain from the intrusion. It's a calming habit of mine, something I find myself doing when the anticipation and nerves start to build the closer I get to my kill.

A noise makes my head lift and peer out the window of my car toward the front door of the house across the street. Harvey Mickels steps out of the opened doorway and heads toward his car parked just a few blocks down. I wait until he's several yards away before turning on my own vehicle, careful to keep the headlights off. Once he has pulled away from the curb, I turn on my lights and begin to follow, keeping enough of a distance so as not to be suspicious.

I've gotten very good at hiding in the shadows over the past eight years. I always had a knack for stealth and have only enhanced my natural ability through disciplined practice. I can follow someone in their car for hours without even the slightest paranoia creeping into their driving.

Thankfully, I know where we are headed is only about 30 minutes away. Which is good as I can feel the need for destruction growing inside more and more with each passing minute. As predicted, Harvey drives straight to the park across from a small apartment complex. I pull up to a stop along the curb a few blocks down and flick off my headlights as I watch my next victim.

He climbs out of the vehicle and begins pulling out items from his trunk. I'm too far away to really see what they are but if I've learned anything from the weeks of hunting this piece of shit, I can guess the contents of his vehicle.

Most likely similar to my own.

The thought causes a chuckle to escape my lips.

Oh Harvey, you should know, there's always a bigger predator.

I wait for a few more moments and then reach over to my passenger seat and gently lift my bag of supplies. Honestly, it's the least you can do to put everything in a bag.

Who tries to kidnap someone with all the materials just awkwardly dangling from your hands? Harvey, that's who.

Another laugh leaves me before I shut it down, settling into hunt mode so as not to spook my prey. I slip out of my car and sling the bag over my shoulder, the only thing still in my hand a small syringe filled with just enough Propofol to knock him out for the short ride.

Harvey nervously looks around and slams his trunk closed. I can't help but roll my eyes, this man is not meant for this line of work. If I weren't about to take him for myself, he would end up getting caught within twenty minutes of attempting to kidnap the child he has his eyes set on. He starts to cross the parking lot toward the park bordering the apartments. Fumbling with his DIY snatcher kit, he doesn't sense my approach.

I creep up behind him and slam my hand over his mouth in the same movement sliding the syringe into his neck. Holding him against my body as the drug begins to take effect, I run over the plan one more time in my mind, pleased with the progress so far. As his arms slip and everything falls to the ground, I know it's safe to remove my hand. I bend over and sling his limp body over my shoulder and jog back to my vehicle, shoving him into the trunk. Softly closing the lid, *because I'm a professional,* I jog back over and scoop up all the items he dropped and throw them into my back seat.

I release a breath as I slide into the driver's seat. Starting the car, I take off, anticipation coursing through my veins. I press down on the gas pedal, ready to satiate my growing need.

"What? Where am I?"

A smile grows across my face as I lean against the wall. Across from me is dear Harvey, straining against the ropes I have tied around his wrists and ankles. His arms dangle from the chain attached to the ceiling, just enough length for him to feel like he has a chance of escape. It's more fun when they have hope. Until they don't.

Finally noticing me, Harvey swings his head in my direction, eyes wide with fear as he tries to glare intimidatingly. "Who are you?" He demands. I chuckle and push off the wall, not answering his questions. Instead I make my way over to the small table set up in the corner. "Where the fuck am I?" When I continue to ignore him, he starts to get angry, voice growing louder with each word. "Answer me dammit! What the fuck is this?"

I pick up a needle, IV bag and rubber tourniquet before turning around. When he sees the items in my hands, his attempts at freeing himself grow more desperate. "Stay–stay away from me! Seriously asshole, I don't know who you are or what you want but I don't do needles, okay?" His voice raises an octave as terror floods his system. "I'm not fucking around. Stop!"

I make my way toward him, still not responding as I stop in front of him. Calmly, I reach up to grip his elbow. He jerks violently against me, trying to loosen my grip. Not that it will do him much good, he's not going anywhere. Sighing dramatically, I tighten my fist and cluck my tongue. "Now, now Harvey. The more you struggle, the harder this will be. Trust me, you want me in a good mood." I turn my head to meet his eyes. He swallows and quickly averts his gaze, stopping his erratic attempts at escape.

I can't quite tell if I'm disappointed or pleased. It's true what I said. It will go much better for him if he doesn't make me angry. But it's so *boring* when they don't fight. Fighting the urge to roll my eyes, I reach up with my other hand and wrap the rubber band around his arm, cutting off circulation and making the insertion of the IV needle easier. "Be an angel and pump your fist for me a few times, yeah?" Harvey whips his head toward me in shock. Meeting my eyes again, whatever he sees there has him immediately obeying and pumping his fist. "What a good boy." I pat his cheek lightly, offering him a smile. Then turn my attention back to my task. "Okay, that's enough. Just relax."

I pull the needle out of its package as I feel around the inside of his elbow for a decent vein. Fucker has deep, rolling veins, I can feel it. Irritation starts to build in me. He's probably dehydrated too, so this is going to take a while. Finally finding a decent spot, I push in the needle and connect the IV bag, pulling off the band once the blood starts to flow out. This is my least favorite part. Yes, the blood is satisfying to watch and it's a necessary tedium, but I enjoy the messy brutality much more than this clinical approach. Rolling my shoulders to release some of the tension, I hang the bag up on a hook next to the chains and step back.

"This part will take some time, but then we can have fun." I wink at him as I discard the trash.

Harvey eyes me wearily, warring emotions flashing across his face before he speaks. "Why are you doing this?" His voice is hardly a whisper, defeat already seeped into his bones.

I shrug in response. "You caught my attention. Honestly, it's completely random. I just go about my day and once someone catches my eye, that's it." Looking him up and down, my mind flashes back to his pathetic kidnapping attempt earlier. "You are a bit of a special case though." Murmuring, deep in thought, I glance away. A soft whimper escapes his lips and I look up to see his attention is focused on the bag of blood.

His blood.

"You do bleed so nicely though, don't you think? Sometimes it takes a minute or so before the flow really starts moving, but look at you! This will be over in no time." Silent sobs rack his body as he tries to look anywhere other than where I'm directing his attention. I tsk at him again, shaking my head. "You know what made you special? You were *almost* like me. Well, you wanted to try to be but you are absolutely awful. Seriously, don't quit your day job." I snicker.

His focus snaps back to me. "This is because of Lucy?" His voice comes out stronger this time, a possessiveness in his tone. "She's mine." He growls at me, finally growing a backbone. I'm almost giddy with excitement. *This* is what I love, a little pushback before the inevitable conclusion.

Even still, I can't help but laugh mockingly. "I don't want a fucking child. And, I hate to break it to you man, she ain't yours. You had your shot but here you are instead. All tied up for me." I wink at him. "Not that you'll put much use to the advice but you should know a few simple rules of the trade." I hold up a hand and count off the fingers with each one.

"Rule number one, make sure you're not being followed. And with that, rule number two, be quiet. Seriously, you were so loud I'm surprised no one else saw us. Which brings us to rule number three, keep your hands free and tools hidden away. You were so busy bumbling around with all that shit you never stood a chance." If looks could kill, the glare Harvey is shooting my way would send me to an early grave. I drop my hand and make my way over to check the bag, seeing it's almost full.

Almost time.

"What the fuck are you on about? You crazy or something?"

Well that's just plain rude.

I scoff, "Here I am, trying to offer you some advice as a seasoned professional and how do you repay me? With insults?" Reaching forward, I violently tug the needle from his arm, causing him to release a startled shout laced with pain. "You really should be careful how you talk to people. And you *really* should watch how you speak to me." My tone dips dangerously low as I take the now full bag of blood and head back to place it onto the table. I grab a pair of pliers and a metal nail file that's been sharpened at the tip. Turning around, I make a show of presenting my tools to Harvey, enjoying the look of confusion and terror spreading across his face.

"What are those for?" He's back to whispering, finally realizing the danger he's in.

"These are where we are going to start. First, I'm going to stab under each of your nail beds to remove your fingernails with this," I hold up the nail file. "Then I am going to remove your teeth one by one with this guy." I gesture with the pliers. "After that, I'm going to grab my torch, cauterize your wounds and then burn off your fingerprints." Harvey's face is so pale he could almost be mistaken for a ghost already. Not yet, but soon.

I make my way over to him and reach up for his hand. Grasping one of his fingers, I work the nail file underneath the fingernail as I continue, "After, I'm going to enjoy cutting up every inch of your body and watching as the last of your blood drains from you. We already know how well you bleed. I'm sure it will be an exquisite sight." With a flick of my wrist, I pop off the first nail, relishing in the scream it elicits. "And *just* before you are going to die of blood loss, I'm going to cauterize your wounds again. I'll give you a bit of a reprieve before using my beautiful blade to stab you over and over as I watch the life drain from your eyes." I groan in anticipation as I continue to pop off his nails one by one. Each causing a cry of pain that satisfies the beast inside of me, feeding on the pain I'm inflicting.

"P-pl-please st-stop." Harvey whimpers in between screams. "P-please don't. You don't need to do this."

I briefly pause my nail extraction and gently pat his cheek. "Oh Harvey, but I do. I really do." And with that I proceed to fulfill every promise I made. Not stopping until the last flicker of life leaves his eyes. Only then do I take a breath, finally feeling like I can breathe again.

This is what I needed.

"Thank you for your sacrifice Harvey." I place a hand over my heart and bow slightly to show my gratitude. Then I begin the clean up.

CHAPTER 4

PAIGE

The Blood Shadow has struck again. We have confirmation that another body has been recovered, just as brutalized as all the others. As with each of the other victims, there is no way to accurately identify the remains due to the disfigurement of the corpse. The only description police were able to provide of the deceased is that this was a Caucasian male in his mid-to-late thirties. The scene has been described as a bloodbath. We will continue to update...

I stop reading, feeling sick to my stomach.

How am I supposed to keep living here with this psychopath around? What if I wasn't just being paranoid that night? What if I'm *next?*

I drop my head down onto the table and try to take deep breaths. It's not going to help anything to have a panic attack right now. I have responsibilities and errands that can't be put off.

I give myself a few more moments of silent panic before straightening, mentally slapping myself, and squaring my shoulders.

I can do this. I am a twenty-nine year old woman, fully capable of going into town without getting murdered.

That's it Paige, hype time.

Feeling slightly more confident, I stand and make my way back to my room to get ready.

Pulling into the parking lot, I make sure to get a spot close to the front and avoid parking next to any vans. My safety tip of the day, *never* park next to a van. It's way too easy to be abducted as you are trying to get into your car if someone decides to slide open the door and yank you inside.

I take a deep breath and slide my keys between my fingers before exiting my car.

Man, I really am on edge.

It makes me feel a little better, though, knowing I can jab a key into someone's eye with my fist if they try something. Giving myself time to grab the pepper spray on my keychain and spray it before running like hell.

Yup, not paranoid at all.

I make it into the store without having to utilize my powers of self defense. Once I grab a cart and make it past the security entrance, I feel safe enough to slip my keys into my jacket pocket - still easy access if needed.

Making my way down the different aisles and grabbing what I need, I'm lost in thought again. My mind keeps wandering back to steel blue eyes. Turning down the next aisle, I stop abruptly and reach up to scrub my face.

Peeking between my fingers, I'm positive I've lost my mind. Or developed the power of manifestation. Because, standing in front of the display of canned beans, is the Greek god-like man I've spent every moment obsessing over since our awkward encounter a few weeks ago.

No way. There's no way *he's here.*

I shake my head and lower my hands. Trying to look less like a crazy person, I make my way down the aisle to grab the next item on my list. Glancing at my note, I groan internally.

kidney beans & black beans

Of course *it's beans.*

Do I really need to make taco salad?

I quickly look over my cart and see I've already got most of the ingredients and *really* don't want to have to put them back. I also can't afford to just be buying food I'm going to have to throw out.

You've got this. Pull up your big girl panties and just grab the beans.

As I'm making my way toward the display, Mick glances up and notices me. He doesn't just look my way. He's full on staring at me, as if he can see into my soul. I've never felt so exposed from just a look. His gaze slowly travels down my body and I can't stop the shiver that runs through me. His mouth ticks up in a smirk as he raises his eyes to mine.

"Hello Paige."

Oh. My. God. He remembered my name?

“Hi.” I whisper, then clear my throat. “Hey Mick.”

His eyes light up at the sound of his name, as if he thought I wouldn’t remember him.

How would that be possible? This man is unforgettable.

I look him over and notice he’s wearing much more casual clothing to-day. Dressed in a pair of basketball shorts, a tight fitting t-shirt, sneakers and a backwards baseball cap.

God, he looks so hot.

I can see the definition of his muscles through the shirt and my mouth waters, imaging what they would look like moving over me. With nothing on. As he thrusts his co-

He coughs and I realize I’ve just been staring at him. My cheeks flame as I quickly look away.

Goddamnit.

Why don’t you just put a sign on your forehead saying “I’M DESPERATE”?

Now fully uncomfortable, I decide to abandon my beans and just hope the salad is still edible without them.

As I start to move, Mick speaks up again. “Did you need something from over here?” Gesturing his hand to the display. I slowly nod. “Pardon me for being in the way.” He ducks his head and shuffles to the side, just far enough for me to walk up but not leaving enough room for the cart. Leaving my new emotional support on wheels, I move over and start grabbing cans. “Would it be rude to ask what you’re making? It looks like it’s going to be good.” He nods to my cart and then glances back at my arms holding the cans, eyes lingering briefly on my chest before looking up again with a soft smile.

My blush deepens and I manage to mumble out a response. “Taco salad. It’s nothing fancy but lasts a few days and is simple, cheap, and tastes good. You know, checks all the boxes for a poor man's diet.”

My eyes widen.

Did I just admit to this man that I'm poor? Good god.

"Not that I'm poor. Well, I kind of am, but it's no big deal. Like, I can pay rent and buy food and have gotten away without food stamps this far." I shrug but can't stop the word vomit. "Not that there's anything wrong with needing the help. I think people should stop shaming others for needing assistance. Especially since everything has gotten so expensive. It's a wonder anyone can survive without a dozen roommates. Not that I have any roommates."

Did you just tell this stranger *that you LIVE ALONE?*

"I mean, I didn't mean...I..."

Stop. Talking.

I let out a half choke, half hysterical laugh and back up to my cart, my mouth still opening and closing soundlessly as I try to think of a way out of this whole interaction.

Mick stares at me intently for a moment, then softly says, "I agree, taco salad is a great meal choice." Reaching toward me, he plucks the cans out of my hands and gently places them into my cart. "I don't really think it's the best idea to admit to people you don't know that you live alone." He throws a pointed look in my direction. "But it is admirable in this economy to be able to afford that luxury." His expression is amused as his eyes shine with what I could swear was pride.

My brain has officially shut down. Thrown up a sign that it's closed for business, good luck and so long.

I continue to stare at him.

What do I say to that? Thank you? Yes, I'm an idiot? Will you come live with me so I'm no longer alone and won't have to worry about panic blurting it out again?

Amused by my silence, his lips turn up again as he reaches forward and tucks a piece of hair behind my ear. "It was good to see you again, Paige. Stay safe." Turning around, he walks away.

I watch in silence as he proceeds to the exit and leaves.

He didn't even buy anything.

Groaning, I drop my face into my hands.

Did I just embarrass him so badly he had to abandon his shopping trip and run away?

I groan again and will the floor to swallow me up whole.

Chapter 5

Mick

I couldn't stay away.

After taking care of Harvey that night, I found myself back at the coffee shop, watching as Paige locked the door and closed up. I knew I shouldn't have been there but something about her drew me in.

A spark of anger flared as I realized she was there alone. It's not safe for a beautiful girl like that to be alone downtown at night. Especially with a serial killer on the loose. Not that she needs to worry about that. At least, not in the way others do. As I had watched her gather up the trash, I noticed that there were no trash cans out front, which meant she would most likely be going into the alley behind the building to dispose of the garbage. I stalked around, sticking to the shadows, and watched. At one point, she must have sensed me as she looked up and straight over in my direction. I held my breath and pushed back into the shadows further. There was no way she could see me but I still needed to be careful. After she darted back inside, I felt the spell break and berated myself. Grumbling angrily as I forced my body to get in the car and drive away.

That night started a daily routine. I would go to her shop and watch as she worked, then follow her home and try to catch a glimpse of her through the windows.

It wasn't healthy but not much about my life could be considered good for the average person. The only times I spent away from her were with Jesse or the occasional fuck with Veronica. Even still, I found myself picturing Paige every time. Her long black hair, amber eyes staring at me, the sound of her saying my name replacing the shrill cries Veronica made.

Earlier today when I saw her leaving the apartment, she looked so nervous I had canceled my plans to make sure she was alright. Following her to the parking lot, I watched as she circled several times until finally choosing a spot close to the front. I parked a few rows over and had every intention of remaining in my vehicle until I noticed the glimmer of keys peeking out between her fingers. Something had spooked her and I needed to make sure she would be safe.

That's how I ended up inside, speaking to her, resisting the urge to laugh and reprimand her stupidity. I knew I had to leave, though, before I did something I would regret. Like kidnapping her. Sure it would keep her safe from anyone else meaning her harm, but I have no intention of killing Paige. She's far too intriguing to snuff out.

My phone buzzes as I reach my car and drop heavily inside.

Jesse

All good bro?

Me

Yeah, sorry to bail. Something just came up that couldn't wait.

Jesse

Naw, you're good. I'm actually gonna hook up with Rik for lunch now anyway. She's really gotten frisky since we started using some of that shit you sent me.

Me

*Awesome man. Have fun *devil emoji**

Jesse

*Fuck yeah *fist pump emoji* *eggplant emoji* *peach emoji**

Chuckling to myself, I exit the chat and pull up my notes.

It's been a while since my encounter with Harvey and I'm starting to get the itch again. I know I won't be able to act on anything for at least a few weeks after I choose so I need to make a decision quickly. Scrolling through the names, I mentally picture each person.

Susan Panitet

Mark Theinnes

Kyle Pretick

Ugh, I hate Kyles. Pretentious, frat boy fuckers. Man deserves to die just for the name alone.

I shake my head, still doesn't feel like the right one.

Natalie Buetl

Becky Hultie

Perfect.

I picture Becky in my head. Long blonde hair pulled back in a high ponytail. Tight leggings, crop top. Obnoxious laughter as she gossips about some poor girl in her psych class. It's been a while since I've gone after a college kid. My restlessness starts to settle as I begin to plan.

Putting my phone down, I return my gaze to the store and wait for Paige to exit.

Once I make sure she is home safely, I'll start my hunt.

"Oh god. Yes. Mick!"

"Yeah, you like that? You're such a slut for my cock." I grunt, thrusting forward. Veronica arches below me, shoving her ass back to meet each of my thrusts.

I really should feel bad about fucking her still while my obsession with Paige only continues to grow. But I don't, I can't. I need some outlet for this pent up sexual frustration. Looking down, I imagine what it would be like to have Paige writhing beneath me while moaning my name. The thought causes my cock to twitch and I thrust harder.

Panting, Veronica reaches between her legs and starts to rub her clit furiously. "Yes...I'm so close. Don't stop." I snake my hand around and grab hold of her throat, squeezing tight, her moans cut off by the pressure. With my other hand I slap her ass.

"You gonna come for me?" She nods her head the best she can, tears leaking down her face as I continue to slap her ass again and again in time with my brutal thrusts. "Good girl. Such a good little whore." I feel her walls start to clamp around my dick. Knowing she's close I pick up my speed, releasing my grip on her throat just enough to allow her to gasp in a breath before squeezing again. "That's it. Come for me. Now." And she explodes, her pussy spasming around me and shudders running through her body.

I don't stop. I drop my hand from her throat and grab hold of her hips, wildly fucking her. Closing my eyes, my vision fills with Paige. Her eyes, her hair, her ass. Groaning, I thrust forward once more and release myself inside of Veronica, filling the condom with my cum. I quickly pull out and remove the condom, tying off the end and tossing it into the wastebasket next to the bed. A handy addition to the room so I can avoid awkwardly carrying around my ejaculation through the house, looking for the closest bin.

I look toward the bed and see that Veronica has collapsed onto her stomach, eyes glazed with post-orgasmic bliss.

See? I'm not that bad of a guy, I still give her the best orgasms of her life. Sure, I have to think of another woman to come, but at least I'm still a good fuck. And that's all our relationship is anyway.

"I gotta head out." Veronica lifts her head and stares at me. I don't know if I quite like the look in her eyes, she almost looks hurt. "That was fun." I gesture to the bed in hopes that the reminder lifts her mood. I might like to inflict pain but it's purely physical. Outside of toying with my victims, I'm not into emotionally damaging folks if I can avoid it.

Rather than bring a smile to her face, my comment darkens her mood further and a scowl forms. "That was fun." She repeats, sarcasm dripping from her tone.

I arch a brow at her.

Did she not enjoy herself? Could have fooled me.

"You used to stay with me after. At least for a while. Now you bolt the second you finish. You know I like being called a whore in the heat of the moment but that doesn't mean I like being treated like one." Sitting up, she pulls the covers around herself.

I stare at her in shock. My mouth opens, then closes. After several long moments of tense silence, I manage to get out, "I thought this was just about sex? I mean, that's all we've ever agreed to and it's not like we really know each other. Or want to get to know each other." I grimace as the words leave my mouth.

Oops, wrong thing to say.

She bolts out of the bed, clutching the blanket tightly around herself. "You are an asshole." She hisses before storming into the bathroom and slamming the door shut.

I stare at the closed door, debating if I should go in after her. She probably wants me to, wants me to chase her and show more of an interest. But that's crossing a line, because I don't want to get more involved. Not with Veronica at least. Letting out a heavy sigh, I turn to the other door leading out to the hall and make my way toward the exit as I pull on my clothes.

I'm going to need to figure something out soon or my hand and I are going to become very well acquainted again.

This is a bad idea.

I've had the same thought at least a dozen times within the last twenty minutes. Yet, here I am still. Grumbling to myself how much of an idiot I am, I exit my car and start toward the apartments.

I know Paige isn't here. I followed her to a friend's house and watched as she climbed out with a bottle of wine in one hand and a stack of DVDs in the other.

Who still watches DVDs anyway?

I couldn't help but feel intrigued by the reason she's not just using a streaming service. That intrigue is what's led me to making yet another careless action. I'm not usually this irrational but every time I think of her, the pull to know her, to take her, to claim her, grows stronger until I can't think straight.

Striding up to the lobby entrance, I walk in behind a young couple who are too distracted with each other to notice my presence. I've found the key to getting into most spaces is to act as if I belong there. People cater to confidence and will do just about anything if you emanate the right aura.

With that in mind, I stride toward the elevators and press the button to reach the third floor. Paige lives in apartment 307. I know this as I stole a piece of mail she had sitting in her car while at work. It was too tempting and easy to pass up the opportunity, and now I am being rewarded for my innovativeness. The elevator dings, the doors sliding open. As I make my way down the hall to the door labeled 307, I discreetly pull out my lock pick and tuck it up into my shirt sleeve. Once in front of the door, a quick glance down each end of the narrow hallway shows I am alone. I make quick work of the simple lock and stamp down the anger that rises at how easy it is to break into her home. It's in my favor right now, but I will need to do something to ensure I'm the only one who gets to slip in and out as they please.

Stepping into the apartment and closing the door behind me, I take a moment to look around. The space is rather small, just larger than a studio with a small bathroom and bedroom tucked away to the left of the doorway. The living room, if you could call it that, sports enough room for a small couch and TV stand. The carpet looks to be at least a decade old with fraying ends and various stains spattered around.

Other than the lackluster space and flooring, the decor gives the apartment a cozy yet lively feel. Soft pastels mix with vibrant splashes of color. Several paintings line the walls of abstract shapes that look more like a drug-induced vision than any defined image. Plants are tucked away in various spots. A large fern in the corner, a few small cacti litter the counters in the kitchen and windowsill, some kind of dangly vine trails from a shelf on the far wall next to several picture frames and small figurines.

Striding farther inside, I look closely at the photographs on the shelves lining the wall. Pictures of Paige in various stages of her life. Her as a teenager giggling with two other girls, Paige in a graduation gown with an older woman who looks to be in her late sixties, a more recent photo that looks to be only a few years old of her nuzzling a small kitten with her eyes closed. I look from picture to picture and try to piece together more of her life. She appears to really care for others, so many smiling faces scattered around, but I haven't seen her with any of the others in the photos in the weeks I've been stalking her. It's possible she just hasn't met up with any of her friends in the photos, but I can't shake the feeling that there's more to it than that.

Turning from the wall, I make my way into her bathroom and start rummaging through the small cabinet below the sink and the hidden cupboard behind the mirror. Nothing untoward coming up, just normal everyday items. Tampons, cleaning supplies, toilet paper, extra shampoo and body wash. Staring at the shampoo, I debate taking it. I need something of her and the scent may be enough to satiate some of the desire inside, at least for a little while.

Giving in to the urge, I snatch one of the extra bottles and rearrange the other items so it's presence isn't missing. It's small enough I can slip it into my pocket without too much of an obvious bulge. Glancing around the room one last time I take in the shower curtain and paintings, similar colors to the living room. The curtain, however, is covered in various water creatures. Turtles, whales, dolphins, fish and even a few octopus and squids fill in the spaces around each other. It's a little busy but, next to the abstract decor throughout the rest of the bathroom, fits in nicely.

Lastly, I make my way into her bedroom. Taking a deep breath, I stand still for a moment, relishing in the scent of her. My cock twitches and I have to adjust myself to relieve some of the uncomfortable pressure. I can already tell the shampoo is not going to be enough.

I need more.

Looking at the space, I observe her queen bed made up with a floral patterned bedspread. Next to the bed are two nightstands, one on either side, both with small lamps. The one on the left is bare other than the lamp and a small coaster. However, the nightstand on the right side of the bed has several books stacked on each other, a small glasses case, a circular phone charger & an empty mug with a used teabag sitting inside. She must sleep on the right side of her bed. I can't help the smile that spreads across my face. She's left open the left side for me, as if she knows that it's my side.

Groaning, I run a hand down my face.

Of course she hasn't left it for me. Why would she?

Now feeling an irritating amount of self pity, I make my way over to her dresser sitting across the room from her bed. Because of the small space, it only takes a few steps before I'm able to start pulling open drawers, taking in the assortment of underwear, bras, socks and pajamas strewn throughout.

After a quick internal debate, I scoop up a couple pairs of panties. Bringing them to my nose, I inhale. They have a hint of her smell mixed with the laundry detergent she uses, but it's not quite enough.

I need more of her smell.

I notice a laundry hamper tucked in between the closet and dresser and quickly snatch a pair of panties sitting on top. This time when I sniff the underwear, I can't stop the guttural groan that escapes my throat.

This is what I needed.

Pure, unclean, unadulterated *her*.

Tossing the unused pairs back into the drawers, I tuck my find into my other pocket and take one more quick peruse of her space before heading back out of the room.

I desperately want to leave her something to remind her of me. It's been too long since our brief encounter at the store and I want her to remember who I am. But, more importantly, I want her to know who *she* is.

Because there is no denying it now. She is mine. Even if she doesn't know it yet.

A few minutes later I make my way out of the apartment and back to my car, smiling to myself as I climb in and start to head home.

Chapter 6

Paige

I know I've had too much to drink but that doesn't stop me from tossing back another shot. Originally, the plan was to just hang out, drink some wine and eat some greasy pizza while watching old movies on the PS4 Taylor's boyfriend has at their place.

Everything was going great until I got a notification on my phone.

When I glanced down, I almost swiped away the message but caught sight of the username listed.

GetSethed

I tried to ignore it, I really did. I had forgotten that I set up for all my socials to notify me with updates about Seth when we split. The decision was made while wallowing in self-pity and drowning in a bottle of rum. Now I'm paying the price.

Lesson learned, never social and drink while depressed, it doesn't end well.

I hold up my hand to the bartender and gesture to my glass, silently requesting another round. She nods my way and comes back to pour more tequila and sets a lime wedge next to my growing pile. I thank her with an incline of my head. Staring at the alcohol sitting in front of me, my hand reaches for my phone and opens up to the post for the hundredth time since getting the alert.

Glaring at the screen, I blink away the tears that form in my eyes, threatening to fall. The picture of my ex-best friend glares back at me. I can feel the pain wash over me again.

How did I never notice?

Blinking again, I reread the status.

BriezzyBeautiful

*OMG guys, I am soooooo excited *praying hands emoji* to announce we're GETTING MARRIED!!! Can you believe it? This stud muffin is going to make an honest *crying laughing emoji* woman out of me. Y'all know what to do if you want an invite. K, love youuuuuu *phone emoji* *envelope emoji* *heart emoji* *wedding ring emoji**

My stomach rolls, I might puke if I keep staring but I can't peel my eyes away.

This is humiliating.

Not only did Seth cheat on me with my best friend, he's now going to marry her instead of me. Sure it's been a few years since I called off our wedding but how could he do this? How could *she* do this?

Brie Carmichael and I used to be inseparable. We did everything together and knew everything about each other. Or at least I thought we did, up until I walked in on the two of them fucking on our bed. Nausea flows through me and I set my phone onto the counter while reaching for the shot glass. Throwing my head back, I wash away my torment with the burn of liquor. Wishing it would permanently scar, cauterize off the bleeding in my heart.

"Babe, I think you've had enough to drink." I shake my head at the sound of Taylor's voice, looking back at my phone. "Yes. You know I love you but this," She gestures to the phone and glass in front of me. "Is not healthy. You deserve so much better than that prick and bimbo." She reaches over and gently hugs my shoulders with one arm. "Why don't we go get some tacos and crash at my place? I'll text Beau to come get us."

I mumble something incoherent, trying to argue so I can stay and drown my troubles in tequila, but Taylor already has her phone out and quickly types out a message before slipping it back into her bag. "Come on P. Let's put away the phone, yeah?" Before I can answer, she's snatched the phone and shoved it in with her own.

I stare miserably down at my hands, shoulders hunching forward.

God, I feel so pathetic.

I'm so angry.

Angry at Seth.

Angry at Brie.

But mostly, I'm furious and disgusted with myself that I still care. I shouldn't let them have this much influence over me, not after all this time. I know part of the problem is I never really moved on. I've had my fair share of hook-ups but no one has caught my attention long enough to even try to get over Seth.

Suddenly blue eyes & blonde curls fill my vision. A small voice in the back of my mind whispers that someone has caught my attention. I shake my head, chiding myself. Mick doesn't know I exist, at least not like that. I've only seen him the two times and, although he made quite the impression on me, I'm positive my babbling the last time we spoke has definitely scared him away.

I drop my head into my hands with a long groan.

Taylor's right, this pity party is doing no good, and tacos do *sound good.*

Peeking up from my hands, I look over at my friend. Her attention is focused on her phone again, tapping away on the screen as the clatter of her acrylics sound with each movement. Her petite figure is wrapped up in a shawl dress, the forest theme of the material contrasts nicely with the rich brown tones of her skin. She reaches up a hand to absentmindedly brush back a wayward lock of hair, the majority of the mocha colored strands tied up in a loose braid.

My heart aches as I watch her. She's been my stability since moving out to New Mexico. We became fast friends and I'm so grateful for her. Even after her and Beau started to get serious, Taylor made sure to make time for me. Overwhelmed with emotion, I blink back more tears and whisper, "Thank you."

She looks over at me with a soft smile, her sea green eyes twinkling. "No thanks needed, babe. I've got you." When she wraps me into a hug, the tears I've been fighting all night pour down my face and a choked sob escapes my throat. She squeezes me tighter, rubbing my back and soothingly shushing me. "It's okay. You're gonna be okay. You are a badass bitch and Seth can go fuck himself." A wet laugh leaves my lips and I lean back, brushing the back of my hand across my eyes.

Grinning at each other, I reply with as much strength as I can force into the words. "Yeah, fuck you Seth and your crooked dick." Which makes us both dissolve into giggles.

We're still laughing when Beau comes in to collect us. And as we make our way to pick up our late night munchies, I can feel my chest lighten. A heaviness I hadn't realized was still there lifts and I take a deep breath.

I am a badass bitch.

After leaving the bar last night, I ended up crashing at Taylor's place and woke up with a massive hangover. Coming to the horrifying realization that I'm almost thirty and can't just drink without consequences like in my early twenties.

I moan again as another sharp pain stabs behind my eyes, the sunglasses glued to my face doing nothing to lessen the assault of sunlight pouring through my windows. I'm tempted to call into my shift today but know I won't because I need the money and I hate to leave Brandi short staffed.

Parking my car, I trudge up to my apartment, keeping my head ducked to avoid as much light as possible. Entering my door, I toss my purse onto the counter and open the fridge to snatch out a bottle of water.

I chug the liquid and throw the empty bottle in the paper bag I keep for recycling and head to my bathroom, hoping a shower will make me feel more human.

By the time I've finished getting ready, I'm running late. I rush out of my room and reach for my purse, freezing when I see something sitting on the counter a few inches past my haphazardly discarded things. Heart pounding, I tiptoe forward until I'm standing flush with the countertop.

Resting on the surface is a small card, about the size of a business card, but there's something about it that makes my stomach roll over. I reach forward with a shaky hand and pick up the invasive piece of cardstock. It's thin and black, the color so dark it seems to suck out the light around it. I turn it back and forth but there is no name or number listed. Only one single line handwritten in white ink.

In blood and flesh, you are mine.

I swallow the lump in my throat and read it over and over.

Where did this come from? What does it mean?

I look around the room to see if there's anything else different but don't notice any other odd cards or any missing items. My eyes slowly drift back to the card, reading it once more.

Someone was in my apartment. Someone wants me.

But for what?

Taylor

What?! Just sitting there?

Me

Yeah, it was on the counter.

I didn't even notice till I was leaving for work.

I glance up at the clock again. We're not really supposed to use our phones at work but we've been dead for the last hour. I've already done all the closing tasks I can until I lock the door and there's still another twenty minutes before I can do that. So I decided to text Taylor about what I found earlier. Obsessing over it in my head during my shift only caused me to grow more anxious and I needed to tell someone else what was happening.

I have no interest in being a feature on one of my favorite true crime podcasts. My horrid story of being a murder victim of some crazed stalker being rehashed in between inappropriate jokes and oddly timed ads for some obscure deodorant company. Hoping to avoid this fate, I decided to take some precautions.

Precaution number one: tell my closest friend some creep broke into my apartment and left a cryptic note.

Taylor

*Babe, I think you should change your locks or something. Or better yet. Move!! That apartment is a *poop emoji* *hole emoji* anyway.*

Taylor

No offense

Snorting, I quickly type out my reply.

Me

Dude, if I could move I would. But I'll look into changing my locks, I don't know if the manager would let me. Or if it would even help. How did they get in anyway? No one else has keys.

Taylor

Ummmmm, did you forget about me? I have a key!

Me

*Oh shit...are you my stalker? *side eye emoji**

Taylor

*Bitch, you wish. You couldn't handle all this *peach emoji**

Me

**laughing emoji* *skull emoji* I love you*

Taylor

Love ya too. Change your locks! And at least look at other apartments.

Me

Yes dear

Taylor

**kissing emoji* Good. I gotta run. CALL ME if anything else happens.*

Me

Byyyyyyeee bitch. Will do.

I slide my phone into my apron pocket and glance at the clock again with a sigh.

Normally, I would be ready to head home but I'm nervous about being alone in my apartment tonight. I really wish I had one of the fancy camera security doorbells so I would at least get notified a few moments before some creep tries to break in. Not that I could afford one. Hell, I'm not even sure I can afford to pay a locksmith to come out and change my locks.

Staring up at the ceiling, I run through my life, trying to figure out what I could have done to avoid ending up here. So many different choices lead up to this moment and, if I'm being totally honest, I don't think I'd have been able to change a single one.

Not that I believe in fate or anything, I just know that I made the decisions I thought were best with the information I was working with at the time. Hindsight is 20/20 and, of course, I can think of things I'd do differently now, but that's just because I have insider knowledge at this point. Like flipping through a book to the middle and reading a few pages then restarting back at the beginning and screaming at the characters to see what was happening.

It doesn't help, won't ever work.

With that thought, I give myself a little shake and decide to start rounding up the trash. At least it'll keep my hands busy and I'll be able to quickly run it out once I lock up. After collecting all the bags, I set them down by the alley door and glance at the clock. Again.

Finding I still have another ten minutes before I can lock up, I pull out my phone. Opening up my contacts, I scroll down to find his name.

I should have deleted it immediately after what happened but I could never quite bring myself to push the button. Even now, after last night, my finger hovers over Seth's name as I will myself to just hit delete.

A loud bang causes my head to whip up and I quickly shove my phone back into my apron. Creeping quietly, I head toward the noise, thinking it might be a stray animal caught in the tables out front. Oddly enough, it wouldn't be the first time that's happened. I try to be more cautious after my mystery visitor this morning. Peeking out the front windows first, I slowly pull the door open and step outside. Glancing around, I don't see anything out of place and am just about to head back inside when another bang goes off to my left.

I scream and jump back, knocking into the patio seating. Losing my footing, I start to tumble backwards, flailing wildly until my hand connects with a sharp piece of metal sticking out of the side of the building. I land heavily on my ass clutching my now bleeding hand to my chest, eyes wildly looking around. I'm both relieved and irritated to find no one else. At least my humiliation isn't being witnessed, but that just means I've worked myself up enough to actually get injured because of a noise.

Huffing a breath, I push up with my uninjured hand and head back inside. Deciding I've been through enough and no one's going to come in the five minutes, I say fuck it and lock the door before heading to the back room and grabbing the first aid kid to tend to my wound. It's not a deep cut but enough to cause a trickle of blood to seep out. I glance down and notice my light shirt has a new stain that looks suspiciously like blood. Narrowing my eyes at my hand, I curse while gingerly cleaning the cut.

Damnit Paige, pull yourself together.

Once my hand is clean, I pull out a small pad of gauze and push it against the cut, wrapping the self-adhesive wrap around my hand to hold the gauze in place. Satisfied with my handiwork, I put away the first aid kit and scoop up the trash bags.

As soon as I'm in the alleyway and heading toward the garbage bin, I start to feel the same prickle down my spine that I felt weeks ago.

Either I'm officially going crazy or someone is fucking with me.

Reminding myself to take deep even breaths, I continue forward.

Deep breathe in, deep breathe out. Now is not the time to have a panic attack. Just keep breathing. In. Out. In. Ou-

My mental pep talk is interrupted by a light scuffling behind me. I freeze, clutching the bags in my hands so tightly my fingers start to cramp. Unsure what to do, I stay frozen to the spot, ears straining for any other noise. A small squeak leaves me as I hear the same sound again, this time followed by the soft pad of footsteps.

That's no animal.

And it's getting closer to me.

Finally breaking out of my stupor, I drop the bags and run.

CHAPTER 7

MICK

Watching the preppy blonde, I find my mind wandering. I've been trying to stay focused on gathering more information on Becky so I can form a solid plan, but have found it difficult to keep my mind on her. Instead, it keeps drifting back to Paige.

Did she find my card? What did she think of it?

I smile, thinking of when she will know it's me to whom she belongs. When she learns how well I can please her, how her body will respond to me. My fingers itch to wrap themselves around her pretty little neck, my mouth waters with the need to taste her.

Soon. I'm going to need to take her very soon.

A high pitched laugh draws me back to where I am.

I need to stay focused.

The quicker I get the information I need, the faster I can get back to my girl.

Becky flips her hair over her shoulder and lightly presses her hand on the chest of the boy in front of her. This is the fourth man I have witnessed her openly flirting with since I began my hunt. Knowing she's not attached to anyone helps make this easier. There's usually an added difficulty when a partner is involved in the routine, another set of eyes to avoid. But, as luck would have it, little miss Becky is a bit of a slut and never stays with one lover longer than a night.

I nearly have enough intel gathered to set my plans in motion, I just need to confirm when she is going to be leaving. It's almost summer break and I've heard Becky mention to several friends that she is planning on taking off to visit her family in Colorado Springs. It's close enough that she can make the trip by car within a day's travel and she feels safe enough to make the trip alone.

Poor girl couldn't be more wrong.

The two say their goodbyes and part ways, Becky heading toward the study hall on the other end of campus. I stay in my seat on the bench, pretending to focus on the textbook in my hands, and wait for her to pass. After she's several feet away, I slowly tuck away the book in the messenger bag slung around my torso before following behind her. Seeing her pull out her phone, I speed up my steps to close the distance a little more. Once I'm in hearing distance, I slow my pace again and pull my own phone out, appearing to absentmindedly scroll as I walk.

"Heyyyyy girl," I force myself not to flinch at the sound of her nasally voice, it's grating and frays my nerves. After a beat, Becky cackles. "Shit! No fucking way. I did not suck off Brandon behind the bookshelves." She pauses before snickering and saying in a low voice, "I blew him under the library table." Whoever she is talking to must have a lot to say in response to that revelation as Becky stays quiet for a long time before letting out a long sigh. "He's not worth it. Seriously, wouldn't you rather know now that he's a cheating asshole before he knocks you up and you're stuck taking care of thing 1 and thing 2 while he's off banging some whore on a 'business trip'?" Another pause, then sigh and I can practically hear her rolling her eyes. "Babe, I did this *for* you. Can't you see that?" More silence. "You know what? *Fuck you.* I'm glad I'm leaving Thursday and won't have to see your pathetic face." Hanging up the call, Becky flips her hair over her shoulder and struts off.

Getting the information I need, I pivot toward the parking lot. Now that I have a date set with Becky on Thursday, I can claim my girl tonight.

I curse under my breath and run a hand through my hair. Watching Paige today has shown me she's not ready to accept the truth. She looks terrified. That's certainly not the response I was wanting. Although, I can objectively see that having someone uninvited into your home could be disconcerting.

Fuck.

I've been hunting for so long I forgot that normal people don't break into potential lovers' homes and leave notes.

"Fuck." I mutter out loud.

Pacing back and forth, I debate my options.

I could go into the shop, say hi and pretend I was never in her home. If I do that, though, she won't realize I've already made my claim on her. Believing there is another out there calling her theirs.

I growl at the thought of anyone else even trying. They wouldn't live long if I found them.

No, playing oblivious won't work. Maybe I could sneak into her apartment again and leave another message?

I pause and ponder this for a moment.

Perhaps not to leave another message but there is merit to entering her space. Opening a window into her world. Possibly giving me an idea on how to further our connection without spooking her.

I gaze back through the shop windows and watch as Paige greets a customer with a bright smile. Her long hair tied back in a braid today, a few strands hanging loose and framing her face. She absentmindedly fiddles with the pen in her hand while listening attentively to whatever the person across the counter is saying.

I narrow my eyes as I watch. I'm about to say fuck it and march inside to end the conversation when she writes on a cup and holds out her hand to take the credit card being offered. After returning the card, she begins to work on making the order and bends to a cupboard below the back wall, showing off her ass in the black leggings she's wearing. The man who placed the order elbows his friend and nods his head toward Paige with a smirk on his face. Rage boils inside as I watch him pull out his phone and snap a photo. He quickly tucks away his phone as she stands and turns back toward the espresso bar, turning to his friend to avoid suspicion.

I take a deep breath and size him up. He's tall, but I still have at least a few inches on him at my 6'4 stature. Though he appears to be in decent shape, I'm sure I could take him. After all, I've handled men much taller and larger with ease. My main concern is his friend. He too is tall but well built, my bet would be he spends most evenings in the gym and mornings out on a run. Probably drinks that green shit and pisses clear. It's going to be difficult to take them both, most likely impossible without drawing attention.

I release the breath, having made my decision. Watching Paige pass over the beverage, the dead man brushes his fingers over hers as he grabs the cup.

Looks like he'll be losing some appendages today as well.

I slink back further into the cover of the building and track the movements of the two men making their way down the street. With one last forlorn look back at my raven haired beauty, I stalk after the man who has just signed his death warrant. Lucky for me, I already have everything set up for my other victim so this will be a simple switch. Who knows, he may even take Becky's place and she can live another day to whore herself around campus.

Maybe.

I've been following the two men for almost an hour. Wherever they are going seems to be a ways out still and I'm starting to get anxious. I want to get back to the shop and...I'm not entirely sure what I'll do when I get there but I need to be near Paige again.

Weaving behind a truck up ahead, their car veers off toward an exit. I slide my vehicle over, keeping two cars in between to avoid suspicion. A quick look shows the rest area sign and I silently say my thanks to whatever power is at work. Rest stops have a bad rap for a reason. I happen to be one of those reasons.

Letting out a dark chuckle, I remember the several victims I have procured at various stops along the highway. I only take the men from these spots, their bravado and arrogance make them easy targets. A woman will be more on guard, more likely to have also given a warning to someone that she was stopping, and where, in case she were to go missing. Men, however, seem to believe they are untouchable.

This is proven again as the dead man and his friend exit their vehicle and split directions. The friend heading toward a vending machine across the lot and my main target entering the restrooms. Deciding it would be quickest to take his friend first, I pull into a spot in the corner, tucked away in the shade of a large tree. I get out and open my trunk to pull out my bag and fill the syringe before throwing the bag around my shoulder and softly closing the trunk lid.

I make my way toward the vending machines and hold my cell phone to my ear as I get close. "No Wendy, I'm almost there. I just had to make a quick stop to grab some snacks and take a piss." Coming up to the snack machine next to him, I throw him a look with a roll of my eyes. He chuckles and shoots me back a sympathetic shrug. "Yes honey, I didn't forget. Okay, I love you too." I pretend to hang up the call and slip my phone into my pocket, muttering, "Women. Am I right?"

"Don't I know it. My bitch won't shut the fuck up." Another roll of his eyes. "Your woman sounds like a real piece of work too. Should put her in her place if you know what I mean." He winks at me and I grind the back of my teeth before forcing a smile.

Chuckling, I slide the syringe into my hand, turning fully toward him. "Yes, I do think I know what you mean." I lunge forward and stab the needle into his neck while covering his mouth with my other hand and shoving him back against the machine. He struggles for a couple minutes before I see his eyes roll back and his body sags. Removing my hands, I lift him by the armpits with a grunt and start dragging him back to my car. Beads of sweat break out as I make my way over, the fucker is heavy.

Finally, I make it to the back of my car and pop open the lid. Setting him half leaning against the edge, half dangling against the ground, I pull out a couple zip ties and cinch his arms and legs before stuffing a sock into his mouth and covering it with duct tape. Once satisfied, I fold his large frame into the bed and close it up, making sure to lock the vehicle before making my way to my real target.

I haven't taken two people at once before and I'm hoping my car will have enough room, otherwise it's going to be an uncomfortable ride with one of them strewn across the backseat hogtied. A flash of another body tied up and waiting for me has me adjusting my cock. Now isn't the time to be thinking of Paige but I can't keep her out of my head. I take a couple deep breaths and try to think unsexy thoughts. It would be rather unfortunate if I go to kidnap this man and he gets the jump on me because my stiff dick gets in the way.

After my half-chub has fully deflated, I push into the restroom and casually stride toward the sinks. The bastard is standing with his back to the mirrors, whistling as he takes a piss. I clench my jaw as I watch his back and wait for him to finish. I have no interest in getting caught in the crossfire of his urine. You only make that mistake once, I swear I could smell the rancid scent for days after. Suppressing a shudder at the memory, I prepare for my moment.

His stream slows and he shakes a little before tucking his dick away and turning toward the doors. I groan internally.

Of course he's a prick that doesn't flush or wash his hands after taking a piss. I may be sick in the head but at least I'm not disgusting.

Not wanting to miss my chance, I rush him and smack his face against the door. Hard. He grunts and jumps back. "What the fuck?" He snaps, holding his piss covered hand to his face. I can't hold back the eye roll. If he wasn't going to be dead in the next few hours, I'm certain he'd have a nasty infection.

Instead of answering him, I reach over and wrap my fingers around his throat and squeeze. The action surprises him enough that I can swiftly kick out my leg and knock his out from under him, causing him to tumble to the ground. I release his throat as he falls and his head smacks against the ground with a satisfying thump. He groans, trying to sit up but I press my foot into his chest and hover over him.

"The fuck man?" He seethes up at me, blood pouring down his face.

Appreciating the sight of the crimson liquid, I glare down at him. "You shouldn't touch what's not yours." He stares up at me in confusion, so I continue. "You also definitely shouldn't take pictures of another man's woman." His confusion fades as he realizes who I'm talking about.

He darts his eyes to the door and then back to me. "Look man, I didn't know, okay?" He licks his lips and nervously shakes his head. "I didn't realize she was someone else's girl. I can delete the photo. Let me get to my phone and I'll delete it right now." I cock my head at him, pretending to consider what he's saying. Encouraged by my silence, he keeps talking. "I mean, how was I supposed to know? She was flirting with me, practically begging for attention." I growl and his eyes widen. "Sorry, I didn't mean...I-"

I don't let him finish whatever bullshit was about to come out of his mouth, swiftly kicking the side of his head and knocking him unconscious. Heaving several breaths, I storm over to the sinks and splash water onto my face. I look up and glare into the mirror as I replay the scene in my head.

Paige standing behind the counter, smiling and fiddling with the pen in her hand. Shyly darting her eyes up and laughing at something the prick said.

I smack my hand against the counter.

That's it, after I take care of these assholes, I'm going to her and I'm going to show her who she is. Who she belongs to.

I make quick work of cleaning up the mess and dragging him back to my car. Once he's tied up, I shove him roughly into the trunk and smoosh them both into the small space before slamming the trunk closed.

My irritation grows as I stomp to the driver door and climb inside. It's a good thing I have something to use up some of this anger. I can't afford to be sloppy now. I need a clear head. Adjusting my mirrors, I head out.

Once I make it to my kill space, I pull the two inside and tie one to the metal chair resting in the middle of the room to the left of the chains I usually use. The other, the main asshole, is strewn up and dangling from said chains.

I go through their pockets and find their wallets, keys and phones.

Unlocking the offender's phone with his finger, I quickly find the photo of Paige's ass and delete it from existence. After that task is complete, I remove the SIM cards from both phones and smash them before also destroying both SIM cards and tossing those into a trash can.

Chucking the keys into a box off to the side filled with other miscellaneous finds from my previous victims, I open the first wallet. This one belonging to the friend.

Adam Engle

Well, at least I can stop referring to him as "the friend" in my head. Though, I don't find Adam quite suits him. I was thinking it would be something more harsh, like Nikolai or Brutus. No wonder he's such a dick, his parents fucked up his name.

I snort, remove the cash, and then chuck his wallet and ID into the box.

Next is the dead man's wallet. Pulling his ID out I chuckle.

Now this name is the perfect fit.

Leslie Clandien

A bitch's name for the king bitch himself.

Finding no cash inside, I deposit his things away and close up the box, spinning the lock. A soft groan behind me draws my attention. I turn around and see Leslie blinking, cringing from the sting of dried blood flaking into his eyes.

"Hello Leslie." He cringes again and glares in my direction but doesn't say anything. "What, cat got your tongue? Usually people's reaction to waking up in my playroom," I gesture around the space. "Is always so predictable. 'Where am I?' 'Who are you?' 'What's happening?'" I mime out with fake horror and a bat of my eyelashes, chuckling at the look of disgust on his face. "Oh come now, you didn't think you were my first, did you?" I wait for a response and grow irritated when he still just stares at me.

Stomping my way over, I jerk back Adam's head, exposing his throat, and watch Leslie's disgusted face morph to horror. I tsk and drop Adam's head before turning and heading to my table in the corner and hum as I look over the options lined out, picking up items to inspect before placing them back down. I had a long time to think on the drive over and already know what I'm going to do, but I also enjoy the added fear when my victims aren't sure what to expect.

Growing a little tired of the game, I reach over and snatch up a hammer and screws, pocketing a few bolt ends as well, and turn back around. Seeing Adam is still passed out, I pick up the smelling salts before sauntering back to him. I shoot a wink in Leslie's direction as I swipe the smelling salts under Adam's nose. His head jerks up and he flinches back against the binds. "What the fuck? Where am I?" His voice grows louder with each question. Looking at me, recognition flares in his eyes. "What's going on?" He demands.

I laugh and call out to his friend, "See! Now *that* is the reaction I was looking for." I give Adam an approving nod as I set down the salts and pick up the hammer and screws. "Welcome back to the living Adam boy. Although, I hate to be the bearer of bad news, you won't be joining us for long." Adam starts to curse at me, pulling harder against the restraints. "Now now, that's no way to act. I suppose I'm going to have to *put you in your place*." His eyes widen as my tone fills with venom on the reminder of his words.

He starts to plead with me as I rest a screw against the back of his hand and raise the hammer. "Please man, don't do this. You don't have to do this." His pleading is silenced as a scream is ripped from his chest. I hammer in the screw forcefully until the end sticks out through the hole I have drilled into the arm of the chair.

This was an addition I was quite proud of when I came up with the idea. Once the screw has been pushed through the body and is on the other side of the hole, I attach one of the bolt heads to the end and it renders the person completely immobile while providing an extra level of agony with each movement. It's quite brilliant if I do say so myself.

I methodically work my way up both Adam's arms and legs until there are five screws lodged into each limb. Clapping my hands, I stand and return my now bloodied hammer to the table and grab the meat cleaver next. I'm not planning on prolonging Adam's torture past my sweet poetic display. I do, however, want to inflict more pain to Leslie via his friend's. Working my way back over to Adam, I tip his head back and force his face toward the man dangling from the ceiling. "Any last words to your friend? Final parting thoughts? I advise you make it good, as you won't be getting a second chance."

Leslie blinks slowly and whispers, "I'm so sorry Adam. I'm so fucking sorry."

As the last word leaves his lips, I swing down the cleaver into Adam's right wrist and sever his hand. His wail turns to gags as he looks down at his detached hand, still fastened to the chair, blood pouring from both sides of the separated wrist. I swiftly repeat the motion on his other side, slicing through his left wrist in another quick movement. The smell of piss and vomit fill the air and I look up in disgust.

I hate it when they can't control their bodily fluids.

I briefly debate whether I want to just end his life to avoid further unpleasant messes but the sounds of gagging behind me and choked sobs remind me of my audience.

Purpose bolstered again, I work over Adam's body. Chopping apart, piece by piece, between each screw until only his knees and elbows up are still attached to his body. Adam passes out somewhere between the fifth and sixth cut and I'd put good money on him not waking up again. Satisfied with my masterpiece, I face Leslie and take in his tear streaked face. He's as pale as a sheet and his eyes show he knows he's next and there's nothing he can do to get out of this. Swallowing, he blinks before whispering, "I didn't know. How-how could I have known?"

Soothingly, I shush him. "I know you aren't entirely to blame Leslie. I will deal with Paige as well." His eyes widen in horror. I shake my head, laughing softly. "Don't be silly, her punishment will be much more enjoyable. For both of us." I discard the cleaver and snatch up an old steel potato peeler. "You know, it's been years since I've peeled off someone's fingerprints." I reminisce, fiddling with the peeler as I walk toward him. "I've gotten quite lazy in just burning them off in recent years. I'm looking forward to returning to my roots."

Once in front of him, I reach up and grasp his wrist, surprised to find no resistance. I cock an eyebrow at him and he grits his teeth, looking away. Having none of that, I grasp his jaw and force his gaze back on me before releasing his face and lining up the peeler with his pointer finger. I slide the blade along his skin and watch the thin layers fall away with each swipe. The deeper I go, the more blood pools, causing some of the removed skin to stick in the wound. Leslie's cries of pain are a beautiful soundtrack to my artwork as I peel off each of his finger pads, stepping back once complete and watching the blood drip onto the floor. His head falls forward as he whimpers.

"That was for touching what's not yours." His only response is another pained whimper. "Next, I am going to cut out your tongue for flirting with my girl." He opens his mouth to beg, pleas falling on deaf ears. I grab a small serrated pocket knife and force his jaw apart. "I'm only going to warn you once, if you try to bite me, I will make this worse. Trust me when I tell you, you do not want that." I wait until he gives a slight nod before reaching in and roughly pulling out his tongue. Holding it firmly in one hand, I saw through the muscle until the last bit detaches. I toss the severed tongue onto the floor and softly pat his cheek. "Good boy."

He stares at me through tears and blood. It's such a beautiful sight. "Because you listened so well and I'm feeling in a better mood after Adam over there." I shrug toward the dismembered corpse beside us. "I'm going to remove your eyes for looking at her. But then I will end your life quickly. It's a mercy and a reward." I smile at him and spin on my heels, snatching up a metal serving spoon and my favorite blade. Shoving the spoon into his left eye, I exert enough pressure to pop it out without rupturing the thin membrane. I gently tug on it until I can see the connective tissue and sever the ball from his face, tossing it down next to his tongue. I repeat the process with his right eye then step back and admire my work.

Walking back up, I reach around and grab hold of his hair, pulling his head back to expose his throat. Softly, I say, "Goodbye Leslie." And slice my blade across his throat.

It's well after dark by the time I make it back to Paige's work. Normally clean up wouldn't take as long but I needed to take extra precautions because of the impulsivity of the murders. Each body had to have all identifying markers removed, be chopped into small pieces, and deposited in the few barrels of lye I have stored away. That shit is expensive and hard to come across discreetly so I use it as a last resort only. It was a long, arduous, and messy process which required a brief stop at home to shower and change.

Under the cover of night, I pull up to the shop and watch through the windows. Feeling another pang of jealousy and fury, I grip the wheel tightly. Paige is standing with her attention on the cell phone in her hand, worry lining her face. At one point she smirks and some of the concern eases from her features.

She really is such a gorgeous thing. A goddess tucked inside a mortal's flesh.

After a few minutes, she slips her phone away and begins working her way throughout the small building, gathering up trash bags. Another wave of anger flows through me as I realize she is, yet again, alone in the shop and will be venturing into the dark alley by herself. I hop out of my vehicle and shut the door more forcefully than I mean to. Stomping toward the entrance I stumble into a patio table, leaping back as it crashes to the ground with a loud bang. I curse as I attempt to quickly right the table. The sound of the door opening causes me to rush back into the shadows and run into another piece of metal furniture.

Fucking hell, where did all these things come from?

Cursing quietly again, I look up and watch in horror as I see Paige lose her balance and begin to fall backward. I reach out uselessly to catch her but I'm still several feet away and won't make it in time even if I run. Helplessly, I'm forced to witness her slice open the palm of her hand before landing with a hard thud on her plump ass. Her eyes dart around with a look of embarrassment as she rushes back to her feet before flying inside and locking the door.

I wait a few heartbeats before sneaking over to the accident scene, looking around for the cause of her pain. I notice a small piece of metal sticking out from the bottom of the window with a few dots of blood. I kick the piece with all the pent up fury pulsing inside me and smugly watch it clatter off in the distance.

Nothing hurts my woman without answering to me, not even a building.

I peek through the window and don't see Paige anywhere. Darting my eyes around the space, I notice the alley door propped open and curse again before making my way around the building. As I round the corner, I'm greeted with the sight of her stiffly walking toward the large garbage bins, clutching the bags in her hands like a smelly shield. I intend to keep my distance but then notice the bandage wrap around her left hand and find my feet moving forward without my permission.

She freezes.

I keep moving.

Her chest rises heavily up and down.

I'm now just a few steps away, hand reaching forward.

Paige drops the bags and darts away, her long braid smacking against her back with each footfall. Sighing in exacerbation, I take off after her. Warring feelings of lust, rage, pride, and worry crash inside of me, building up a tumultuous storm.

This woman is going to be the death of me, I can already feel it. But what a sweet and glorious end. I would choose to lay down my life a thousand times over just for a moment with her existence.

May the devil help the world once I have a taste of her.

Chapter 8

Paige

Breathing heavily, I curse myself for skipping leg day. Okay, fine, skipping everything day. I don't work out, and I'm *really* starting to regret that.

At first I was relieved because I didn't hear anyone behind me but when I had to pause to heave in a breath, the sound of pounding footsteps much to close filled my ears and I took off again. Sobs keep trying to build but I shove them down with everything I have. If I start crying, I'm going to trip and fall. I need to keep a level head and figure a way out of this. There's got to be something.

My eyes dart back and forth across the empty streets. All the stores have already closed and employees left for the evening. A desperate noise leaves me, eyes still searching for anywhere I can duck away and hide.

I don't want to die, I'm not ready. I just got my life back and, sure, I haven't exactly been living but I can. If I make it through this. God? Goddess? I don't know, Buddha? Anyone? I would really, really, really *appreciate it if you helped me not die tonight at the hand of some crazy person. I don't know what to offer but I can promise I'll try to do something more with my life if you help me out of this alive.*

Huffing, I feel the tears prick at the corners of my eyes and know I won't be able to hold them off much longer.

Then, up ahead, I see a bar lit up. I swear there's a glow around the entrance, like a beam of holy light inviting me in answer to my desperate pleas. I sob and send out a silent thank you and push my legs harder. Waving my arms desperately as I get closer in hopes someone will step out and come to my aid.

I run harder, pushing with all of my remaining strength, closing the distance.

I'm only a few blocks away now. I've got this. I can make it. I'll run inside and call for help. Just a little farth-

A scream is ripped from my throat as arms encircle my waist and yank me back into a hard body, the sound abruptly cut off as a large hand clamps over my mouth. I twist and kick, flinging my body around, futilely trying to free myself. Despair washes over me, snuffing out any remaining hope I had as I slump in defeat. The hand on my mouth shifts up and two fingers pinch my nose while still covering my lips. My eyes bulge as I try to drag in a breath, but it's useless. This stranger is too big, too strong, too determined.

With one last attempt to free myself, I jerk against the hold.

Darkness clouds my vision and I slip away.

I wake with a gasp and suck in a large breath.

I'm alive.

Relief only lasts for a few seconds as I try to sit up and find my body won't move. Panic sets in as I start yanking my arms and legs only to meet resistance. I lift my head and look down at my body. My legs are stretched apart and each ankle strapped to a bedpost. A quick glance shows my arms are similarly bound. My heart rate accelerates and my breaths speed up.

I'm chained to a bed. I'm fucking strapped down on some psychos bed.

I notice that my clothes are still intact but can't find it in myself to feel any relief at the realization.

I wildly look around the room. It's a large room with minimal decorations. Dark neutral tones of black and gray make up the majority of the space with speckles of deep red scattered throughout. Craning my head back, I see a large painting hanging above the bed and suck in a harsh breath. It's beautiful but something about it makes a shudder run through my body. I'm transfixed on the image, a familiarity tugging at the back of my mind.

The frame is midnight black, the canvas itself stark white. Speckles of crimson decorate the canvas. Several larger spots fill the center, a depth to them with darker hues running inside the pools.

As I continue staring at the disconcerting painting, I realize why it looks so familiar.

All the larger pools form around each other to build a heart. An anatomical human heart.

My eyes widen further.

This is sick. Like, needs professional help, sick. And I'm stuck here with the person who decided to hang a bloody heart painting above their bed, tied up to said bed.

Fully hyperventilating, I desperately yank at the binds, sobbing as fear consumes me. The restraints don't give even an inch. Hopelessness crushes me as I fall back and cry.

I'm not sure how long I've laid in the bed alone. After a while, my tears dried up and I just stared up at the ceiling. I have moved past hysteria and find only emptiness now, resigned to my fate.

When I hear the door creak open, I keep my gaze fixed, still staring at the ceiling. Footsteps make their way up to the side of the bed. The sound of something being set down next to my head precedes a soft clinking noise. I feel the depression in the bed as the kidnapper sits on the mattress next to me.

My eyes remain trained up, mentally tracing the various patterns. I hear the sound of someone clearing their throat and what sounds like hands rubbing against fabric.

Am I making you uncomfortable? Ha!

I fight to keep my face neutral at the thought.

Another throat clearing then a firm, "Paige." I squeeze my eyes shut.

I know that voice. I know *that voice. But from where?*

"Paige, look at me." I shake my head, still trying to place the sound. A sigh precedes the feeling of a hand gripping my jaw. I flinch away but the hand only tightens and forces my head to face my captor. "Open your eyes. Look at me." I peek open one eyelid and gasp, blinking several times then fixing a wide eyed stare at the man sitting before me.

What. The. FUCK.

"Mick?" My voice is barely a whisper and I curse myself for how shaky it sounds. Mick watches me intently, hand still firmly grasping my chin. He nods and shifts his hand so he can stroke my cheek with this thumb. He's still as breathtaking as the last time I saw him. His beard has grown at least another inch but his curly blonde hair has been trimmed back so the soft locks fall to the middle of his forehead rather than his eyeline.

My eyes trail down and I can't help but fixate on his mouth as his tongue flicks out and licks along the bottom lip.

The image of him putting those lips on me, the feel of them as he kisses and licks my pussy, invade my thoughts. I try to clench my thighs together against the flood of heat they cause but find the straps don't allow for the movement. Mentally cursing at myself, I flick my eyes back up and see that the motion didn't escape his attention. His eyes have darkened with lust, a hunger reflecting back at me before they rake down my body. I swallow the lump in my throat and try to keep my voice even as I ask, "Mick, why am I here?"

He looks back up and replies confidently, "Because you are mine." He says it with such conviction, like he's stating a well-known fact rather than an insane declaration.

My brain stutters.

I'm sorry, what?

I laugh out loud, I really can't help but laugh.

He's joking, this is some twisted prank. Fucked up and we are going to have to have a long talk and maybe a piece of paper that says he can't get within five hundred feet of me, but he can't *be serious.*

The look he gives me causes the laughter to die in my throat. "What?" I squeak. "I'm not yours."

He reaches out with his other hand and softly brushes back the hair surrounding my face, having fallen from my braid in my struggle to get free. He leans forward, his face only a few inches from mine as he whispers, "Yes, you are, little bird." I suck in a breath but he continues. "You are mine and now that I've caught you, I won't ever let you go." His breath washes over my face as we stare at each other, neither of us blinking or looking away.

A small voice in the back of my mind is screaming at me to move, to do something to get away from this deranged man. I can't move, though,

I'm transfixed by the deadly creature staring at me. I know I need to say something to convince him to let me go but I find myself leaning in instead, responding to the desire in his eyes.

His breaths become heavy and his lids start to droop, heavy with lust. The hand on my hair tightens its hold and pulls back, causing me to suck in a sharp breath. He hums his approval and leans away, glancing down to my pebbled nipples pressing against the thin material of my shirt. Dragging his eyes back up, he smirks and wets his lips again. "Perfect. So fucking perfect."

I force down the moan that tries to escape and glare at him. His smirk deepens and he leans forward, trapping a nipple between his teeth. Applying enough pressure that a twinge of pain flashes before pleasure shoots straight through my core. I can't stop the moan this time and my back arches into him at the same time I pull against the restraints again. He releases my nipple and moves up, placing a kiss against my throat before licking the length of my jaw and nipping at the skin on my pulse point. Another wave of desire floods me, overwhelming any rational thoughts I have.

Aware of the reactions he's causing, he continues to kiss, lick and nip along my throat. Taking my earlobe between his teeth, the pressure of his mouth and the sound of his heavy breathing thundering so close to my ear elicit another throaty moan out of me. He growls in response, removes his teeth, and leans back so he can look down at me. "You are mine. But I can't allow you to have too much pleasure yet. You need a punishment for your actions first." I stare up at him in confusion, shaking my head. He growls again. "Yes. You have been such a naughty girl, little bird." He runs his hand down my face, fingers gliding past my throat, between my breasts, and landing on my stomach. "You caused me to be rather sloppy today, and I don't enjoy taking unnecessary risks." He presses his hand down. "Two men died today because you flaunted this body for someone else." His fingers snake under the hem of my shirt and curl around the waistband of my leggings. "Showed off your lucious ass to a couple of assholes."

My brain is too far lost to terror and lust to understand what he's saying. I gasp as he yanks his hand down, ripping the material apart. He continues to pull at my leggings until they're pooled around my ankles. My mind finally sharpens and I'm about to demand what he's doing when he slips out a small knife and moves down between my feet. I still, terrified of making the wrong move.

"No one else gets to enjoy this body. No one else gets to have your smiles. You. Are. *Mine*." He punctuates the last word by slicing through the material and ripping off what's left of the leggings, tossing them to the side of the room. I whimper and press harder into the mattress. This only seems to make him more angry. He shoves the blade behind him. Returning, he runs both his hands up my bound legs, fingers digging into my skin as he approaches my center.

I stare at him, mouth parted and panting.

I'm so confused, I shouldn't be this turned on by the man who kidnapped me, tied me to a bed and...wait, did he just say two people died? Because of me?

"What do you mean two people are dead?" I demand, proud that my voice came out stronger than I expected.

He chuckles as he pauses his ascent, sliding his hands inward so he's gripping my inner thighs. "I killed them." I let out a sound I'm not entirely sure is human.

He killed them? He murdered two people and is just admitting it? Who the fuck is this man?

He darts his eyes up to meet mine as he pushes apart my legs farther. "I told you, no one else gets you. They had to pay for their actions, as do you." He leans forward and pulls my panties to the side with his teeth before returning and taking my pussy with his mouth. I cry out as his warm tongue circles my clit.

I should tell him to stop, I need *to tell him to stop but his mouth is working miracles.*

He runs his tongue back down through my slit and plunges inside my pussy, fingers tightening on my thighs. I moan and cry, writhing against his hold as he devours me. His nose brushes against my clit and I can feel my orgasm building inside.

No. You cannot come on the face of the man that just admitted to murdering two people in cold blood.

"Stop." I beg, even as I push further against him. "Don't. Please, stop." I'm panting as the pressure continues to build. He ignores my pleas and continues his assault on my pussy, pushing me closer and closer to climax. "No!" I scream as I come. Tears pour down my face, my body jerking through the most intense orgasm I've ever experienced.

Even as I start to come down, Mick keeps his face buried in my pussy. Peppering kisses against my lips, lingering briefly on my clit before turning and biting the skin of my thigh. I gasp and try to pull away, more tears falling. He finally pulls back and sits up, licking his lips. "Hmm. Even more delicious than I imagined." He takes in my tear-streaked face and leans forward, hovering dangerously close, only a few inches separating our lips now. "I'm already addicted to you." He leans forward to kiss me and I jerk my head to the side so his lips land on my cheek instead.

With a sound of angry frustration, he yanks my face back and forcefully presses his lips against mine. His tongue darts out and pries apart my lips so he can devour my mouth with as much ferocity as he did my pussy. His kiss is hungry, demanding and claiming. I fight against him as hard as I am fighting against myself.

After several long moments, he releases me and backs up so he is sitting between my legs. I pull my arms again, knowing it's useless but

I need to do something. I need to keep reminding myself that I am in danger and I can't give into my body's demands to beg Mick to fuck me. The sting of rope rubbing against my raw skin brings back enough clarity to fight the urge and bite down on my tongue.

Undeterred by my escape attempts, he reaches behind him and grabs hold of the knife again. I watch in horror as he brings the blade down to my skin, pressing lightly. I lock my muscles and remain as still as possible while he glides the blade across my exposed legs. His hand slides up slowly until the tip of the knife slips under the side of my thong. With a flick of his wrist, he slices through the thin material on one side and moves the blade across my skin over to the other side, cutting it as well. Mick tears the destroyed fabric from me and shoves them into his pocket with a wicked smile.

I'm frozen, watching and silently begging him to stop. He doesn't.

Pushing up my shirt, he exposes my bra before continuing his slow ascent. He circles the knife tip along my belly button then moves farther upward. Reaching my chest, he angles the blade under the center of my bra and slices it apart. My heavy breaths push the cups off, exposing most of my breasts. Still not enough for him, Mick uses his other hand to free both fully from the padding.

He stares down at me, a look of adoration and wonder on his face. He gently massages one of my breasts while moving the blade to my other. Circling my nipple with the sharp point, he adjusts his wrist and pushes the flat side of the knife against my aching nipple. Pressing down firmly with the blade, he pinches the other between his fingers and I moan, fighting against the urge to arch into the sensation. Heat floods me again and the ache between my legs demands attention.

Mick focuses on my chest, lightly rolling the nipple between his fingers before leaning forward and replacing them with his mouth. Groaning, my hips lift in desperate search of relief. He slides his now free hand down my side, gripping my hip roughly and pressing down harder with the knife still on my breast. I make a noise of pleasure, pain, and need as I press my head back into the bed. He squeezes my hip and then moves his hand again, gliding across my stomach, moving down until I feel his fingers slip between my thighs. I cry out in relief when he begins circling my clit, causing a groan of approval to leave him.

He sucks on my nipple and pushes two fingers inside of me. I arch into his touch and gasp as I feel a sharp pain on my chest. Quickly lifting my head, I glance down to see the knife has penetrated my skin, small trails of blood leaking down each side of the sharp blade. I look over and see Mick's attention also on the knife with a look I can't decipher. When he gazes up at me, I whimper as I realize the look in his eyes is past hunger.

He's ravenous. And now that he's caught the scent of my blood, he wants more.

Gently removing the blade from my skin, he pulls his fingers from my pussy. Shifting, he lowers his mouth over my injured breast at the same time he shoves his fingers back inside of me. I scream and lift up from the bed. He doesn't stop. His tongue lapping at my bleeding nipple and fingers fucking me, hitting a spot inside that's causing stars to fill my vision.

Just as I think I'm going to pass out, his thumb presses against my clit and I explode. My mouth falls open in a silent scream, my whole body tensing as waves of pleasure overwhelm me.

Mick pulls his fingers from me with a loud squishing noise that makes me cringe. Pressing a kiss to my injury, he leans back again before slipping his fingers into his mouth. Eyes locked on mine, he sucks my arousal off his fingers and groans.

I start to pant.

Fuck. Why is that so hot?

Groaning again, he pulls his fingers from his mouth and adjusts his cock. I had been too focused on everything else before to notice the stiff peak in his sweatpants. I notice now, and I really notice because *holy shit,* it's massive.

Lifting my eyes, I find Mick smirking back at me and feel my face flush from embarrassment. Shifting once more, he kneels between my legs. "I want to fuck you so badly Paige." His voice is strained, eyes zeroed in on my dripping pussy. "I want to claim you with my cock. Mark you on the inside." Running a hand down his face, he lets out a pained sigh.

I'm caught between the intense desire for him and the rational part of me that knows this has already gone too far and I need to find a way to stop it. Mick appears to be having his own internal war as he fiddles with the knife still in his other hand.

That voice in my head continues screaming at me to get away, reminding me of the danger I'm in.

It's not like I can do anything to stop it. I'm literally tied up.

I pull against the rope again to accentuate the thought. The voice doesn't let up, continuing its assault on my brain.

Great, I've lost it. I'm literally arguing with myself while a man is staring at my pussy. I'm dreaming, right? Maybe this is what an acid trip is like. Did I take drugs and not realize it? Huh, that would make more sense than this. *Okay, think. What will get me to wake up? I can't pinch myself. Screaming obviously didn't help. Umm, maybe if I just tell myself to wake up? Okay. Wake up. WAKE up. WAKE UP.*

I don't realize I'm yelling until I feel a hand clamp down on my mouth.

"I would appreciate you not screaming, little bird." Mick pauses and chuckles. "Well, not like that." He peers down at me, stroking my cheek. "You're not asleep. There's nothing to wake up from." Tears fill my eyes as I look up at him, reality crashing into me again. "Shh. It's okay. I'll take care of you." Stroking my cheek one more time, he shifts back and grasps the end of the knife blade, releasing the handle. I watch in horror as he reaches up and begins pushing the hilt inside of me. "There you go. Take my knife like a good girl." Groaning, he works the knife in and out of my pussy, holding tightly to the blade.

I gasp as I feel each inch of the cold, hard material sliding inside of me. My walls clench around the intrusion, the feeling of arousal heightened by fear, knowing the smallest slip of his hand will cut into my sensitive flesh. My breast pulses, a reminder of the real possibility that poses.

Mick pushes the blade further inside until I feel the edge of the hilt hit my lips. He stills his hand and I can feel a slight shifting before he resumes the motions, fucking me with the knife.

"Please stop." I whisper, voice cracking in fear.

He shushes me again and speeds up his movement. The wet sounds coming from the movement grow louder as my core flames with heat and my traitorous body becomes more aroused. "No." I try again, not sure if I'm saying it more to Mick or to myself.

I can feel myself getting close again and try to fight against the approaching orgasm.

I've already let this man take so much from me, I can't let this happen. I won't.

Squeezing my eyes shut, I try to disconnect from the sensations, pushing against the pleasure spreading through me.

I hear a ruffle of clothing then a grunt. Opening my eyes, I look down to see Mick has pulled his cock out and is furiously jerking himself in time with the thrust of his blade.

Any hope I had of staving off my impending release disappears as I watch his hand slide up and down, thumb flicking over the head. I cry out as another earth shattering orgasm rips through my body. Mick roars out his own release and I feel the splash of warmth from his cum landing on my leg. The knife is pulled from me and I wince at the loss. Shame floods me as I watch him tuck away his dick before rising from the bed.

Returning to staring at the ceiling, I will myself not to cry. Not yet. But no matter how much I fight against them, I can't keep the silent tears from rolling down the side of my face.

I don't look when Mick returns and wipes me clean with a warm cloth. I don't react when he cleans my breast and pulls my shirt down again. I don't say anything when he lays a blanket over my body.

I continue to stare at the ceiling long after he leaves the room. Only one thought repeating over and over inside my head.

I am so fucked.

Chapter 9

Mick

Fuck. Shit. Fuck.

Running a hand over my face, I drop my head between my knees. I didn't mean to take things as far as I did with Paige last night. I had intended on going in there and scaring her, planning to dole out her punishment later. But the sight of her tied up on my bed, and when she looked at me, said my name.

Fuck.

I lost myself to her. Her body called to me in a way I've never known.

She was so responsive too. Even as she begged me to stop with her words, her body screamed for me to keep going. Her dripping cunt at the mixture of pleasure and pain I was delivering almost had me throwing all sense to the wind and fucking her. It wasn't until I heard her yelling to wake up that I regained any control again.

Paige needed to be punished, not rewarded with my cock. She earned my knife as much as the two men currently dissolving in my kill room. Smirking, I remember how her orgasm racked her body around my blade. It would seem my raven-haired girl is as fucked up as I am.

Groaning, I run my hand through my hair and sit up while adjusting my now hard dick. I look at the door to my room with longing, debating if I have enough time to go visit her and find out how much more depraved she is.

My phone dings, reminding me I'm already late. I sigh and push off the couch. Snatching my keys, I head toward the door and pull out my phone to see the message.

Rick

You on your way?

Me

Heading out now.

Rick

Good. We can't afford to mess this up.

Rolling my eyes, I remind myself for the thousandth time why I need the little prick. The only reason he's still breathing, despite the pain in my ass he's proven to be.

Me

Yeah, got it. Be there soon.

Sliding my phone in my pocket, I make sure the front door is locked before jogging to my car. I'm not usually worried about someone breaking into my home but can't risk anyone stumbling on my sweet little captive while I'm away.

I can't stop the smile spreading across my face as I think of her again and imagine all the things I'm going to do to her when I get home.

Just wait, little bird. You'll really see what it means to be mine soon.

"As you can see, we have planned for any possible contingencies. The market can be rather unpredictable and right now is the perfect time to break ground on a new renovation." I keep my irritated groan inside as Rick continues with his spiel. He really is such a kissass and it grates at my nerves. It is, however, also why I keep him on as my top sales employee.

If you ask me, reputation should be enough and potential clients should come to us. Recent years have seen a shift in the market, though, that has required more and more of these menial sales pitches to obtain new contracts.

When I started my construction business years ago, it was just me and a few buddies working on bids by word of mouth. We did a really good fucking job, so we quickly outgrew just the few of us and I started expanding the business. Now I own one of the most successful construction businesses in the Santa Fe area. The fact that we still have to have these meetings makes my teeth grind, even as I keep a neutral expression on my face and periodically nod encouragement.

Rick gestures to the folders in front of the handful of men and women in the room. "Inside the packets we have prepared are quotes lining out the estimated costs of material, labor, and time. As well as some examples of recent projects we have completed so you are able to get a visual idea of how we are able to accommodate various designs." He smiles widely and clasps his hands together, signaling the end of his pitch.

I clear my throat and all eyes turn to me. "Thank you Rick." He inclines his head to me before taking a seat. I look around and make sure to meet every person in the eye before continuing. "I have been the owner of Mickstruction since day one and built my company from the ground up with my bare hands. I take great pride in providing quality results and not fucking with your time or money." A few chuckles sound, I smirk.

It's important to emphasize we won't just run away with their money. The industry has left a bad taste in many people's mouths due to contractors neglecting their work. "With all that being said, I won't bend over or beg for your business." Rick's eyes widen and he lets out a nervous laugh. Ignoring him, I press on, not in the mood to deal with this bullshit. "You'll see the good work we do in those packets and if you ask anyone who has previously hired us, they are all more than pleased." I stand up and tuck my hands into my pockets. "I look forward to hearing from you." I nod my head and, without looking around the room again, I leave.

Heading out, I greet Rachel, the company receptionist. She tucks a lock of hair behind her ear and glances down quickly. Laughing softly, I press the button for the elevator and climb inside. Rachel looks up and sends an awkward wave and calls out, "Have a good night, Mr. Pullson." I nod at her as the elevator doors close.

The elevator dings open to the parking lot and I stride toward my car, my thoughts again drifting to the woman in my bed. Whistling, I slide into my car and pull out onto the street. My dashboard lights up with an incoming call and I let out a heavy sigh before clicking to answer. "What do you want Veronica?"

She huffs before answering. "Really Mick? That's what you have to say to me after fucking me, running out, and then ghosting me for weeks?"

I forgot how whiny her voice is. What did I ever find desirable about this woman?

The sound of Paige saying my name fills my head and I shift in my seat. I debate hanging up but decide I might as well get this conversation over with and, hopefully, put a stop to the incessant texts. "What do you want Veronica? I'm kind of busy."

"I want you, Mick." She whines. "I miss you. I'm really sorry for those things I said, I don't care if you leave right after. I just need you."

Taking a deep breath to resist snapping at her, I slowly let it out before replying. "In case my silence wasn't enough of a hint." *Which apparently it wasn't.* "I'm done Veronica. We had our fun and now it's over. Time to move on." I hear her sniffling on the other end of the line and roll my eyes. It was a mistake to ever get involved with this woman. I usually just stuck to one-night stands but had found her to be a decent enough fuck. I also enjoyed the convenience of having her just a text away and the no-strings situationship we were in. At least I had thought that's what it was.

She sniffles again. "What did I do wrong?" She sounds so pathetic I can't help but sigh.

"Nothing. It's just over."

"But-"

"No buts. We're done. I won't repeat myself again." I end the call before she can say anything else. I can feel the anger burning underneath my skin. The release from Adam and Leslie had staved off the itch but between the bullshit of that meeting, Veronica, and not being able to fully claim my woman, I can feel the need for blood growing again.

I glance at the clock and note it's just about 4pm. I have enough time to swing by my spot to restock the supplies I used before picking up food for myself and Paige. With a quick spin of the wheel, I turn and head off, pressing my foot on the gas to speed up.

The quicker I can get home, the quicker I can look into those mesmerizing amber eyes and release some of this tension.

Entering the front door, a frustrated cry reaches me. I quickly drop everything on the counter and fly to the bedroom, flinging open the door. Paige lies on the bed, yanking against the binds on her arms, letting out a growl as the rope rubs against her raw flesh. She does this several times before flinging her head back and releasing an angry scream.

I lean against the doorframe and let out a chuckle, my eyes raking over her. She's kicked off most of the blanket, exposing her bare body. The shirt she still has on has ridden up so the underside of her breasts are also on display. I reach up and rub my jaw, licking my lips as I gaze at her.

Hearing me, she whips her head in my direction and fixes me with a heated glare. I stare right back at her, amusement barely contained. Still glaring at me, she purses her lips and spits in my direction. I watch as the saliva flies out and lands just past the bed, quirking an eyebrow. Unperturbed by the failed attempt, Paige shuffles her arms and flips me off with both hands. After a brief second of stunned silence, I burst out laughing.

Angered further, Paige lets out another angry shriek. "This isn't funny asshole!" I laugh harder, earning me another glare. "Do you have any idea how terrible it is to be left strapped to a bed all day? Not to mention the shit you pulled last night." My laughter dies off as memories of just that flash through my mind. Realizing her mistake, she quickly continues, but this time her angry shouts have slipped to an embarrassed whisper. "Or how awful it is to have to use the bathroom but you can't move?" After a small pause, she mutters, barely loud enough for me to hear, "I'm lucky I haven't soiled the bed." Her cheeks flame and she averts her gaze back to the ceiling.

I've noticed this has become a habit for her and glance up to the ceiling as well, curious what she finds comfort in to keep returning her attention to the spot.

When she doesn't continue, I push off the door and quietly make my way to the bed. Sitting down on the mattress, I gently push her hair back out of her face. She flinches away but keeps her gaze up, refusing to look my way. "Paige." When she doesn't react, the familiar anger burns again. Gripping her jaw, I force her face toward me but the stubborn woman keeps her eyes averted. "Look at me." I growl, squeezing my fingers.

I wait until she finally shifts her gaze to meet mine. It takes me a moment before I can say anything else, getting lost in her eyes. I clear my throat, trying to regain a little composure. "I'm not sorry for tying you up." She tries to say something but I squeeze my fingers again in warning and she quickly shuts her lips. Nodding my approval, I continue. "Nor am I sorry for giving you the best orgasms of your life." Her eyes twinkle with rage but she can't deny what I said was true and we both know it. My tone softens, "I am sorry. Truly sorry, for not realizing you would need to relieve yourself. I won't make that mistake again. I promise."

Paige stares up at me, conflicting emotions warring across her face. I continue to hold her chin a few more moments before stroking my thumb across her lower lip. She parts her lips and inhales a heavy breath. Unable to help myself, I push my thumb into her mouth, grunting as she bites down hard. "This mouth is divine. I'm dying to get these pretty lips spread over my cock." She tries to hide the whimper my words cause and I smirk, tugging my thumb out of her mouth. Glancing at it, I can see she has broken the skin and a small line of blood has formed on the imprints her teeth left. "I suppose we'll have to wait for that though. I'm quite fond of my dick and worried you might try to bite it off at the present." I wink at her and the look she gives me confirms she would, in fact, try to do just that.

I push off the bed with a sigh, "If I remove these binds so you can use the bathroom, can I trust you not to run?" I watch her face closely and see the moment she realizes that, even if she were to try to run, I would catch her.

That's right, little bird. I'll always catch you. You fell into my trap and I have your scent now. There's nowhere you can run, nowhere you can hide, that I won't seek you out.

She finally gives me a sharp nod and a wide grin stretches across my face. "Perfect. Let me just help you with these pesky things then." I go to the dresser and pull out my knife, my cock twitching as memories of where it was last replay.

I adjust myself before heading to the foot of the bed. Gripping her foot, I pause before cutting off the rope. "I'm sure I don't need to tell you, but just so we're clear. If you try anything, I will tie you back up with chains and you will not be given another opportunity. You'll have to live in your piss and shit until I decide to fuck you again. At which point, I will drag your chained body to the shower to clean off your filth before making you dirty again." I look up into her horrified eyes. "You think I'm evil. You think what I've done to you is terrible. But I can assure you, little bird, this is nothing. You do not want me to become angry with you. Am I clear?" I cock an eyebrow at her and wait for her response.

She whimpers as a tear slides down her cheek. I track the movement before returning my gaze to meet her watery eyes. She nods again and whispers, "Yes. I understand." Returning her nod, I make quick work of releasing her from the restraints.

Paige sits up and rubs her wrists, staring down at the floor and worrying her bottom lip. I round the bed again and place my fingers under her chin, lifting her head up. "Good girl." She bites her lip harder. "Now let me show you the restroom." I step back and gesture for her to rise. Once she has stood, I place my hand under her elbow and gently guide her out of the room.

While she relieves herself, I make quick work to set up the table with the food I picked up on the way home. Humming to myself, I can't remember the last time I felt like this. The emotion is almost foreign and hard to place.

It's not until I see Paige exit the bathroom, dressed in one of my shirts and a pair of my sweats, hair tied up in a messy bun. Biting her bottom lip and wringing her hands, while looking up at me through her lashes.

It's not until I see her that the word hits me.

Happiness.

Jesse

Dude what the fuck?

I try to keep my irritation down, I knew I was going to hear from Jesse eventually after the meeting earlier. Honestly, I'm surprised it took so long for Rick to run his whiny ass over to tell on me. Not that I have to answer to anyone, it's the reason I started my own goddamn company. I don't play well with others and I really don't do well with people telling me what to do. Pushing down my frustration, I type out a response.

Me

What?

I stifle a laugh, knowing it's just going to piss him off more. The little bubbles pop up and disappear several times and I can't stop the chuckle at the image of Jesse wringing the phone imaging it's my neck.

At the sound, I glance over to make sure I haven't awoken Paige.

I was surprised when she fell asleep on the couch, though I suppose she felt just as safe there as anywhere else in my home. That is to say, not at all.

I feel bad about threatening her earlier but I really can't afford her trying to escape. My plans for tomorrow cannot be put off, it's my only clean window and I can't wait the several weeks it would take to secure another victim.

I reach over and tenderly brush the back of my hand across her forehead, stilling as she shifts in her sleep. She's breathtaking, even without makeup and a little drool spilling out the side of her mouth. My eyes trail down her body again, hidden underneath my clothes. I never thought I'd find a woman wearing my things so hot, but the desire to rip them off of her and plunge my cock inside of her wet cunt nearly overtakes me every time I look at her. The sight of her in the clothes feels like another way of claiming her as my own.

My phone dings again and I force myself to look away from the goddess lying next to me.

Jesse

Don't be a dick. You know what I'm talking about. Those were huge clients. They could have brought in millions of dollars worth of business Mick. Millions.

I roll my eyes and am about to reply when I see the text bubbles pop up again.

Jesse

*I know this is your company *eye roll emoji* but you gotta think about other people too dude. The world has changed and we have to play the game now just like everyone else.*

Jesse

I swear I'm just trying to help.

I scrub a hand over my face, I know Jesse is right but I still fucking hate it. Deciding I can't deal with anymore of this shit tonight, I respond with something I know will placate him and at least get him off my back for now.

Me

I know man. I know. Look, it's been a long day,
let's talk about it tomorrow, yeah?

Jesse's reply is instant. A simple "k".

I groan and put my phone down. Very few people could speak to me the way Jesse can without ending up six feet underground. It's the reason he has to play mediator a lot and is my second hand at Mickstruction. Not that anyone is aware of my extracurricular activities, but one look at me when I'm in a mood is clearly enough to warn people to stay the fuck away.

My mind wanders to my plans for tomorrow, running through each detail again to make sure it's solid. It's the first time in years that I've felt a twinge of nervousness. I have to make sure everything goes off without a hitch so I can return to my girl.

My gaze trails over again to the girl in question and a soft smile pulls up my lips.

I'll always come back to her.

CHAPTER 10

PAIGE

Filthy. There's no other word to describe how I feel right now. Even after showering and changing into new clothes.

At first I wanted to refuse to put on the shirt and sweats Mick had placed on the counter for me, but I knew if I didn't wear them I'd have to walk around naked and that was so much worse. Even still, when I opened the door and saw him standing there, staring at me with a possessive heated look, I almost ripped the clothes off and chucked them at his stupid face. Instead, I settled for flipping him off again.

I know it's childish but the little act of defiance made me feel better. And there wasn't much more I could do, he made it very clear things could and would be worse for me if I tried anything. With this in mind, I was good and dutifully ate the food he had brought for me in silence. I only grumbled a little when he insisted on watching a movie together on the couch, like we were on a date or something. I'm really beginning to think the man is unhinged. At the very least he's deluded.

I'm not sure at what point I fell asleep but I must have as I woke up in the bed. Alone, thankfully.

True to his word, Mick didn't tie me up again. However, when I tried to exit the bedroom, I found the door wouldn't open. I had pounded on it until I was certain there was no one else in the house to let me out and, after several more minutes of tugging and kicking proved fruitless, I slumped against the wood and hiccuped a sob.

I let myself stand there and cry for a while until I can't hold off my bladder any longer. Going to the adjoined bathroom, I'm grateful to find this door unlocked. I push inside and fly to the toilet, sighing as I pee.

Think Paige. What are you going to do? You can't just stay locked up in this room waiting for him to return and do god-knows what.

I have a pretty good inkling I know what that is, especially given the look in Mick's eyes every time I had glanced his way last night.

Quickly cleaning myself, I walk to the sink and wash my hands before looking around the counter. There's not much on there, an electric toothbrush, bottle of mouthwash, deodorant and cologne. Along with some hand soap and a small dish off to the side that's probably for his watch or something as I hadn't noticed any jewelry.

Well, at least he's not married. Not that I care. Because I don't, obviously.

Returning to my search, I start pulling open drawers and still find only basic men's bathroom supplies. A comb, some hand towels, a few razors, a beard trimmer. On the third drawer I let out a triumphant shout, plucking out the unopened pack of travel toothbrushes.

Grinning, I rip open the package and quickly squeeze toothpaste on the bristles before aggressively scrubbing my teeth. After brushing my teeth, I swish some mouthwash and turn my gaze to the deodorant sitting on the counter. Glancing at myself in the mirror, I take in my state. My hair is a mess, even thrown up in the bun, several pieces have fallen out around my head. My face is bare of makeup and my eyes are bloodshot from hours of screaming and crying.

Trailing my eyes down, I look at the oversized shirt tucked into the waist of the sweatpants I have cinched to keep them up, the hem pooling at my feet. Mick has already marked me in ways I can't begin to fully process without another breakdown, plus I already smell like him by using his shampoo and body wash. I shrug at my reflection before mumbling "fuck it" and snatching the deodorant. I do a couple quick swipes under both arms and set it back down. Giving myself one last quick look in the mirror, I turn and leave the bathroom, returning to my jail room.

Now that I'm not strapped to the bed, I can really take in the space. It seems even bigger standing in the corner looking around. I note the closet on the far side, a couple end tables on both sides of the bed, and a dresser directly across the bed. My eyes snap back to the dresser and I remember seeing Mick pull the knife out of the top drawer.

He wouldn't have left it there, would he?

Hesitantly, I sneak toward the dresser, glancing around as if someone can see what I'm doing. I take a deep breath and yank open the drawer. Staring down, I blink several times. I reach in with a shaky hand and pull out the small black card sitting atop the clothes. White ink scrawled along it.

Tsk, tsk. Naughty little bird.

I drop the card and shove the drawer closed. My breathing becomes heavy and I slam my hands over my eyes.

This can't be happening. Why is this happening?

With nothing else to do, I crawl back onto the bed and curl up under the covers.

It's not till after dark that I hear the front door slam open and closed. I jolt upright and clutch the blanket to my chest. I'm not sure why but he sounds angry and I'm scared of what that means for me.

I hear the sound of him fiddling with something on the door, then a lock clicks and he pushes it open. My eyes widen at the sight of him.

Mick stands in the doorway, breathing heavily. His hair is pushed back and sticking up in a few spots, damp with something I can't quite make out. His clothes are disheveled and it takes me a moment to realize they're also covered. I narrow my eyes, staring at the stains on his shirt.

Sucking in a breath, my hand flies to my mouth. "Is that...is that blood?"

Mick doesn't say anything, instead he strides into the room and doesn't stop until he's towering over me. His eyes blaze as he stares at me and I shrink back further into the bed. His face flickers before he darts out his hand, wrapping his fingers around my throat. I gasp again and claw at his hand but he only tightens his grip in response. With his other hand, he reaches out and rips the blanket off of me and onto the floor. I curl up and try to distance myself from him as far as I can with my throat still held captive.

Growling, he grips my hip and yanks me back toward him, sliding his hand around to the ties of the sweatpants. With a flick of his wrist, he pulls the tie loose and reaches inside the waistband. I yelp as his fingers roughly brush my clit. He keeps his eyes on mine as he pushes his hand down further and plunges a finger inside of me. I can't move, I can't think. I'm trapped. His prey.

As if he can hear my thoughts, Mick bears his teeth at me and pushes in another finger, stretching me open. I whimper as he begins to scissor his fingers and slowly pull them out before roughly shoving them back in. His fingers flex around my throat, his eyes flashing. I can feel myself growing wetter with each pump of his wrist and curse myself for how much I want this. How much I want *him*. Even after everything, my body responds to him with a growing need.

He leans forward and flicks his tongue out, licking up the side of my face. Stopping to whisper gruffly in my ear, "So ready for me. So goddamn wet. Your pussy is just begging for my cock. Isn't it, little bird?" I whimper again and he chuckles darkly. He nips my ear before pulling back and gazing down at me. My eyes trail up and with his closeness, I can now see that his hair is matted with blood, the blonde locks stained pink from the crimson liquid. I gag at the thought of why he's covered in blood.

At the sound, Mick squeezes his fingers again and groans. My eyes fly back to his and I can see that his pupils have dilated so much there's almost no blue left. It's terrifying, making him look like the predator he really is inside. I'm frozen, my mind racing as I think about the blood covering him and the sound of him saying last night *"I killed them"* replays in my head over and over again.

This man in front of me is a monster, a murderer.

He stares back at me. I'm not sure for how long, it could have been a second or an hour. Time seems to have stopped, the only sound in the room is our heavy breathing and his fingers working in and out of my pussy.

Mick eventually breaks the spell and looks down at my lips, licking his own. He leans in and captures my bottom lip between his teeth, biting down hard. I cry out when he breaks the skin, keeping pressure then releasing and lapping at the wound with his tongue. I groan and he shifts quickly, taking my mouth and shoving his tongue inside. He controls the kiss and commands submission with his rough strokes. I moan into the kiss and chase his tongue with my own, losing myself to the sensations and forgetting why I shouldn't want this.

My hands fly up around his neck and he removes his fingers from inside me. I whimper at the loss and then suck in a sharp breath as he yanks the sweats down, the force he uses pulls them straight off.

Without breaking the kiss, he releases my throat and starts fiddling with his belt before unzipping his pants and shoving them down. Pulling back slightly, I feel him step out of his clothes and climb onto the bed so he's hovering over me. I gaze up at him and try to remind myself of who he is, that I should stop this.

All thoughts flee as I feel the head of his cock sliding across my slit. I arch back as he runs the smooth skin over my clit and back down through the folds, teasing me.

He trails kisses down my face and along my jaw, nipping at my throat before sucking on the sensitive flesh. I'm writhing under him, lost in my desire. I need him to fuck me, I need him more than I've needed anyone. I feel him notch up to my entrance a second before he shoves inside in one brutal thrust. I cry out in relief and pain, dragging my nails down his neck. He grunts, pulling back before slamming back into me.

I'm a blubbering mess, mumbling nonsense and raising my hips to meet him with each thrust. Mick continues his punishing rhythm, making little noise except for the grunts escaping him. It's so unlike how he was the last time he used my body. This feels more like a primal need he's satisfying instead of pleasure. I can feel myself getting wound up, that familiar pressure building inside. Mick senses it too as he moves his head lower to capture my stiff nipple between his teeth.

I cry out as the pain mixes with the pleasure and I'm close, I'm so close to falling over the edge. Tears are falling down my face and I'm begging to let go. "Please. God, fuck. Please Mick." He growls against my skin and slips a hand between us, finding my clit and rubbing quick circles. "Yes. Yes! Oh fuck, I'm so close." I pant, my eyes squeezed tight.

Mick releases my nipple and props himself up with his elbow, using his free hand he grips my jaw and forces my eyes on his. He looks deeply into my eyes and commands, "Come. Now." And I scream, my eyes rolling back as I shatter around him. He groans and pushes into me, fucking me through my orgasm.

As the last tremors begin to subside, he moves again. Gripping both of my hips, he slams into me so hard the bed shakes. After several punishing thrusts, Mick throws his head back and drives deep inside of me, moaning my name as he finishes.

He remains like that, breathing heavily. After several long heartbeats, he leans forward and collapses. Once our breaths have returned to normal, he pushes off of me and rolls off the bed. Without a word, he heads into the bathroom and slams the door shut behind him.

I'm left laying on the bed, staring at the closed door and wondering how the fuck I'm going to get away.

A small part of me, a part I'm not willing to admit, wonders if I really want to.

Chapter 11

Mick

Holy fucking hell. That woman has a divine pussy.

Standing under the hot water, I can feel my cock already beginning to harden at just the memory of her wrapped around me. I slam my hand against the wall and curse myself. I've already become too obsessed with her. The whole time I was hunting down Becky and slicing up her skin, my mind kept wandering back to the woman waiting for me at home.

I've never rushed through a killing before like I did tonight and it's only served to piss me off. I work too damn hard to select the perfect victim and coordinate the most opportune timing to execute my destruction to be this distracted. I needed the release today too that only bloodshed can give me.

Jesse was waiting for me outside my office the second I walked into the building and proceeded to run through all the ways I fucked up the meeting. By the time I left, my hand was trembling with the need to hack something apart.

Waiting for Becky to get her perky ass on the road was torture. A level of torture I happily returned the favor of once she was secured in my kill room. Her screams did little to quiet the chaos inside of me. I sliced, chopped, ripped and plucked every inch of her in an attempt to regain some calm amongst the unrest inside of me. Even as I dumped her mutilated corpse off and set up the display to match the others, the anger rolled inside, demanding more.

When I returned home to silence, my only thought was that Paige had somehow escaped. I could see the locks on my bedroom door that I had installed before leaving in the morning but it didn't stop the fear coursing through my veins. I had slammed the front door and quickly strode across the room, struggling momentarily with the locks before throwing open the door. My heart stopped when I peered inside and caught sight of her lying in my bed, in my clothes, waiting for me.

I stood there in silence, trapped in her spell. When she gasped and whispered, horrified by the blood on me, I moved. I didn't think, I wasn't in control any longer. The monster inside of me clawed its way out and demanded I claim this woman while covered in the blood of its victim.

As I had begun to expect, Paige's inner demons called to mine and responded in ways that took my breath away. When she pleaded to let go, calling out my name, I lost it. It took everything in me to hold off for her to finish, and the feeling of her walls pulsating around my cock was beyond words. Addictive, necessary. I now needed to feel it again and again. A desperate need that mirrors the bloodlust that consumes me.

I reach down and pinch the end of my dick, the pressure building deep has me concerned I'm going to come again just from the ghost of her haunting my thoughts. Cursing again, I make quick work of cleaning the remaining evidence off my skin and hair before stepping out of the shower and wrapping a towel around my waist. I step up to the sink and quickly brush my teeth, my eyes drawing down to the toothbrush laying next to my toothpaste.

I spit into the sink and set my own down and pick up the new brush, bringing it to my lips. She went through my things, found a way to bring comfort, made herself at home. I look into the mirror and find my reflection looking back at me, a wicked grin covering my face.

Paige may try to pretend that she doesn't want to be here, doesn't want me, but she can't lie to herself. She's already coming to accept who she is and who she belongs to.

Slowly setting down the toothbrush, I turn and head back into the bedroom, ready to show her just how much she wants me.

I stretch my arm out and panic when I feel the space beside me is empty. Patting around, I feel that the mattress is cold, meaning it's been empty for a while.

Shooting upright, I look around and don't see Paige anywhere in the room. My eyes narrow on the open bedroom door.

No, she wouldn't dare. I told her what would happen.

A low rumble sounds deep in my chest as I fling back the covers and stalk out of the room. A quick search proves that she did, in fact, dare.

My black-haired beauty has flown away.

Slowly, I make my way back to the bedroom and pull on clothes, steadying myself with deep breaths.

She may have run, but I will find her. When I do, she'll learn that there's no escaping me, not now that I've touched her, tasted her. She's screamed, come and bled for me. There is no longer a her without me and there won't ever again be a me without her.

I step into the bathroom and my attention is immediately drawn to the mirror. Across the glass, scrawled in toothpaste, Paige has left me a message.

I belong to no one.

Chuckling, I relieve myself and finish cleaning up, rereading the note over and over.

As I step out of the house, keys in hand, I feel an excited anticipation building for my hunt.

My little bird thinks she can fly free, we'll see about that.

Chapter 12

Paige

I stumble again, cursing as I scrape my knees and hands before righting myself. I've been at this for hours, trying to find my way back somewhere familiar. I had no idea where Mick had put my phone and couldn't risk searching around to try and find it.

Now I'm wishing I had spent at least a few minutes looking because I'm completely useless without the device. I knew I needed my phone but I didn't realize how dependent I am on the stupid little thing.

UGH. If I get out of this, I'm teaching myself geography, or at least how to read a fucking map.

Not that that particular skill would help me right now, since I don't actually have a map. But it still seems like something I should know how to do for the next time a psychotic, murdering Greek god decides to kidnap me and lock me away in his bedroom to use as his own personal fuck toy.

I groan and scrub my hands across my face, willing the sensations of how he used my body to go away. The amount of shame I feel with myself rivals the resentment I have toward the man.

I think I'm going to need some serious therapy to work through some of these issues. What would they call it? Stockholm syndrome doesn't quite fit because I still loathe the man, it's just my pussy that has fallen head over heels for his dick.

I groan again and smack my face.

Looking up, I see that I've come up on a small diner. I glance around before ducking inside and beelining for the older woman working behind the counter. She looks up with a startled expression before schooling her features and plastering on a smile. "Hi darlin' what can I get for you?"

Trying to push back the embarrassment of my appearance, I lean forward and rush out, "I need to use your phone please. I've been kidnapped and need to call someone to come get me, quickly. Before he wakes up and finds me." I stare at her in desperation as she looks back at me in stunned horror. Reaching forward, I lightly grasp her hand resting on the counter. "Please." I plead, heart hammering.

Shaking herself, the woman extracts her hand from my grip and turns around. Snatching up a phone against the wall, she moves to hand it to me. "Here you go, make your call and we can hide you away in back until your friend is able to come get you." Nodding to me in encouragement, she presses the phone into my hand. I offer her a shaky smile in return.

Turning my attention to the phone, I stare at it, my mind a complete blank.

Motherfucking, stupid, piece of shit, dependent on a cell phone, millennial ass. Why don't you know a single person's phone number?

I glare at the plastic lifeline, mentally berating myself while racking my brain for a phone number. Any number.

I close my eyes and try to picture the screen when I pull up contacts. It's got to be in there somewhere.

Come on Paige. Your life literally depends on you remembering ten digits. Don't let yourself get chained up in your own piss and shit because you can't recall-

My eyes fly open in triumph and I quickly dial the number, slamming the phone against my ear. I'm gripping it so tightly my fingers scream at me. Pleading under my breath for the call to pick up, a sob leaves me as I hear a tentative, "Hello?"

"Taylor!" I scream, making the poor woman in front of me jump. I give her an apologetic look before returning to my call.

"Oh my god, is that you Paige? Where have you been? Everyone has been so worried." I can hear the panic in her tone laced with a twinge of frustration. I feel guilty for worrying her but I'm so grateful to hear her voice that the feeling overpowers any others.

I sob again and try to pull myself together enough to answer. "Tay-Taylor. He kidnapped me." Another sob. "I was at work and he chased me. I was so close to getting away but he was too fast. And then I was tied to a bed. And there was blood, so much blood. And he...he..." I can't get the words to come out of my mouth.

I can hear Taylor's horrified gasp on the other end of the line and her whispering something hurriedly to someone else. "Where are you babe? Beau and I are going to come get you but we need to know where you are."

I glance at the woman again and mouth the question. She responds and I relay it to my friend, more tears falling as she promises they will be here as quickly as possible. With shaky hands, I hang up the phone and fall into the stool next to me.

"Thank you." I whisper, dropping my head into my hands as I break down. "Thank you." I repeat over and over, sobbing the words.

The kind woman pats my back reassuringly, murmuring that I'm safe now. I want to believe her, I want to believe that I'm safe but my ears keep ringing with his words.

"Yes, you are, little bird. You are mine and now that I've caught you, I won't ever let you go."

Taylor and Beau pull up to the diner about forty minutes later and I run into her arms the moment I see her. Tears flowing down both of our faces as we cling to each other.

Beau looks around the small diner, protectively hovering near us. His lanky stature wouldn't fare well against Mick but the rigid tension in his muscles gives hope he'd at least put up a decent fight.

I've never been so thankful for my friend having a steady and stable boyfriend. I'm usually all for being a strong woman and needing no man, but in this moment, when I've been stripped of all my power, I'm grateful to have someone else to lean on.

Pulling back from the embrace, Taylor runs her hands over my hair and frames my face, peering into my eyes. "Babe, we need to get out of here. And, know how much this pains me because you know how I feel about them, and I know how you do too. But...I think we need to call the police." I'm already shaking my head furiously. *No way.* She sighs and places a tender kiss on my forehead. "Okay, let's at least get you home, yeah?"

I look back at her, sniffling. "Can, can I come stay with you guys?" Her eyes soften and I quickly continue in a hushed tone. "He knows where I live, Tay. He broke into my apartment. I know it was him because he left another card for me when I was at his house, it was the same black card with a cryptic handwritten note on it. I can't...I can't go back there and be alone. I can't..." I start crying again and she shushes me, rubbing her hands down my back.

"Of course, P. You can stay with me and Beau for as long as you need." She promises. I see her glance at her boyfriend and feel a twinge of guilt at the concern in her eyes. I wish I didn't need to put them in danger, but I don't have anywhere else to turn.

We stand there for a few moments longer before she ushers me to the door toward their car. I call a thank you to the woman who helped to save me. She smiles back at me with kind eyes and waves me on.

The drive back to their place is quiet. I stare silently out the window while Taylor and Beau have a hushed conversation in the front. Tuning them out, I run over everything that's happened again and cringe. The space between my thighs throbs, an unwelcome memory of all the ways Mick claimed my body last night. I screw my eyes shut and try to will away the memories of how my body claimed him back.

A throat clearing brings my attention back to the present and I turn my head toward my friend. She offers me a soft smile. "Hey, we thought you might be a little hungry, do you feel up to eating if we swing through somewhere and pick up some food?" I nod mutely and her smile widens a little. "Okay. What do you think? I feel like this calls for our hangover cure. It might not be liquor that caused it but I have a feeling you're going to have one hell of a headache." She winks at me and I feel a weak smile spread across my face.

"That sounds great." I whisper, tears pricking my eyes again. I blink them away and wipe the back of my hand against my eyes. The movement causes me to glance down and I realize I'm still wearing Mick's clothes. A choked sob rushes out as I start clawing at the clothing, desperate to get it off my skin.

I faintly hear Taylor calling my name but I can't respond. I can't do anything except get this man off of me. Rough hands gently cover mine and I swing around violently, screaming. The hands retreat and I blink a few times before my eyes focus and disheveled auburn hair fills my vision. Shaking my head to clear away the haze of panic, I meet Beau's worried russet brown eyes. Concern creases his forehead as they dart between Taylor and me, his hands fluttering helplessly, uncertain what to do.

"I'm s-sorry." I sob, rubbing my hands aggressively against my face. "I thought...I thought you were him." I glance up and meet Beau's worried gaze again. "I'm okay. I just, I need to change." I look away again and worry my bottom lip, willing myself to pull it together.

Taylor reaches back and squeezes my knee. "Of course babe, we'll get you home first and then Beau can run for our food while you and I find you something of mine to wear. That sound okay?" I look toward my friend and give her a grateful smile, nodding my head. She glances at her boyfriend and he nods before closing my door and sliding back into the driver's seat. Pulling back onto the road, he speeds up.

The rest of the drive, Taylor speaks softly to me, telling me about nothing and everything. A funny moment at her work, the newest celebrity gossip, a restaurant that is going to be opening in a few months that's been all the talk over social media. I relax into the seat and listen to her voice, letting it lull me into a sense of security. At least for now, I'm safe.

The next few days are filled with phone calls and gestures of sympathy and concern. My boss reached out after Taylor left her a message with a brief explanation on what had happened.

Brandi was concerned when she had come into work the next day and found my bag still in the building, the alley door open, and the trash abandoned a few feet from the garbage bin. She had tried to reach out to me but said my phone kept going straight to voicemail. I had Taylor listed as my emergency contact and when she didn't have any answers either, Brandi grew more concerned and contacted the police. Much to my annoyance.

I couldn't be too upset that she cared, but I had a bad history with law enforcement and no desire to have them sniffing around my life.

After assuring her several times that I was okay and just needed a few days off to readjust, Brandi insisted that I take all the time I needed and to reach out if I needed anything else. She also let me know she would contact the detective in charge and to expect a visit from him. I thanked her and ended the call.

The rest of the calls coming in were from various friends and family expressing their gratitude that I had been found safe. Word had spread thanks to the official missing persons report. I didn't go into detail with any of them on what happened but thanked them each for their concern.

When my mother called me, she was more hysterical than I had been. I had to reassure her that I was alive and okay and force her to agree not to fly out. She spent half the call reminding me that she never thought it was a good idea for me to move out here alone and that she wasn't surprised something had happened.

Taylor had to take the phone from me at that point as I started crying again. I'm not sure what she said because of my own thunderous thoughts but the tone of her voice made it clear she was not happy. After hanging up the call with my horrid mother, Taylor insisted we have ice cream sundaes and binge watch cheesy nineties movies. I gave her a watery smile and agreed. We had then spent the rest of the day doing just that.

It's now been about a week since I escaped Mick's house and the events are starting to feel like a dream. Even when the detective came by to get my statement, I felt disconnected, like I was recalling a movie rather than relaying my own experiences. I'm not sure if I feel grateful or worried at how I feel, but there's not much I can do to change it.

"Miss Greene, just a couple more questions." Detective Lary had droned on. I suppressed a sigh, exhausted from the hours of questioning.

Who knew you'd be treated like a criminal when you were the one that was kidnapped. *Not the one doing the kidnapping!*

Fiddling with my sleeve, I waited for the detective to ask his, what I was hoping to be, last questions. Flipping through the small notepad in his hands, Detective Lary cleared his throat. "Okay. You said you didn't get a good look at the perp." He paused, giving me a look that implied he did not believe that. I fidgeted in my seat at the reminder of the lie.

There was no way I could tell anyone how intimately I came to know my captor.

Biting my lip, I looked away, careful to look up and to the left *not* the right, giving myself a mental pat on the back.

I knew that the time binge watching crime shows would pay off one day, I thought bitterly before straightening my spine.

"Yes, that's right." My voice sounded strange to me, lifeless and disconnected.

"Hmm." I chanced a look back in his direction, catching his eyes roaming over my body when he thought I wasn't looking. My stomach recoiled as disgust filled me.

Okay, I am so done with this. I did not escape a depraved psychotic man to be leered at by a gross detective.

Realizing he had been caught, Detective Lary abruptly stood up, snapping the notepad closed. "Thank you for your time, Miss Greene.

We'll be in touch if we have any further questions." I nodded mutely, avoiding his gaze as he made his way out the door.

Taylor distracted me with another round of sweets and alcohol as we talked about everything but the giant elephant in the room. This became our normal as I recouped under her roof, reminding me so much of when I first moved to New Mexico and all the times we spent together while I barely held my shit together.

God, I love her so much.

However, no matter how much I adore my best friend, I'm looking forward to going back to my apartment. My apartment manager agreed to change the locks and Beau even installed a new camera and security system for me so I feel safer staying there alone.

I take a deep breath as I head to my car, shouldering the small bag of things I've accumulated in my short stay at Taylor's. I owe her big time and I already know I'm going to plan a huge thank you present.

Maybe we can take a girl's cruise. To the Caribbean.

I smile as I picture the two of us sipping on exotic drinks and sunbathing on the cruise deck.

Oh, yes, I am so going to do that.

I'm still smiling as I pull up to my apartment building. It's not until I step out of the elevator and stand outside the door to my apartment that my smile falls away. I stare at the door handle, too afraid to reach forward and open it.

I can't shake the feeling that he's going to be in there waiting for me. It's stupid. I know he's not and multiple people have assured me that they've seen no sign of my elusive kidnapper.

Taking a deep breath, I reach a shaky hand forward and unlock the door, pushing it inward and jumping back. When no one reaches out for me, I take a tentative step forward and peer inside. It's shocking to me how everything is still the same, almost like there should be a physical change in my home after the things that happened.

Squaring my shoulders, I stomp in and shut the door behind me, making sure to lock it and set the new security alarm before venturing farther inside. I glance toward my kitchen and let out a breath of relief when there are no black cards waiting for me.

Huffing a laugh, I shake my head, "That's right Paige, there's no one else here. No one has been here that you haven't given permission to be."

Nodding to myself and embracing my completely normal habit of speaking my thoughts out loud, I make my way to my room and deposit the bag next to my bed. I throw myself down on the mattress and heave a sigh of relief. *I missed this bed.* I'm not a mattress snob but I had paid good money to get the one I liked and being forced to sleep in foreign beds over the last couple weeks had really bummed me out. I close my eyes and allow myself to fully relax.

Life could finally start to get back to normal.

I'm my own person. I get to decide who I belong to. And the only person who can lay claim on me is myself.

Sending a mental middle finger toward the asshole who disrupted my life, I settle into the covers and let my mind drift off to sleep.The words reverberate through my head, a reassuring lullaby as I fade away to a place full of dreams and free from monsters.

I belong to no one.

Chapter 13

Mick

One week. Seven days. One hundred and sixty-eight hours.

That's how long I've had to exist without my little bird. I've bid my time, watched her and waited for the perfect moment to snatch her away again. The woman has not been alone the entire time. My jaw aches from the constant pressure of my teeth grinding as I see her just outside of my reach.

I almost snapped when that man showed up at her apartment and installed a new security system. *I'm* the only man she needs to protect her. My fingers twitched as I slipped into the building behind him and watched him saunter up to her door and stride inside like he owned the place. I would have killed him then and there if the apartment manager hadn't come by to check on the progress. To avoid doing anything reckless, I had stormed away and returned to watching Paige at her friend's condo.

She was so despondent the first few days it made my chest ache. I wanted nothing more than to get to her, offer her comfort, and reassure her that she was safe. But the need to punish her for leaving me outweighed the desire to assuage her despair. She needed to learn that there was no escape from me. Her and I belonged together and I would tear the world apart to prove it to her. These thoughts circled my head endlessly. Plans of how I would bring her to heel played a continuous background in my mind as I watched her.

Thankfully, I have set up my company so that I can disappear for days on end without it causing a hazard to production. After the stunt in my last meeting, I've been banned from meeting with potential clients anyway. Jesse has picked up the slack on that end so he hasn't had time to badger me on my absence. I left a few messages with Rachel over the days, saying I had a personal concern come up and to reschedule any appointments, giving strict instructions to only contact me in the case of an emergency that could not be otherwise handled.

I'm now parked again outside of Paige's apartment building. This time, however, my little bird has returned to her home. Alone. I can feel the devilish grin on my face as I prepare to move forward with taking her back.

I'm just about to step out of the car when someone whips into the parking lot and screeches to a halt. Intrigued, I watch as a man in his early thirties flings open his car door, slams it, and takes off in a sprint for the building. Looking around to make sure no one else sees me, I climb out of my vehicle and make my way inside. I come up behind him as the man repeatedly jabs his finger into the elevator button, mumbling under his breath. Waiting silently, I observe him.

His hair is trimmed short, dark and thick. He has a five o'clock shadow lining his jaw and bags under his eyes from several restless nights. Glancing down, I take in the disheveled appearance of his clothes. His shirt is wrinkled and bunched. The jeans hugging his legs have several creases and stains, looking like he has spent at least the last few days in the same clothes.

The man continues to jam his finger away at the abused button and I stifle my amusement, wiping my face to a neutral expression before clearing my throat. He whips around, eyes darting wildly until his gaze lands on me. The man runs a hand down his face and shakes his shoulders a little to loosen up some of the tension. When he looks back at me, I lift the corner of my lips into a smirk and gesture to the elevator. "I'm not sure that's helping make it come any faster."

He looks sheepishly at the elevator then back at me, blowing out a breath of laughter. "Yeah. Sorry man, I'm just in a hurry." Looking around again, his shoulders slump before continuing. "I got some terrible news about my girl and I need to make sure she's okay."

I nod my understanding, after all, I'm here for the same. "I hope she is." He gives me a small smile and whips around as the elevator doors ding open.

Reaching his hand out he holds open the door. "You coming?" I shake my head and wave him on. I can't have a witness for what I'm planning. He gives me a slight nod and retracts his hand as he clambers inside. "Thanks man." He mutters before the doors close.

I wait patiently for a few minutes before pressing the button for the elevator to return and can't help but smile as I step inside the empty lift. Pressing the button for Paige's floor, I start humming.

Ready or not, here I come.

CHAPTER 14

PAIGE

I'm awoken by a sharp pounding on my door. I jolt upright, heart thudding in my chest. Fumbling around, I grab my new phone and pull up the app for the camera with shaky hands.

It's not him. It's not him. I repeat to myself over and over.

The last few days have been wonderful, I've returned to my old routine and even been able to work a few shifts. The nights have been the scariest alone in my apartment, but nothing has happened and the added security measures have helped me to be able to at least sleep. I'm now reconsidering all of that as I wait for the video feed to load so I can see who the intruder is standing outside my apartment.

When the video finally catches up, I gasp. Pressing the button to speak, my voice comes out shaky. "Seth?" At the mention of his name,

Seth whips his head around, looking erratically up and down the hall until his eyes land on the camera. He gives me a half wave and a small smile. "Seth?" I repeat. "What the fuck are you doing here?"

I'm so shocked I can't be entirely certain I haven't lost my mind. That would be a plausible explanation for my cheating ex-fiancé suddenly appearing at my doorstep. Shaking my head, I push off the bed with weak legs and make my way to the front door. It takes a few moments to turn off the alarm and unlock the door. By the time I have it opened, Seth is standing there wringing his hands. His eyes shoot to me and he rakes his gaze up and down several times before rushing forward and pulling me into his embrace. I'm frozen in shock. He says something but it's muffled against my hair.

Seth squeezes tightly before loosening his grip and holding me back at arms length, looking me over again. "Paige," He breathes. "Fuck. I'm so glad you're okay. I was so worried." His eyes sharpen again as he peers into my eyes. "You are okay, right?" I just stare at him, dumbfounded.

How is this happening? What is happening right now?

He gives me a little shake and repeats, "Paige?"

I blink and finally snap back to reality. Pushing against him, I pull back from his embrace and wrap my arms around myself. "Seth, what are you doing here?" I glance behind him, half-expecting Brie to pop up. Crazier shit has happened. When I don't see anyone else, I look back at him and sigh heavily. "Shit. Okay, come inside. I don't want to stand here with the door open." Seth stares down at me, concern etched into his face. I pull his arm inside and glance around the hall again quickly before slamming the door, twisting the lock, and resetting the alarm. I turn around and find Seth's gaze intently on me, his jaw set in a hard line and expression unreadable. I let out another sigh and gesture for the living area. "Do you want something to drink?"

He nods. "Water would be great. Or a beer if you have one." He runs a hand up the back of his head before heading to the couch and plopping down. I go to the kitchen and pull out a couple beers, popping the caps. Glancing at the clock I shrug, this conversation is going to need some help and it's five o'clock somewhere. Even if it is only nine-thirty in the morning here.

Walking toward the couch, I take in Seth's appearance. He looks like shit, to put it kindly. His hair is trimmed short but he has a shadow of a beard running along his jaw. His clothes look like he hasn't changed them in several days. If I didn't know any better, I'd guess he had driven all the way here.

Looking intently at his face as I hand him the beer, I notice the bags under his eyes and the exhaustion lining his features. "Seth. Did you drive here?" He looks away sheepishly and shrugs. I stare at him, mouth hanging open as I choke out, "Why?"

When he looks back at me, his hazel eyes blaze with an intensity that makes me fidget. "You were in trouble. As soon as I got your call, I started reaching out to contacts in the area. No one had heard anything but then Kristoph got back to me and told me an investigation had been opened into your disappearance. I dropped everything and drove out here. I got the call on the way that you had made it back but I needed to see you to make sure." Seth reaches his hand out and gently brushes against my cheek. I blink at him, absorbing his words. "You are okay, aren't you baby girl?"

The endearment leaving his lips is what finally snaps me from my stupor and I jerk back like he slapped me. Wincing, he lowers his hand and eyes. Glaring at him, I grit out the words. "I'm not your baby girl. Not anymore." Seth winces again but keeps his gaze averted. "You fucking cheated on me, Seth. With my best friend. Where is she, by the why? No, better yet. Why are *you* here?" My mind is racing, none of this makes sense. I didn't call Seth. I'm not sure how he found out but I know for a fact I did not call him. I don't understand why he's here and I really don't understand why he's lying to me, but I just need him to leave. I already have one delusional man to worry about, I don't need another one. "You need to leave." I demand as I come to the decision.

Seth shoots his eyes back up to mine, pleading with me to reconsider. I glare back and don't say anything, arms crossed protectively over my chest. After a long while, he sighs and slumps against the couch. "Okay, I'll leave. I really did just need to make sure you were okay ba-Paige." He closes his eyes and rubs the bridge of his nose.

Goddamnit, I'm not going to cave. I need to hold up my anger.

When he opens his eyes and I see the worry reflected back at me, I lose my hold on the tenuous hostility toward him. No matter what happened between us, this man just drove halfway across the country just to make sure I was okay. Letting out an exacerbated breath, I roll my eyes. "Fine. You can stay here." I hold up a finger as he opens his mouth to speak. "For one night. That's it. Then you need to get your ass back to Pennsylvania and stay out of *my life*." I spit out the last two words and he winces again but nods his agreement.

"Thanks Paige." Reaching out, he grabs my hand and rubs his thumb along the back of it.

My eyes are glued to the connection as I murmur, "Why did you lie?"

His thumb freezes for a second before continuing its circular pattern. "About what?"

At least he has the decency not to deny it, I think bitterly.

"About me calling you. I never called you." I can hear the suspicion in my voice and it helps me focus on who this man really is despite his gentle touch.

Seth reaches out with his other hand and nudges my chin so I look up at him. "You did Paige. I think it was the night you were taken." I suck in a sharp breath, searching his eyes as he continues. "I was so surprised to see your name pop up that I answered immediately. All I could hear was some shuffling and then you screamed." His eyes tighten as if pained by the memory. "I heard you scream and then the call went dead. I've never been so afraid in my life." He brokenly whispers, squeezing my hand and huffing out a breath.

I stare at him, replaying the night in my head.

I was at the shop, texting Taylor. I pulled out my phone and was going to delete his contact.

My eyes widen as I realize what must have happened and I burst into laughter. Seth stares at me, clearly worried about my sanity. I only laugh harder at his expression. "Paige. *Paige.* This isn't funny." He snaps. "I was really scared for you. Why are you laughing?"

I hold my side and gasp in breaths, trying to get my hysterical emotions under control. "I didn't mean to call you. I was actually trying to delete your number from my phone." Seth sucks in a breath through his teeth and leans back. Shaking my head, I continue, "I must have hit the call button on accident when I slid my phone into my pocket. An animal had run into some tables or something out front and I had gone out to investigate. The scream you heard was because I startled myself and fell over." He's staring at me with a look of pained amusement.

Sure, it was the same night that Mick took me, but that all happened after I apparently called my ex. As I was in the middle of deleting him from my life.

I break out laughing again as the irony of it all hits me.

After a few moments, Seth chuckles as well and brushes my cheek with his fingers. "I'm so happy to hear that sound again." His voice is soft and I bristle at the gentle touch.

"Don't Seth." I warn, pushing up from my seat. Heading to the kitchen, I throw my empty bottle into the recycling. A soft sound outside the door catches my attention momentarily before I hear Seth approach behind me.

His breath ghosts my neck and I shiver as he reaches around me to throw his bottle into the bag. Lingering briefly, he breathes against me before backing away. I let out my own breath before turning around. Seth peers down at me and whispers, "I miss you baby girl."

My eyes well up with tears and I shake my head, pushing past him.

This man already broke my heart once, I can't deal with this. Not now.

Without turning around I say, "I'm going to grab you some blankets. Get some sleep. You leave first thing tomorrow morning."

I don't wait for his response as I head out of the room.

"What?" Taylor shrieks in my ear. I flinch and cover the receiver of my cell, holding it away from me.

Bringing it back to my ear I keep my voice low. "Shhh. He's sleeping in my living room right now. And can you please not scream in my ear?" I can hear her trying to calm herself and can't help but grin. At least I'm not the only one freaking out about all of this.

After a few moments, Taylor's voice comes through again, much quieter this time. "God, I'm sorry. But...seriously, what the fuck Paige? Why did your ex show up at your door?"

I shrug as if she can see me. "I dunno. He drove all the way over here." Glancing at my bedroom door, I lower my tone so it's a hushed whisper. "Tay, he called me baby girl." Taylor shrieks in my ear again and I pull the phone away. "Taylor," I growl, "Can you *please* stop doing that."

"Sorry sorry." Her voice is breathless and comes out in puffs. "Seriously, this is just...a lot."

I roll my eyes. "Tell me about it. Like one psycho isn't enough." I laugh and the other end of the line goes eerily silent. Pulling my phone away, I make sure the call didn't get disconnected. "You good?"

She mumbles something but I don't quite catch what she says before she lets out a heavy sigh. "I'm coming over." She declares.

"What? No! You don't have to do that. Seriously, I'm okay."

"No arguments babe. I'm heading your way right now. And I'm bringing wine and chocolate. Fuck your ex, we can kick him out to the hall if we need to. You need some Tay-Tay time and to get away from these crazy ass men." I smile, despite having tried to stop her.

I love this girl so fucking much.

Taylor comes barging in thirty minutes later, arms full and expression stern. I barely have time to get the door open before she rushes inside. I follow her over to the kitchen and between the two of us, we get everything lined up on the counter.

Once our arms are free, I wrap her in a hug and whisper a thank you in her ear. Taylor pats me on the back and gives me a squeeze. Pulling away, I look over the supplies she's brought and decide to tackle the large bag of chocolates first. Behind me, I hear a throat clear and look up to find Taylor glowering. Rolling my eyes, I turn around, mouth full of gooey decadence. "What Seth?" I grumble around my bite.

He stares at me for a moment before his eyes dart to Taylor and then back. "Um," He clears his throat again, rubbing his chest. "Do you mind if I take a quick shower and maybe do a load of laundry." He gestures down at his rumpled clothes and gives me a shy smile. "I feel pretty disgusting."

Behind me, I hear Taylor grumble, "That's cause you *are* disgusting, cheating slimeball." I snort and start coughing as I choke on the chocolate. Taylor pats my back with a wicked grin on her face.

I shoot her a warning look and nod Seth toward my bathroom. "There's towels in the cupboard under the sink. I don't have any clothes to fit you but you're free to run yours through the wash. Just make sure to secure your towel really well. I've seen enough of your dick for a lifetime." This time Taylor snorts and then falls into giggles. Seth gives me a scathing look before turning and heading off to shower.

Regaining some of her composure, Taylor lightly smacks my shoulder. "Bitch, I love you." I beam back at her and return to my snacks as she pulls down a couple wine glasses and starts pouring.

We spend the next hour chatting about how things have been since I returned to my apartment. I ask her to pass on my gratitude to Beau for installing my security system. She tries to wave me off, only promising to say something after I insist several times and explain that it's helped me to be able to sleep. I blink back some tears and her face softens as she finally agrees to pass on my thanks.

Seth stumbles out of the bathroom at some point and makes himself at home, snatching another beer from the fridge and lounging on the couch. I keep sneaking peeks at him, trying to decipher what his angle is and why he's not back home with Brie. I know I saw the announcement, I can remember the sharp pain I felt. It was nothing compared to what happened later, but still seared into my memory.

Seth catches me looking at one point and smirks as he lifts his bottle to his lips, pulling slowly while maintaining eye contact as he swallows. It's most likely the wine but I can't stop staring at his throat as his Adam's apple moves with each swallow. My eyes wander to the tight grip he has on the neck of the bottle and I stifle a gasp as his fingers tighten around the glass. Seth's eyes rake down my body as he lowers his drink and licks his lips. I bite my bottom lip as I stare at his.

I'm vaguely aware of Taylor saying something but my mind has checked out. The ache between my legs grows again but as I continue watching him, my mind wanders to another man. Blue eyes and blonde hair fill my vision and my nipples pebble at the memory of his rough beard scraping against them before sucking into his mouth and biting. I stifle the moan that tries to escape by taking a large swig of wine. I should not be having thoughts about that. About either of them. Trying to distract myself, I turn back to my friend and listen to what she's saying.

"-ou wouldn't believe the size of it! I'm serious, it was as big as my head!" She laughs, so I do too. I have no idea what she's talking about but I bask in her joy. It's so rare for me these days. I swallow more wine and push back that depressing reminder. Taylor's eyes are glassy and she's clearly had too much to drink.

I smile at her and reach out, grabbing her hand with a squeeze. She stops, looking down at our hands. "I think you should stay the night. You're drunk dear." I smirk at her as she looks offended.

"I am not drunk." She hops up from her seat, wobbling as she lands on her feet. "See, I'll prove it. Hey, you!" She shouts at Seth who's still lost staring at me with desire burning in his eyes. "Yo, Detective O'lanne. Helloooooo." She waves her arms and sways, grasping the counter to steady herself with a giggle.

Seth finally moves his attention from me and looks toward my inebriated friend. "Hmm?"

Throwing her hands on her hips, Taylor juts out her chin. "I need you to give me a sobariety. Wait, sobrietery. No, that's not right, umm..." I burst out laughing as she taps her chin, thinking hard. "Sobriety!" She exclaims, finger pointing at the ceiling in triumph. "I need you to give me a sobriety test so I can show my friend here I'm not drunk."

I'm laughing so hard my side hurts as Seth stands with a chuckle. "Okay, Miss...?"

"Hauve." Taylor hiccups in response.

"Miss Hauve," Seth repeats as he swaggers over to us, amusement fading from his expression and replaced by a serious scowl. Stopping when he's a few steps away, he crosses his arms and peers down his nose at her. "Have you had anything to drink?"

Indignant, Taylor lifts her head. "No, sir, officer." I giggle behind my hand.

Seth raises an eyebrow, clearly not impressed. "Mmhmm. Let's see about that. Please put your arms to your sides and raise one foot up." Taylor slaps her arms down and lifts a leg. Swaying unsteadily, she gloats at him as she regains her balance. "Perfect, now keep your leg up and your eyes on your elevated foot as you count up from one thousand until I tell you to stop."

Taylor starts counting and wobbles, giggling before righting herself and staring at her foot in angry determination. She starts again and begins to fall, flailing to catch herself. Seth strides forward and catches her, gently helping her back to her seat. Taylor crosses her arms and pouts. "This proves nothing." She grumbles, glaring at the counter.

I snicker and look between the two of them, raising an eyebrow. "Well, officer? How did my friend do."

Seth stares off contemplatively. Lifting his hand, he rubs his chin before humming softly and clucking his tongue. "I'm sorry to report, but it would appear Miss Hauve has had too much to drink to safely operate a motor vehicle."

Taylor's indignant expression and Seth's obnoxious formality have me doubling over in laughter. I lose my balance and land on the floor, rolling to my side giggling. They both stare at me in shock before dissolving into their own laughter. I gasp for breath and look up, a smile spread across my face.

I'm hit with a pang of melancholy. This could have been my life if Seth hadn't fucked it all up. Swatting away the pity party, I choose to enjoy the evening, regardless of how strange it is to be in the same room with my ex-fiancé and my best friend after running away from a murderous kidnapper set on making me his.

At least there's wine.

Chapter 15

Mick

I've never wanted to kill someone as much as I do right now. When the elevator doors opened and I saw that disheveled man be pulled into Paige's apartment and her dart her head out before slamming the door, I saw red. There were no longer thoughts, there was only fury.

His girl. He called her his *girl.*

I clench my teeth and crack my knuckles.

I need to get inside of that apartment. I need to pull that man away from my woman. His screams of agony are going to be the only acceptable payment for this treachery. If I had known...

I shake my head, there's no use in thinking like that, there's only what I do now.

The only reason I haven't broken down the door yet is I heard Paige tell him off shortly after he arrived. I wished she had kicked the asshole out but at least my girl has remained faithful to me. I watched her friend sneak in with arms full of food and wine.

That was hours ago, and she still hasn't left either.

Releasing a breath, I rub my forehead. At least with her friend there, I know for sure there's nothing else going on between that man and Paige. Leaning my head back against the headrest, I close my eyes.

I'm so tired. I haven't had a decent sleep since she left.

Scrubbing my face with my hands, I look up and see the light for the apartment is still on. I let out a heavy sigh and lean back in my seat.

Might as well try and get a little rest while I wait.

I wake with a start and look around.

The sun is shining and most of the parking lot has emptied of vehicles. A quick inspection shows Paige's friend and mystery guest have both left. I notice Paige's car is also gone.

Scooting my seat up, I start the engine and back out, heading toward town. If she's not at home, she's most likely at work. That's fine, I can handle a challenge.

One thing's for certain, I'm tired of waiting.

It's time to catch my little bird.

Chapter 16

Paige

"One large Caramel macchiato for Bentley." I call out, setting the espresso down.

A young man walks up and smiles, grabbing the drink. Looking away quickly, I walk back to the coffee bar and get started on the next order. Brandi has already mentioned my attitude towards customers, especially male customers. I can't shake the feeling of being watched, though, and the knowledge that two people are dead because I smiled at them makes me extra cautious in my interactions.

I know it's not my fault what happened, but I have to do everything I can to avoid being the reason behind any more deaths. I shudder as I pick up the next cup. Prepping the shots, my mind wanders to Seth.

What would happen to him if Mick found out? Why do I feel guilty?

Regardless of what he claims, I do not belong to Mick, which means I can do whatever I want with whoever I want.

Not that I want to do that with Seth.

Sucking in a breath, I hold it for a few heartbeats before slowly releasing the air from my lungs. My life has gotten so complicated and all because stupid men think they can do whatever they want without any consequences. I grit my teeth as I steam the milk, imagining what I'd like to do to both men in question.

Would they be so cocky if they were missing a couple dangly bits?

I stifle a laugh and then feel horrified.

I cannot believe I just laughed at the thought of mutilating someone. Sure they deserve it, but still, that's not me.

Or is it?

Angry, I push the thought away and pour steamed milk over the shots, creating a simple leaf on top with the foam. Gently carrying the drink over, I set it down and look up to call out the order when my breath catches in my throat. My eyes widen and I take a half step back. Staring back at me are a pair of steel blue eyes, twinkling with barely concealed fury. I raise a trembling hand to my throat and back up another step.

"No," I whisper, shaking my head.

I look around and see people all around with mixed expressions ranging from concerned to bored. I look back at the man that has haunted my dreams and watch as he slowly lifts a finger to his lips, shaking his head almost imperceptibly while gesturing around with his other hand, eyebrows raised. I look around again and see all the faces surrounding us. There are a few couples, an elderly woman, some teenagers, and a few other patrons scattered throughout the space. I look back and the expression on Mick's face leaves no question as to his intention. If I make a scene, at least some, if not all, of the innocent people around us will be paying the price. And if I've come to know him correctly, I'd bet that price would be their lives.

I gulp down the scream that's trying to force its way out of my throat and take a shaky step back toward the counter. "Vanilla l-lat-latte for Jessica." I manage to stammer out, my voice trembling as my gaze stays fixated on Mick. Someone comes and snatches the drink with a quiet thanks. I smile robotically and turn back to the bar to start on the next drink.

Fine, if the asshole is going to come threaten me at work, he's going to have to wait while I do my job.

I give myself a mental pat on the back for the small act of defiance and continue on through the rush.

Orders start to slow down and my palms get sweaty. I'm terrified of what's going to happen when everyone leaves. I don't see how I'm going to get out of this. Mick has continued to watch me, not saying anything. He doesn't need to, I can see his intentions burning in his eyes. He told me what would happen if I left, and I did it anyway. And then I just went back to my life like nothing had happened.

Stupid, stupid, stupid! What were you thinking? You should have run far, far away, not stayed here like a pretty little sitting duck. I close my eyes and breathe. *I just need to think.*

The sound of the door chiming has my eyes opening and I'm overwhelmed with relief. Until I glance at Mick and see the murderous look in his eyes.

Oh fuck.

"Hey Paige!" Seth calls as he strolls in.

I wildly swing my eyes back between him and Mick. Seth seems relaxed and happy, completely unaware of the danger he's in. How this man is supposed to be a detective when he has the observation skills of a golden retriever is beyond me. I snort and quickly cover my mouth when Mick turns his glare on me, shoulders tense and lips thin.

I shift my focus back to Seth and try to plead with him through my eyes to leave but he doesn't notice. Instead he walks straight up to the counter and leans over. "So, I know you said to leave this morning but Kristoph asked to meet me first and we thought we'd swing by and grab a coffee. If that's cool?" He starts to look a little sheepish as he finally takes in my expression, obviously misreading it as a reaction to him being here. Straightening, he shoves his hands in his pockets and turns around mumbling, "Sorry, I know. I'll just leave." Seth's shoulders slump and he starts heading to the door when he freezes, gaze locked with Mick.

No. No, no, no. Just keep walking Seth.

I have to keep both hands over my mouth to avoid shouting at him as I watch everything in slow motion. Seth squares his shoulders, pulls his hand out of his pocket, strides forward to Mick and...shakes his hand?

What the fuck?

Laughing, Seth claps Mick on the shoulder. "Hey man! I can't believe I ran into you again. Sorry for my appearance last time, I've had a chance to clean up since." Seth chuckles and drops Mick's hand, still oblivious to the thunder cloud floating over his new friend's head. "Have you met my girl?" Seth gestures to me and I stiffen. Mick's eyes narrow to slits and I rush forward.

"I'm not your girl, Seth." I snap, more harshly than I mean too but, seriously, does the man have a death wish?

Waving me off, Seth returns to his conversation. "Yeah, yeah. I know. Anyway, it's good to see you man." He claps Mick on the shoulder once more before brushing past and greeting another man walking in. My eyes widen even farther as I recognize the detective I spoke with shortly after returning to Taylor's condo. "Kristoph!" Seth calls loudly.

The older man shakes his hand, inclining his head. "Detective O'lanne."

Seth waves him off. "Dude, I told you. Call me Seth. I'm off duty." He chuckles.

Kristoph grumbles and looks over, seeing me paralyzed behind the counter. His eyes narrow and I have a feeling his observation abilities are a little better than my ex's. I straighten my spine and drop my hands, trying not to fidget with my apron, a familiar churning in my stomach as I remember the way his eyes raked over my body the last time we spoke. Kristoph makes his way toward me and nods his head in greeting. "Hello Miss Greene. How are you?"

I swallow and force my eyes to stay on him as I reply. "Fine." It comes out more of a squeak so I clear my throat and try again. "I mean, I'm fine. Thank you for asking." His eyes burn into mine, trying to pull out my secrets and I mentally curse myself.

I want to scream "It's him! He's right behind you!" But I can't, not if it would endanger other people. And I know there's not enough evidence to really do anything but make Mick mad. When it came down to it, it would be a he said, she said situation. I don't know much about him, but Mick gives off an air of authority that I don't think I'd stand a chance against. It's one of the reasons I never gave a name or description to anyone about who had taken me. So, instead, I plaster a smile on my face and ask, "What can I get started for you?"

Seth and Kristoph order and make small talk as I work on their drinks. Once I've handed them over, the two men go to head off and I let out a relieved sigh. Just when they're about to leave, Seth turns around and strides back toward me, an intense look covering his face. Stopping in front of the counter again, he murmurs, "I'll be in touch." He reaches over, meaning to brush my cheek with his fingers, and I flinch back, shaking my head.

"You should go Seth. Really, it was very sweet of you to come all this way to check on me but we're over. You need to get back to Brie and let me live my life." I stare at him, pushing all of my emotion into my expression and willing him to listen. I know, without him having to say anything, that Mick is going to kill Seth. I can't bear that. Even though he hurt me deeply, he still holds a piece of my heart.

After an agonizing pause, Seth's shoulders slump and he nods. "Yeah, you're right." He looks up at me. "Stay safe Paige. And don't hesitate to call if you need me." He gives me one last lingering look before leaving.

I watch his retreating figure and force back the tears threatening to spill. My eyes slowly drift to Mick. He's staring after Seth as well but as he feels my gaze on him, he turns his head to meet my eyes. I suck in a breath and watch as he takes a step toward me.

I don't know why I ever thought I could get away from this man. One look from him and I'm trapped. My body pulls toward him even as my mind screams to run away.

Even if I fight it every moment of the rest of my existence, one thing has become very clear.

I *am* his, because he's never going to let me go.

Chapter 17

Mick

Seth O'lanne. Detective Seth O'lanne.

My mind is a swirl of thoughts as I watch Paige talking to the man determined to invoke my wrath. I had planned on capturing my girl first and then looking for him but then he waltzed right into the shop. Observing the rise and fall of her chest, the clench of her jaw and the small beads of sweat on her forehead, it's obvious she's nervous. I tilt my head as I contemplate the reason behind her concerns. She keeps glancing at me and swiftly away, fiddling with the edge of her apron. I turn my gaze to the intruder.

Seth.

He looks relaxed, happy. He's babbling about some nonsense to Paige and the other man standing next to him. I recognized Detective Kristoph

Lary immediately and had to flex my fingers to avoid strangling him when he turned his attention to Paige. The fact that he knew her made my teeth snap together and blinding hatred overwhelmed me.

I listen to the conversation and subtly crack my knuckles as I glare holes into the back of the two men's heads. I don't know much about Seth but I know Kristoph. I may be a monster, but at least I don't hide behind a false morality. Despite his public image, Kristoph is as bad as I am. He makes corrupt cops look like saints, his sins are a dark stain on him. If Seth treats him with such camaraderie, I can only guess at how blackened his own soul is.

Seth and Kristoph are wise enough to leave after obtaining their drinks. I have to grip the back of the chair next to me to physically restrain myself so I don't lunge when Seth tries to touch Paige. She pulls back and tells him to leave, for good, and my lips twitch as I fight to keep the smile off my face. She won't have to worry about him bothering her for much longer. Not with what I have planned for him. For both of them.

I feel Paige's eyes on me as I focus on the men climbing into a vehicle and pulling away from the curb. I slowly turn my head to meet her gaze and find my feet moving, magnetized to her. She gasps softly but doesn't move. My eyes stay on hers as I amble toward the counter. I stop when my hips hit the surface and don't miss the way her body leans toward me.

Smirking at her, I watch her face flare with rage even as she has to grip the countertop to keep from leaning further into me.

Oh my little bird, your body yearns for me. Your mind may try to lie to you, but your body knows who you belong to and soon, so will the rest of you.

Paige's lips part as I reach forward and brush my fingers across her cheek before grasping her chin. "You've been very bad." I shake my head and tsk. "Do you know what happens to bad girls?" She doesn't say anything but her eyes widen as she stares at me, transfixed. I lean forward so my lips press against her ear and purr, "They are punished."

Paige trembles under me and lets out a choked noise, trying to pull out of my grip. I tighten my fingers and stick my tongue into her ear before growling, "Don't try to run again, little bird. Or I'll make sure you never come again." She whimpers and presses her thighs together. I press a soft kiss on her temple and lean back, keeping hold of her face. "Now be a good girl and finish up, we have some things to discuss." I release her and stroll back to the table, sitting down and crossing an ankle over my knee. Slinging my arm behind the back of the chair, I stretch out and stare her down. One eyebrow raised, daring her to test me.

After several long moments, Paige visibly shakes herself and cleans up the mess from the rush of customers. I look around and am relieved to see the lobby is mostly empty. Only a couple of college age kids with their heads tucked into laptops, headphones covering their ears. I wouldn't have cared if someone had witnessed the interaction but this makes my clean up much easier. Returning my gaze to the center of my devotion, I watch her finish up then turn and walk toward the back.

I move to push up from the seat, my expression becoming thunderous, when Paige freezes and glances around. When she's certain no one can hear her, she licks her lips and mutters just loud enough for me to hear. "I have to tell my boss I'm leaving early." Her head tilts toward the door leading farther back into the building. "Her office is back there. I'll be quick." She lowers her head and raises just her eyes, peering at me through her long lashes.

Forcing back my desire to rush to her and throw her over my shoulder to take away any possibility of her running, I rub my jaw and incline my head. "Be quick." It's not a request, it's a command and she would do well to heed it. Nodding stiffly, Paige takes off.

I wait patiently, well as patiently as a predator stalking his prey can wait, staring at the door she disappeared into. Glancing at my watch, I grind my teeth, my control beginning to slip as I watch the minutes tick by. I'm about to rise and storm back to find her when I hear the door swing and look up to see Paige stride through, her purse slung over her shoulder.

She glances around and then rushes to me, stopping a few steps away with her eyes on the floor. I study her as she stands before me, taking in her beauty. She has her hair pulled up into another messy bun, light makeup on her face and a simple pair of earrings in. Her t-shirt is stretched tight across her chest and ends just shy of the hem of her dark jeans. My jaw works as I take in the amount of skin showing on her stomach and through the massive tears in the jeans she's wearing.

Slowly rising, I take a step forward and slide my hand to her exposed midriff. Paige stiffens but doesn't move or look up. I run my fingers over her skin and watch as goosebumps rise in response to the touch. In a low voice, I speak while continuing my patterned movement. "Did you wear this to make me angry, little bird?" She sucks in a breath and shakes her head. I hum, fingers moving further down and brushing against the top of her jeans. "If that's not it, did you wear this to turn me on?" Her eyes flick up to mine and then quickly return to the floor as she shakes her head again. "You sure? Because I think you wore this in hopes you would run into me." I lean over her and undo the button, slipping my fingers into the top of her pants. "You know what you do to me and you wanted me to find you." She gasps as my fingers drift over her clit. "This drenched pussy of yours is desperate for my cock. Isn't it?" It's not really a question as I roughly grab hold of her pussy and squeeze.

The feeling of her damp panties against my palm has me stifling a groan. She whimpers as I squeeze harder and I have to bite my lip to keep the noise from escaping my throat. "Fuck Paige. I'm so goddamn hard." I roll my hips into her, showing her just what she's doing to me. "I'm going to fuck this tight cunt and remind you who it belongs to." I promise as I release her. Pulling my hand out of her pants, the smell of her arousal emanates from my damp fingers.

Looking at her, I'm filled with fury again.

This woman left me. I warned her. I showed her who she is and what I can do to her. For *her. Yet she still fled.*

Growling, I roughly lift her face and spit my command at her. "Fix your clothes so we can leave." I push away from her and wait while her fingers clumsily adjust her clothes and rebutton her jeans.

Once she's done, I grip her elbow and guide her out of the shop. As we are leaving, I glance up and see a woman staring at us from the doorway leading to the backroom. Narrowing my eyes, I challenge her to say something. Rather than rise to my unspoken threat, she looks between Paige and me before spinning on her heel and storming to the back.

I'm not sure what she's going to do but I can tell there's going to be an issue I need to take care of sooner than later. I look back at Paige stumbling along beside me and speed up my steps.

Yes, I need to solve whatever problem that is but I need to address my girl's betrayal first.

The drive back to my house is quiet. I keep my focus straight ahead, knowing if I look at her too much, I'm going to pull over the car and fuck her on the side of the road. I shift in my seat, pushing the visual out of my head and press down harder on the gas pedal.

Paige hasn't said anything. I was mildly surprised when she climbed into my car with no hint of an argument. She didn't react as I reached across her and buckled the seat belt, pulling on the belt to ensure it was secure. After I had rounded the vehicle and climbed into the driver's seat, she had averted her gaze out the window and hasn't moved since.

The dash lights up with an incoming call and I give Paige a warning look before pressing the button to answer.

"Where have you been?" Jesse's voice filters through the speakers. I roll my eyes and work to keep my voice even.

"Aww, you worried about me hunny?"

Jesse scoffs on the other end of the line and I swipe the side of my mouth to hide the smirk. "You know I always worry about you *sweetie*." I can hear the laughter trying to break through his irritated tone and give up on my attempts to hide my own humor. "Seriously though, you've been MIA for a week. Rachel said you pushed all your appointments and refused calls from anyone. What's going on with you man?"

I shift my eyes to Paige as I answer. "Something came up that I had to take care of. I shouldn't be gone much longer and you can catch me up on everything I missed."

Jesse grunts and clucks his tongue. "Sometimes it feels like I'm the one running the company and you're just the pretty face on the brochures." I bark a laugh, he's not wrong.

"Gee thanks sugar plum, I love it when you say such sweet things to me."

I can practically hear Jesse rolling his eyes as he grumbles his response. "Yeah, whatever, you know what I mean. I really do need you to start acting like the boss, though, or give me a new title or something." I contemplate his words. It wouldn't be such a bad idea to put Jesse in charge and take a step back. I had started the business to avoid having to work for others and the necessity of money to pay bills. With our continued success, I've more than accomplished both those goals.

A familiar anxiety creeps up at the possibility of relinquishing control and it resulting in disaster. We never had money when I was a kid and I have no interest in living that way again. Especially when money helps to grease palms and open doors to make my hobby easier. My mind wanders back to the man responsible for our lack of stability and finances growing up. The knot in my chest tightens more and I grip the steering wheel harder. I long ago dealt with the heartless fucker and refuse to think about him.

The sound of material shifting brings me back to the present and I glance over to my raven-haired beauty sitting in the passenger seat, nibbling on her thumb. I narrow my eyes at the expression on her face. Deciding it's best to end the call quickly before she acts on the thoughts I can see running through her mind, I tell Jesse I'll text him later to let him know when I plan on heading to the office.

I end the call and shoot a look at Paige. She looks back with false innocence, lowering her hand to her lap. Shaking my head, I return my attention back to the road. Looks like I have more work to do, because this woman, my woman, still doesn't understand.

There's no one who can save her now.

We arrive at my house and I guide Paige inside by the elbow again, depositing her on the couch. Her eyes flick nervously around the space and she presses her lips tightly together. I study her momentarily before locking the door and striding into the kitchen.

Pulling out the ingredients for a simple sandwich, I make quick work of lunches for us both. Throwing some chips on the plate, I grab a couple cans of soda before making my way to the couch. Depositing the food on the coffee table, I slump into the sofa and kick my feet up as I grab my plate and shove half the sandwich into my mouth.

Paige watches me slack-jawed, suspicion marring her features as she reaches forward to pick up her drink. The sound of the seal breaking is loud in the otherwise silent room and she flinches before bringing the can to her lips. Taking another bite, I watch with rapt attention as she swallows down the soda, head tipped back and eyes nearly shut. I lick my lips, fixated on hers wrapped around the small hole in the aluminum.

Sensing my gaze, Paige looks at me and slowly lowers the drink, wiping her mouth with the back of her hand. I indicate she should eat by tilting my head toward her plate of food. Following my direction, she leans forward and grabs the sandwich, taking a tentative bite. I can't peel my eyes away from her, darting between her lips and throat as she chews and swallows.

Encouraged that I haven't poisoned her food, she dives in for another bite and manages to cause a large dollop of mustard to land on the skin peeking out from the top of her shirt. She reaches to wipe away the mess but I snap my hand out and grip her wrist, stilling the movement. Her eyes meet mine in confusion that shifts to fear as I lean forward. My lips seal over the wayward condiment and I suck, my cock twitching as Paige softly moans.

I snake my other hand up and knead her breast as I continue to suck on her exposed chest. She lets out a husky moan and tries to pull away. I growl and tighten my fingers, gripping her breast hard enough I'm sure it's painful. Releasing her wrist with my other hand, I reach up to push her down into the cushion. She falls back without resistance, her body craving me as much as I crave her.

Her breaths come out in puffs as she tries to speak past her lust filled haze. "Sandwich." She pants.

I lift my head and look down at her with amusement. My eyes drift to the sandwich grasped tightly in her hand. Leaning forward, I take the last of her food in my mouth. My teeth brush against her fingers and cause a shudder to run through her body. With my eyes on hers, I work my jaw to chew around the large mouthful. Swallowing, I return to lick her fingers clean before sucking them into my mouth and gently biting down. Her back arches as her lids become heavy.

Drawing back, I release her fingers with a pop before returning my lips to her chest. I trail kisses along her collarbone, working my way up her throat. My hands continue massaging her breasts and tugging on her hardened nipples through the material of her shirt and bra. I pinch them with a twist of my fingers, causing her to gasp and lift her hips into me.

There's too many layers between us and my patience has worn thin.

Sitting up, I whip off my shirt before reaching for her jeans. Making quick work of the button and zipper, I grip the hem of her pants and underwear, tearing them off of her body. Paige lets out a squeak at the sudden movement but I don't stop. Reaching forward, I grasp the top of her shirt and rip it apart, exposing her bra. I let out a growl when I see the black lacy material resting on her pale skin.

Glowering, I raise my eyes to hers. "Who did you wear this for?" I snarl. Paige whimpers but doesn't reply. Glancing down again at the transparent bra, I push off of her, my ire increasing as I stalk over to my bag on the kitchen table.

Retrieving a knife, I march back to her. Paige's eyes are wide as she notices the blade gripped in my hand. I catch the shift of her thighs as I grow closer. Seeking friction, she continues to rub them together. I smirk at her and hold up the knife. "Remembering the fun we had with this?" Her cheeks flame and she glares at me but presses her lips together. She can't deny me, not when I'm right. "Don't worry, little bird. We can have fun with my blade again soon. But not now. Right now I need to be inside you."

Covering the remaining distance, I lift her bra. "First, I need to make sure you can never wear this for someone else again." She gasps as I slice through the thin material in the middle and each strap, rendering it useless.

There. That's better.

With the knife still in my hand, I cut up the intact material of her shirt. The ruined top slides off, pooling on her sides and leaving her completely bare before me.

I stare down at her, taking in the smooth skin, pebbled nipples, small bulge in her stomach showing she enjoys a good meal, the thickness of her thighs, her shaved pussy.

This woman is a walking wet dream.

My cock aches to be inside of her again and I'm not about to argue.

I hurry to return the knife to the bag. Can't have her getting any ideas of stabbing me while I'm buried in her, at least not with the hate shining in her eyes right now.

Stripping out of my pants and boxers, I make my way back to the couch and lower myself over her body. Taking one of her nipples between my teeth, I bite down, just the way she likes. Paige cries out and I reach my hand up to encircle her throat, squeezing as I rotate my hips into her. With my eyes on hers, I snake my other hand down and push two fingers inside of her, groaning as she squeezes around them. Opening her mouth in a silent cry, she leans her head back into the cushions.

Releasing her nipple, I shift up so I'm lined up with her entrance as my fingers pump in and out. "You're so wet, baby. So needy for my cock." I squeeze her throat tighter and she whimpers, tears running down her face.

I can see she wants to fight me, to fight against the desires threatening to consume her. But I won't let her. She wants this, even if she won't admit it yet.

Pulling my fingers out of her, I bring them to my lips, flexing my other hand so she opens her eyes and looks at me as I slide them into my mouth. "Hmmm. I missed this." I groan as her flavor explodes on my tongue. "You are the most delicious thing I've ever tasted." Her pupils dilate as she watches me run my tongue over my fingers, cleaning the juices from them.

I pull my fingers out of my mouth and grip her hip, adjusting her position on the couch. With her eyes still locked on me, I slam my cock inside of her, groaning at how tight she feels. The heat of her pussy warms up my cold soul. I won't ever let my small ray of sunlight disappear. Never again.

I pull back until just the head of my cock is still inside and thrust forward harder than the first time. I continue pummeling her with violent thrusts that push her farther up the couch, her tits bouncing with each movement. "You are *mine*, little bird." I plow into her, groaning as I declare, "This pussy belongs to me." Removing my hand from her hip, I slap her breast. "These tits belong to me." Hovering over her, I grip her chin. "*You* belong to me." Tears are flowing down her face as she tries to shake her head. "Yes." I grunt, thrusting into her. Releasing her chin, I slap her other breast. "Say it." I demand as I fuck her mercilessly. She shakes her head again and I squeeze my hand on her throat, cutting off her oxygen. "Say. It." I growl, leaning forward so I'm inches away from her face.

She opens her mouth but nothing comes out. I relax my grip and she sucks in a breath. Glaring up at me, she whispers, "I belong to no one."

I laugh as I lean back, releasing her throat and pulling out of her. I don't give her a chance to react before gripping her hips and flipping her over. Now on her hands and knees, her ass points up in the air. I grab hold of her hips again, lining my cock against her opening. With a firm grip on her, I slam back into her soaking pussy and tug her back into me in the same movement.

Resuming my punishing rhythm, each thrust allows me to sink deeper. I move one hand down and massage her ass cheek. Paige moans and writhes beneath me, shoving back to meet my thrusts. I withdraw my hand and bring it down hard against her ass. She cries out and tips her head back, hair falling loose from the bun.

I continue to land blows on her, my hand coming down over and over to redden her skin as I reach up to grip her hair. Yanking her head back, her body bends farther to fight the pressure. "You can deny it all you want." I pant between thrusts, slapping her again. "But your body doesn't lie. You were made for me." I give her hair a sharp tug, causing her to cry out.

Stopping my blows, I snake my hand around her body and pinch both of her nipples before sliding my hand down to her pussy. Brushing my fingers over where we're connected, I search out her clit. Applying just enough pressure to turn her cries into pleas, I circle the sensitive bud. "You want to come?" I tease as my fingers work her closer to climax. "You want me to make you come on this cock, baby?"

She tries to nod but my grip on her hair prevents the movement. Pushing against me, she begs, "Please. Oh god, please let me come." The sound of her begging is my new favorite sound. But it's not enough to give her what she wants. I need her delirious with the desperation for release. I need to remind her that I own her pleasure. "Mick." She cries out, body trembling with need. "Mick, please. I need to, I can't. Please."

Tugging her hair, I lean forward and lick the side of her face before whispering in her ear. "You know what to say if you want to come, little bird." I release her hair and grip her throat again, pounding into her hard enough her ass jiggles from the movements.

Sobbing, Paige drops her head forward. The loose strands of hair cover her face. I flex my hand around her throat. Stretching a finger upward, I force her lips apart and shove it inside. She sucks on my finger, pulling a low groan from my chest. Removing my hold on her throat, I plunge two more fingers into her mouth, pushing them far enough she gags. Keeping them as far back as I can, I slam into her from behind.

I grit my teeth as I feel my impending orgasm approaching. Withdrawing my hand from her clit, she whimpers at the loss. The sound opens her throat and allows my fingers to slip deeper, causing her to gag around the intrusion. I slide my free hand up her body to her breast. Taking her nipple between two fingers, I pinch and twist. Paige's cry is muffled around my hand. Her arms and legs shake as she grows closer with each added sensation.

Between clenched teeth, I demand one last time. "Say it Paige. If you want to come, you need to say it." I extract my fingers from her mouth and grip her other breast in my hand. Paige sniffles, her body tightening. The increased tension causes her walls to clench around me, strangling my dick. If she doesn't give me what I want soon, I'm not going to be able to hold off any longer.

Sensing she's running out of time, Paige looks back at me. Tear streaks mixed with her running mascara cover her face. The lipstick she had on has smeared around her mouth from my fingers and she has snot dripping from her nose.

She's never looked more beautiful.

I groan and still, trying to stave off the near unbearable need for release. Paige chokes on a sob before giving me what I want. Her voice wavers as she whispers, "I'm yours, Mick. My body belongs to you." I remain frozen, soaking in her words.

Ready to give my girl the pleasure only I can, I slip a hand between her legs. Slapping her pussy, I shift and rub tight circles on her clit. My hand on her breast alternates between the two, pinching and tugging on her hardened nipples. I resume my thrusts and adjust the angle until I see her eyes roll back in her head when I find *that spot*. It only takes a few more thrusts and she explodes around me, screaming my name. My own orgasm is ripped from me as her pulsating walls milk my cock.

Collapsing against her, I moan her name as the sensations work their way through our bodies. When I can breathe again, I sit up and watch as my dick slips out of her pussy, drenched with our combined cum. Paige's legs are still shaking so I stand and scoop her up, heading into the bathroom. I gently wash her body and hair before quickly cleaning myself. Climbing out of the shower, I towel her dry and dress her in one of my shirts, wrapping a towel around my waist. Her eyes remain closed, not willing to look at me after her admission. Once finished, I scoop her up again and stride into the bedroom.

She still doesn't open her eyes until the first click. The sound causes her to snap them open and look at me in horror. She slowly lowers her gaze to her arm as I work my way over to the other side. "What are you doing?" She demands, terror filling her voice. I snap the other side closed and grip her chin, forcing her to look up at me.

Holding her horrified gaze, I state, "I told you what would happen if you ran, little bird. You should know, I don't make idle threats. And I always keep my promises." I drop her face and I turn away.

Striding out of the room, I leave her chained to the wall on top of a tarp I've secured to the floor.

Chapter 18

Paige

I don't know how long I've been chained up in Mick's bedroom. He keeps the curtains closed and doesn't sleep in here. The food and water he brings me are always sporadic and never hint at the time of day.

I spent a long time crying, screaming and calling him every name I could think of and making up new ones when I ran out of ammunition. My fists ache from pounding on the wall and my nails are ripped apart from trying to pry open the metal cuffs. He gave me enough slack in the chain that I can lay down and stretch but not much more than that.

At first, I didn't understand why he had attached a tarp to the floor below me. It wasn't until I had sobbed for him to let me use the restroom during one of his brief visits that I realized. He had just stood there and arched an eyebrow at me, not saying a word as I repeatedly begged. The realization slammed into me and I was filled with horror.

He had warned me I would have to live in my own filth, and he intended on fulfilling that threat, just like all the others.

I had stared at him, opening and closing my mouth, silenced by the lack of basic human decency this man possessed. Mick just smirked at me and turned around to leave the room. Screeching at him, I chucked the glass full of water at his head, screaming louder when I missed and it shattered against the wall. He didn't get me a replacement glass that day, or night, I'm not sure which. Either way, by the time he came with something for me to drink, I snatched it out of his hand and quickly guzzled it down.

I lasted as long as I could without having to relieve myself. When my body wouldn't allow me to put it off any longer, I tried to get as far away as the chains allowed before squatting and pissing on the tarp. I cried the entire time and didn't stop crying until I fell asleep.

I can't say I've gotten used to my bed and bathroom being the same small space, but the part of me that revolts against my new reality has died. A lot of me has died during my time in captivity. I've spent hours contemplating ways out of this situation and have resigned to the fact that there are only two solutions, each one just as horrible as the other.

I've never thought of taking my own life before but the life Mick has forced me into has me imagining all the ways I can end this torment. Grimly, I acknowledge to myself it's either that or give myself to him entirely and beg for his forgiveness. My stomach rolls and threatens to purge the small amount of food I've been given at the thought of allowing him to touch me again willingly.

My only small solace is Mick has not been interested in fucking me again since chaining me up. Not that I'm not surprised. I'm more animal than human now. But I know it will happen.

The only question is, will I let it happen, or will I push him until he ends this.

Ends me.

My awareness returns before I'm able to move. I can hear someone softly murmuring and brushing the hair back from my face. For a brief, blissful moment, I forget where I am. Then everything comes crashing back into me and I flinch away from the hand.

Opening my eyes, I see Mick peering down at me, his eyes soft as he looks me over. I try to scoot as far away as I can and curl up in myself, refusing to take my eyes off of his movements. Mick drags his gaze up and down my body and I can see the warring feelings of desire and disgust on his face. I sneer at him and his expression hardens. He's on his feet before I can blink and I push harder against the wall, tightening my arms around my bent knees. Muttering something to himself, he turns and stalks over to the bathroom. I hear him rummaging around and then the sound of water spraying causes tears to prick the backs of my eyes.

I want to be clean so badly but I also know what it means that he's running a shower for me.

"*I'll clean you of your filth just to get you dirty again.*"

His words echo in my mind.

I didn't believe him then, didn't take his threats seriously. I know differently now. *I'm* different now.

When Mick returns and unlocks the metal cuffs on my wrists, I can't stop the whimper as my raw skin is exposed to the air. He curses under his breath and reaches down. Yanking me to my feet, I stumble behind him as he drags me to the shower. I don't protest as he pulls the soiled shirt off me nor when he pushes me into the falling water. The second the warm water hits my skin I groan, tipping my head back and enjoying the feeling. After a few moments, I peek my eyes open and see Mick staring at me with undeniable hunger and I can't help but shudder under his intense gaze.

I try to cover myself with my arms but he grabs my wrists and yanks them back down. I cry out as the rough treatment reopens the wounds, biting my lip to stop from reacting more. I'm not sure what has caused him to want me again, but from the look in his eyes, my cries are only going to make this worse for me.

Mick drops my wrists and reaches over my head, grabbing the bottle of his body wash. Lathering his hands, he meticulously washes every part of my body. I watch him as his hands glide over my skin with a surprising tenderness, stiffening as he passes his hands between my legs. He proceeds without a reaction, almost clinical in his movements. He washes every inch of my body thoroughly twice before putting the bottle back on the shelf. Spinning me around, he massages shampoo into my hair. I bite my lip to hold back the moan as his fingers work my scalp.

I can't marry the man in the shower with me to the man who has had me inhumanely chained to his wall. This man seems to care about me, the other would step on me as if I were nothing more than a bug.

I'm lost in my thoughts as I hear the water switch off. I immediately stiffen, terrified of what's going to happen next. Mick doesn't say anything as he grabs a towel and dries me off. I stay as still as possible as he pulls another of his oversized shirts over my head, leaving me bare again from the waist down.

When he stills, I look up at him.

Mick has his eyes closed and is breathing heavily through his nose. I watch as his chest rises and falls with each breath. I'm unable to tell what he's thinking but something about his obvious discomfort causes a tiny bud of hope to bloom in my chest. I rub my fingernails against my skin to distract myself.

I can't let those emotions start, it will only make it worse when he decides to let his monster out again.

Slowly, I turn to face him and he opens his eyes. I'm conflicted as I stare at him.

Come on Paige, you know what you have to do.

I will myself to move my arms but no matter how much I try, they remain fastened to my sides. Changing directions, I open my mouth to say something but nothing comes out. Closing and opening it several times, I can't seem to get anything past my lips. Tears fill my eyes as I stand in front of the man who holds the key to my freedom, no matter how little it may be.

I can't do this.

The thought floats through my head and the truth of it hits me.

Even if I have to live the rest of my life chained up like a wild animal, I can't beg this demon for forgiveness that I don't need. I can't lay myself at his feet.

I feel the fires of rage building inside of me, consuming all the pity and self doubt. It's in this moment that I realize what I need to do.

I need to kill the killer.

Chapter 19

Mick

She's staring at me and I watch as the brokenness diminishes, replaced by a fiery determination. I don't know what she's thinking but the look in her eyes makes me want her. Want her more than ever.

I have spent the last few weeks warring with myself over my decision to follow through with chaining her up. I nearly broke when she sobbed for me to let her use the restroom. But I had to stay strong. She needs to know how serious I am about this bond between the two of us. So, instead of giving in, I turned and walked out.

Something broke in her that day and I think she finally started to really understand. I can be the master of her pleasure, but I can also be the executor of her pain. Even still, I left her like that for a while longer.

When I came home today and saw her sleeping, I knew I needed to end this punishment. She had experienced the consequences of leaving me and now I wanted to reward her for surviving them. I was already planning on letting her free of the chains but now I can see her bloodlust shining through, a mirror of my own. My plans for her new freedom are already shifting.

I wonder just how far she's willing to go?

A wicked smile covers my face and I reach out, pushing her hair behind her ear. Looking into her eyes, I murmur, "How would you like to stay out of the chains, beautiful?" Paige grimaces at the endearment and glances at herself before looking back up at me. Mistrust and timid hope filling her eyes, she slowly nods her head. I hum in response, moving my hand to her cheek and rubbing the pad of my thumb over her damp skin. She tries to stay still but I see the slight flinch at my touch and a small burst of anger hits me, causing the thumb to freeze.

Breathing through my nose, I push the emotion down. I resume my gentle strokes, holding her gaze while softly asking her the question that will grant her freedom or imprison her again. "Who are you?"

She peers up at me, eyes flickering and I catch another brief glimpse of that fire in her before she stamps it down. When I'm about to demand she answer the question, Paige parts her lips and lets out her answer on a breath. "Yours."

My chest aches at her whispered word and I groan as I swiftly pull her into my arms, kissing the top of her head. "That's right baby. You are mine. My little bird." I lean back and pepper kisses over her face as she closes her eyes and digs her fingers into my flesh, clinging to me. I move my lips to meet hers and when she parts her lips, allowing my tongue access to taste her, I dive in.

She moans as I kiss her with all the pent up desire and passion I've kept at bay while she has been here. My own self inflicted torture, having her so close but not being able to touch her, taste her. I move my hands into her hair and tug, causing her to gasp into me. Swallowing the noise, I groan, losing myself in her.

I only pull away when we are both gasping for air, leaning my forehead against hers. Stealing another soft kiss, I release her before turning for the bedroom door. Paige takes a step to follow me and I shoot a warning glance over my shoulder. She freezes mid step and cocks her head. Clucking my tongue, I shake my head. "Someone's been a dirty girl and I need to clean up the mess. You'll wait here." I chuckle as the sound of something hitting the wall by my head follows me out of the room.

Oh yes, I think we can have some fun together. Just need to work on her aim first.

Chapter 20

Paige

I never thought I would be so happy to sleep on a couch. Following the strange interaction after the shower, Mick cleaned up the bedroom and it was as if my torment never happened. I can't stay in there, though. Every time I enter the room a wave of nausea hits me and I lose the ability to breathe until I walk out again. I probably have some version of PTSD after the weeks spent in the room living my own version of hell.

When Mick sheepishly admitted how long he had kept me locked up, I went into screaming fit, throwing everything I could get my hands on. He shielded his head and his junk and just laughed, letting me work out my anger by destroying his possessions. It wasn't enough but it damped the desire to stab him in his stupid face.

I've spent every night out on the couch, watching shows and planning my revenge. If Mick suspects anything, he hasn't let on. He has given me space to adjust to the new normal and is gone most days, returning at night exhausted and sweaty. I pushed off the curiosity as long as I could until the fourth night in a row. I broke down and asked where he goes all day. All he replied was "work" and didn't elaborate beyond that. To pass the time, I try to guess what kind of "work" he may be involved in. I've narrowed it down to stripping or the mob, but I can't bring myself to ask if I'm right. Plus, he's not covered in nearly enough body glitter to be a stripper and his clothes are suspiciously less bloody than I would expect a mobster's to be, so I'm probably wrong anyway.

Fiddling with the TV remote, I stare at the screen, not paying attention to whatever movie I had put on to fill the silence. My mind is on how I'm going to get my revenge. I still feel queasy thinking about ending someone else's life, but it's his or mine. Call me selfish, but I'm choosing me.

Giving up on the TV, I click the button to turn it off and wander to the kitchen, rummaging through the cupboards to find a snack. It's starting to get late and Mick will be home soon, most likely with some form of takeout for dinner. As I've picked up the unfortunate habit of drowning my sorrows in wine, I need a little food to go with it and I don't want to wait for him to show up to start pouring.

Settling on crackers and cheese, I set up a small plate and snatch my half full bottle of wine out of the fridge, taking a swig from the neck as I pull down a glass. I pour a good amount out and stare at the glass, loneliness and despair filling me as my mind wanders back to the last time I enjoyed wine before all this. Tears prick at my eyes as I think about Taylor and remember laughing with her so hard we cried. I miss that. I miss when tears could be from happiness too. Blinking furiously, I push the emotions down and pick up my food and drink, plopping down at the table. I know what I have to do to get back to that life, and I'm going to do it, I just have to figure out how.

I've finished my cheese crackers and refilled my glass of wine by the time Mick barrels in the door. I don't look up immediately, lost in thought. When I hear the door slam, my eyes lift. I stiffen as I take in the state of the man in front of me. The sight is familiar and my mind flashes back to me being tied up to the bed as he stormed in, covered in red and breathing heavily while he stared at me like he was starving. The image in my brain dissolves and reveals the man before me, in much of the same state.

Mick stands there, chest heaving, eyes on fire. His face and clothes are covered in blood. My eyes move slowly up and down until meeting his gaze. He doesn't take a step toward me, instead he slowly shrugs out of his shirt, dropping it to the floor. I lick my lips as I watch the fabric flutter down and land pooled next to his bloody boots. He kicks those off next, along with his socks. Reaching around, he unbuttons his jeans and pulls the zipper down achingly slowly. I can feel the movement of his fingers as if he's caressing my skin.

I shudder and bring my glass to my lips, taking a large gulp. Mick watches the motion of my throat as I swallow, his eyes darkening. Lowering the glass down, I set it on the table with a loud thud, the remaining liquid splashing around. He rakes his eyes over my body, gazing at each inch of my skin with a growing hunger. When he lifts his eyes back to mine, I stare him down, muster all of the courage I have, and shake my head.

The reaction is immediate.

Mick moves so fast I almost don't get out of the chair in time before he's crashing into the table. I shriek and throw the rest of my drink into his face. He howls in rage, wiping his eyes to remove the alcohol. Taking the opportunity, I sprint toward the small bathroom on the other side of the living room and kick the door shut behind me. I fling myself against the door as I hear him come barreling over.

"Open this door right now, Paige." He thunders, fist pounding against the wood.

I'm shaking so hard my teeth are rattling but I won't do this again. I'm not going to allow him to use my body as some reward to whatever fucked up shit he's involved in. Sucking in a breath, I will my voice to sound strong. "No. Fuck off Mick." I snap.

He roars and pounds on the door again. "I'm serious, sweetheart. Open this door now or face the consequences." I gulp. I'm still recovering from his last punishment but I refuse to give in. Not in this. "Paige." He warns again.

Shaking my head, I slump back against the door, sinking to the floor and bracing my feet against the vanity. "No! Take your mobster ass back out and find someone else to fuck out your bloody victory."

Mick stops pounding on the door and it goes eerily silent. I hold my breath, afraid of what he's going to do. I didn't mean for that to come out, but he did come home bloody again, so my stripper theory is basically out the window.

Unless he's a secret assassin stripper. Well, fuck, I didn't think of that and now I have to stand by what I said.

Abruptly, I hear Mick burst out in laughter. There's a thump on the other side of the door and the laughter grows. I stand and creak open the door, gripping the handle and keeping my body shielded behind the wood. Peaking out I see Mick slumped on the ground, hand on his stomach as he laughs and laughs. Feeling embarrassed and irritated, I slip out and place my hands on my hips. "What's so damn funny?" I demand, glaring down at him.

Mick looks up at me and wipes tears away with his hand, face lit up with amusement. "Fuck Paige. I'm not part of the mob." He chuckles,

"Where did that even come from?" Raising both his eyebrows he peers up at me, a grin on his face.

My lips twitch in response as I force back a smile. I shrug, "I dunno. You always come home sweaty and exhausted. I've had a lot of time on my hands so I've been trying to figure out what you do all day. I had narrowed it down to a stripper," Mick's laughter returns in full force and I huff, waiting for him to calm down. He waves a hand in apology and gestures for me to continue. "Like I was saying, either a stripper or a mobster." I shrug again. "I didn't think you were glittery enough for a stripper and not bloody enough for being part of the mob but then you showed up like this," I gesture toward his bloodied appearance and the discarded clothes by the door, "And remembered the last time you showed up like that and, well, you know. It made the most sense." I look away, wringing my hands.

If that's not it, what is he doing? And why does it involve so much blood?

Mick pushes himself to his feet and walks to me, wrapping his arms around my waist. "You have quite the imagination." He snickers, eyes alight with mirth. "But I can promise you, I'm not dancing or killing for money. And I don't belong to any organized crime or answer to anyone for that matter." He presses a kiss to my hair and inhales.

I tilt my head back, gazing up at him. "What do you do then?" I whisper, unsure if I want the answer.

He studies me, debating his response. I can see the moment he decides to give in. Sighing, he squeezes me before answering. "My day job is construction. I actually own the company so I don't always do the hard labor but have found a need to use some of this pent up tension and the guys can always use another set of hands."

I consider the information and give a nod of my head as I deem it plausible. Mick stares at the wall, avoiding looking directly at me. Nudging his arm, I bring his attention back to me as I urge him to continue. "And the blood?" I quietly question.

Mick's muscles tense as he tightens his arms. The grip he has makes me wonder if he thinks the answer will make me run away if given the chance. I have a feeling he may be right.

Looking at the ceiling, he takes a deep breath then snaps his focus back to me and blurts out in a rush, "That's for me. To satisfy my...needs." I look at him quizzically, waiting for an explanation. "I have this...need. For blood. I first discovered it on accident years ago and have since perfected my ability to seek people out and ease the hunger." My eyes widen and my body freezes. An uneasy feeling begins to slither under my skin, the hairs on my arm prickling in response. "It's a long process and can take weeks and lots of careful planning. I set everything up and wait for the perfect moment to act when no one will be able to tie anything back to me. It's worked for me so far." He shrugs.

I'm pretty sure he's admitting to being a serial killer and the fucker fucking *shrugs.*

Sensing he's losing me, Mick quickly continues. "I'm careful, you don't have to worry about someone coming here or asking questions. I'm so good I've been given my own nickname." He smirks, smugness emanating from him as he divulges the name. "The Blood Shadow."

I choke on my breath.

He's the Blood Shadow? The man who kidnapped me, tortured me, and has given my body so much pleasure is the Blood Shadow?

Shaking my head furiously, I refuse to believe it.

Serial killers are social pariahs and have missing teeth or like a third eye or something. Mick seems too normal. Too well-adjusted. Aside from all the fucked up shit he's pulled with me.

I extract myself from his arms and start pacing.

It does kind of make sense. And would explain a lot. But...

I stop and look over at him.

What's the reasoning? All the people, the victims, *were random. At least according to the newspapers. But he's saying he plans them out for weeks. It doesn't make any sense.*

"Why?" I finally ask out loud.

He tilts his head, "I already told you, I have a need-"

I wave him off. "No, I know, I heard that part. But why them? Why kill those people? What did they do to you?"

He shrugs and nonchalantly states, "Nothing."

"Nothing?" I squeak.

He regards me for a moment before coming and enveloping me in his arms again, "We all die at some point, little bird. Their time just happened to be then." He nuzzles my neck but I shove against him.

"What gives you the right to decide that? Who told you that you can just...kill people?" I force out the words.

This can't be real. I can't be having this conversation right now.

"I did." He grips my face and forces me to look at him. "*I* decided. I grew up with a shitty father in an equally shitty place and discovered that life doesn't mean anything. There's no heaven, no hell, no higher power pulling the strings. No one to come to the rescue or provide what we need." His voice cracks in anguish.

I picture a young Mick crying out for someone to help and, much like my own prayers, met with silence. My heart aches at the image.

"There's only you and I and every other fucked up human being on this planet stumbling through life." He peers into my eyes, begging me to understand. "We have to take our pleasure where we can. To satisfy our needs, our desires, in order to truly live. And that's what I'm doing, Paige. Other's lives have been forfeited so that *I* can *live*." He crushes his mouth against mine. I struggle against him but he doesn't let up. True to his word, Mick takes what he needs from me.

My mind whirls as I replay his words. I still don't understand how he came to the conclusion that his life is somehow worth more than another's. A sickening feeling settles in my stomach as it dawns on me that I was just thinking the same earlier when it was his life or mine in question.

I open my eyes as he devours my mouth and let the feeling settle over me. An anguished acceptance engulfs my being.

At this moment, he and I aren't that different.

And, because I'm choosing myself too, I close my eyes and lean into the kiss.

Mick and I settle into a comfortable routine. He sleeps in his bedroom while I crash on the couch. By the time I wake up, he's gone and returns late at night with food. Since our talk, he's much more relaxed around me, like he's let go of a heavy weight that has been tying him down and now he can freely exist. I spend a lot of time replaying what he said in my mind, mulling it over now that I'm not dulled by the effects of alcohol.

One thing has become clear, I don't know myself anymore. Maybe I never really did.

The desire to hurt him back for what he did to me is still there, simmering under the surface, but I no longer want him dead. Instead, I find myself curious, wanting to know more about the man who has discovered how to live for his own enjoyment. So that's what I do. Every night as we eat dinner at the table, I badger him with endless questions. He's usually open and willing to provide answers. The only subject he shies away from is his childhood and family. I don't push him on it, not yet at least.

We're currently mowing down on Chinese takeout. I'm asking questions around mouthfuls of mar far chicken and lo mein, oddly at ease with the man who I wanted to stab not that long ago. He looks up at me as I've paused my attack on the food and smiles, "Any other questions tonight?" His tone has a hint of amusement as he leans back and raps his knuckles on the table.

I study him before asking something that's been plaguing my mind for a while but haven't yet had the courage to broach. "You said you own your own company?" He nods in encouragement as I pause. Clearing my throat I stammer, "What, um, what's the name of it?"

Mick doesn't respond immediately, raising his hand to rub his chin. I pick at the remaining food on my plate as the seconds tick by. "Why do you want to know?" He finally asks.

I can understand his hesitation. The more details I know about him, the more dangerous it is if I ever get free again.

I shrug and shove another piece of chicken in my mouth, buying time as I chew. Swallowing, I admit the truth. "Honestly, I'm curious and I...I want to get to know you more." I look down at the table, avoiding his gaze. I feel shame wash over me at the admission. I shouldn't want to know more about him, I should be trying to run away again. But the way he has been with me since our conversations...I find myself intrigued and drawn to him in a way I can't rationalize.

Mick's fingers gently tug on my chin, lifting my face so he can look at me. His eyes are soft as he studies me in silence before stroking his thumb over my lip and pulling his hand away. Leaning back, he takes a drink and clears his throat, setting the glass back on the table. He averts his eyes and looks almost embarrassed as he answers. "Mickstruction." He mumbles. "The name of my business is Mickstruction."

Watching his face closely, I wait for the joke. That name, it's truly awful. When he doesn't say anything else, I laugh. He whips his head toward me, a scowl on his gorgeous face. I laugh harder and shake my head. Grumbling, he picks up his chopsticks and stabs a piece of chicken. "It's not that funny."

Gasping, I try to regain my composure. "Mick, that name is so bad." He glares at me and another laugh pushes past my defenses. "Truly terrible. How does anyone take you seriously?" I giggle and take a drink of water, watching him over the rim.

Sighing heavily, Mick drops his hands to the table and glowers at me. "They take us serious because we are damn good at what we do. The best really." He taps his finger on the table to accentuate the claim. I resist rolling my eyes at the blatant narcissism. "And, to be perfectly honest, it started as a joke." He shrugs, a hint of a smile ghosting his lips. "My buddies and I talked about starting the business but none of them had the guts to move forward with it. So, we all got drunk one night and the name was thrown out, and my dumbass decided to file for the business license that night while a fifth of whiskey deep." A grin breaks across his face as he recalls the memory. "It was too late at that point, and I was too prideful to back out, so I stuck with it." He joins in when I start to laugh again, looking at me with a joyful freedom shining in his eyes. "Honestly, the ridiculousness of it worked. Helped clients remember us when we were first starting out. Also made us seem more approachable and down to earth, which people really gravitate towards."

I smile at him, imagining him with his friends, all joking and carefree. My smile fades as I think of Taylor and the familiar ache returns. Softly rubbing my chest, I gulp down more water. Mick takes my free hand and soothes his thumb over my palm. "What is it, little bird?"

Studying his face, I take a deep breath.

Here goes nothing.

"Please don't get angry, I'm not running again, okay?" I look away as he stiffens. Sucking in another breath, I continue. "I miss my life, Mick.

I miss my friends. My bed." I glance over to the couch and sigh, rubbing the kink in my neck. "I don't want to get locked up again but...I can't live like this either." I turn back to him, imploring him to understand.

Mick stares at me for so long I start to fidget.

Fuck, I shouldn't have said anything. I should have just been grateful to not be chained up anymore. At least now I can use the bathroom and watch shitty TV to pass the time.

Fuck. Stupid Paige.

Finally, Mick releases my hand and leans back, nodding. "I understand." His eyes drift to the wall, expression far away.

I watch him, holding my breath. When he continues his deep contemplation, I whisper, terrified of the answer. "You're not angry? No more chains?"

He focuses back on me and I see guilt burning in his eyes. "No more chains, baby. I promise." Mick takes both of my hands in his and pulls me closer to him. Bringing the clasped hands to his face, he places a soft kiss on my knuckles. "You can go back to your life," I suck in a breath as he continues. "But you're going to need to do something for me first."

I look at him and the next word comes out without me deciding to say it.

If I had really taken a moment to think beyond the possibility of getting to go home, I would have slapped a hand over my mouth to keep it inside, but that's not what happens.

Instead, I open my mouth and breathe out the one thing I should never say.

"Anything."

It's been several days since my promise to Mick and I'm growing impatient. He hasn't mentioned me leaving again and hasn't made any hints as to what he wants me to do in return.

I climb out of the shower and scream as I run into a wall of muscles. Mick reaches out and steadies me, his eyes focused on my hardened nipples from the change in temperature. I put a hand on my chest, attempting to steady my breathing. "Um, what are you doing in here?" I ask nervously, hunting for my towel.

We haven't had sex since before he chained me up and the tension in the air is so thick you could slice it with a knife.

There's a few other things I'd like him to do with a knife.

I scold myself for the thought, my cheeks flaming. I've had to take matters into my own hands a few times now from memories of Mick sliding the smooth end of his blade inside of me.

Stop it, Paige. Not the time.

Seeing my towel hanging on a hook to my left, I quickly snatch it and wrap up my body, arms folded over my chest.

Mick doesn't say anything, just watches as I cover myself. Once my breasts are concealed, he shakes himself and looks up at my face. In a low tone, he says, "We need to go somewhere. I've gotten you some clothes and put them on the couch. Get dressed, we need to leave in ten minutes." Without waiting for me to respond, he spins on his heel and exits the bathroom.

I stare after him for a brief moment before getting into action. Wiping the steam from the mirror, I study my reflection. Unsure where we are going or how nice I need to try and make myself look, I quickly brush my teeth and slather on some of Mick's deodorant. He still hasn't gotten me one of my own and I have a suspicion he likes that I smell like him. I'd rather smell like a man than an old onion, so I haven't complained yet.

Leaving the towel around me, I exit the small bathroom and beeline for the couch. Folded on the cushions are a pair of black leggings, socks, a bra, a black cropped tank and a black zip up hoodie. Leaning against the couch on the floor is a pair of combat boots, also in black.

I see we have a theme going on.

I grab the clothes and look around, trying to find where the underwear must have fallen. When I don't see any, I call out to Mick. "Hey, I'm missing underwear. Where is it?" Mick doesn't respond but peeks his head out of his room and shoots me a wink before retreating again.

Rolling my eyes, I head into the bathroom and get dressed.

Guess I'm going commando on this adventure.

The mirror has fogged up again and I wipe it clean, staring at myself. I chew on my thumb and decide to braid my hair, figuring I don't need anything fancy if the clothes are any indicator.

As I braid, I try to guess where we are going. This will be the first time I'll have left the house since he took me again. My stomach flutters with nervous anticipation. This has to have something to do with my payment for getting to go home, I just hope it's something I can live with myself afterwards.

With one last look in the mirror, I head out and flop onto the couch, shoving my feet into the boots. The sound of quiet footsteps draws my eyes up and I see Mick standing in the doorway to his room, dressed in his own black ensemble. He's wearing steel-toed boots, a pair of jeans that mold to his muscular thighs and a button up shirt that he has rolled the sleeves up, showing off his forearms.

I lick my lips as I look at him. This man could make a nun sin, he's so delectable.

Easy girl, this man is also a murderer. A serial killer. And he's already tortured you once. You need to calm down and keep your pussy in check.

At the brief attention, I feel heat flood between my legs and press my thighs together. It's that moment I'm reminded again I have no underwear on.

Great, just great. Make yourself soak through your leggings. At least they're black, I guess.

Dragging my thoughts out of the gutter, I nervously smile up at Mick and push off the couch. Rocking on the balls of my feet, I ask, "Soooo, where are we going?" Mick still doesn't say anything, instead grunting and gesturing for the front door.

Geez, wonder what's gotten into him. Cat got his tongue? I have a kitty that could take his tongue for him.

Goodness, I am in so much trouble. Apparently living with this fallen god has my hormones in overdrive. Following behind him, I watch his ass in his jeans and groan internally.

Yup, that is so *not helping.*

Walking awkwardly, I shift to ease some of the tension between my legs and jog to catch up with his long strides. Mick opens the passenger door to his car and I clamber inside. He leans in and buckles my seat belt, tugging it to make sure it's secure. He did this last time too and my body aches to lean forward and close the space between us.

Mick pauses to gaze down at me before pulling away and striding around the car. He slips into his seat and starts the engine, backing up. I watch his hand as he spins the wheel with his palm, fingers splayed.

Ugh, even that is hot as fuck.

I close my eyes and turn my head, only opening them once I'm facing away.

I stare out the window and ease into the silence, mind running as I contemplate where we are going.

The drive takes almost an hour and my anxiety continues to grow as we head deeper into the wooded area, leaving any civilization far behind us. I worry my bottom lip as we pull off the road onto a bumpy trail, my hand holding the door in a death grip.

Mick has kept up his silent routine and I have given up on getting an answer from him. So, even though I'm eighty percent sure he's driving me somewhere to finally finish the job and kill me, I don't say anything. That fear heightens as we pull up to a small building and Mick slows to a stop. I scramble for the handle and climb out, clutching my arms around myself and looking around.

I feel Mick walk up behind me and I tremble, whispering, "Where are we?" Not surprisingly, I get no response.

I feel the pressure of his hand on my lower back as he guides me toward the intimidating building. It's not the building itself that's so worrisome, it's the aura emanating from the space. Even with lights shining from the top and side, sporadically placed around the brick, there's a darkness that shrouds it. Something about this place feels really, really wrong.

I hold my breath as Mick reaches into his pocket and pulls out a key. He drops his hand from my back and walks to the door, unlocking it and pushing inward. I'm surprised it doesn't creak. There's a haunted feeling that gusts out of the open space and I take an involuntary step back. Mick looks back at me, motioning his head toward the entry. "Come." His tone is low and full of authority. My legs tremble as I obey and wobble inside. He follows behind me and shuts the door with a loud thud.

I blink several times as my eyes adjust to the bright lights, a stark difference to the darkness outside. The first thing I notice are the rows of tools lining the walls. There are so many, all various types. A cursory glance shows different kinds of hammers, screws, and other things you'd expect to find in a tool shed. As I continue looking, I see there are more sinister and deadly items lined up as well. A collection of knives, whips, guns, even a couple spiked maces.

I'm so confused by what I'm seeing, I look to Mick for an explanation, only he's not looking at me. My head moves to see what's got his attention and I suck in a breath, my hands flying to my mouth.

Time freezes.

I shake my head and blink, rapidly opening and closing my eyes to dispel the image in front of me. Silently begging for this to be some horrible dream or a hallucination. No one answers my unspoken pleas.

In front of me, dangling from chains that look all too familiar, a man hangs with his head between his shoulders. His arms are pulled up and his shoulders strain under the weight of his body. The man doesn't have anything on his torso but his legs are still covered by a dirty pair of jeans. His bare feet dangle on the ground.

My muscles begin to unfreeze as the initial shock wears off and I look rapidly between Mick and the man in front of us. "Mick? What's going on? Who is that?" I don't recognize my voice as I ask the questions.

Mick turns his focus to me, his pupils dilated and lips parted. He reaches out a hand to brush along my cheek and I flinch away. Narrowing his eyes, he grips the braid at the nape of my neck. "This is how you earn your freedom, little bird." I'm shaking my head, refusing to accept what he's saying. He jerks my head back roughly by my hair. "You wanted to go home, this is how you do it. How you show me I can trust you." He softens his tone but keeps a firm grip on me. "There's no more running, baby. You either let your demon out to play with me, or we return to my home and I let mine out to play with you."

I stare back at him, desperately trying to think of a way out of this situation.

No, no, no. You did it again. You let his sweet words and good looks lull you into a false sense of security. This man is evil, he's pure evil, and you wanted to "get to know him better".

I close my eyes and feel a tear trail down my cheek.

Maybe I deserve this, I obviously don't have any self preservation skills. I let myself fall in his trap. Again.

I choke back a sob as I feel the finality of this moment.

It's him or me.

Opening my eyes, I look hard at the man hanging unconscious in the too bright room.

It's him or me.

Chapter 21

Mick

I have never been so turned on in my life.

Bringing Paige here tonight is a decision I've been struggling with since our conversation. I know there's darkness inside of her. I can sense it, calling out to the darkness in me. I just need to get her to realize that societal morals don't matter. That she can have true happiness if she gives in to her baser instincts.

I watch her fighting against herself, my hand wrapped around the long braid draped down her back. My thoughts keep returning to the fact that she's not wearing any panties. That was intentional on my part. I know if she gives in tonight, I won't be able to hold back from claiming her body again. I've allowed guilt over what I did to hold me back but bringing her here, seeing her stand before our victim...

Fuck. I need this woman.

Paige steadies herself and squares her shoulders, determination filling her eyes. She turns my direction and gives me a nod. Quietly, she whispers, "Okay." The simple word is like a shot of pure ecstasy to my veins.

Yanking her toward me, I slam my mouth against hers. My kiss isn't gentle. It's hard, unforgiving and desperate. She claws at my back as I tug her hair, arching her neck. I pull my lips from hers and kiss down her face to the exposed skin of her throat. Sinking my teeth into her flesh, she moans as I lick the bite to soothe the sting. My cock is painfully hard, twitching in my pants and begging to plunge inside of her.

I can't wait any longer.

With my hand still gripping her hair, I tug Paige away from me and push her to her knees. She sinks down and grips my thighs, peering up at me with bruised lips. I run my thumb along her swollen bottom lip. "So beautiful." I push my thumb between her lips as I demand, "Suck." She obeys immediately.

Closing her plump lips, she hollows her cheeks. My chest rumbles as I groan, "Fuck, baby. I need you. Now." She hums, licking along my fingertip and softly biting down. Her eyes still locked with mine, she pushes forward, taking the rest of my thumb into her mouth. I return my other hand to the back of her head and take hold of her braid. Pulling sharply, my thumb slips out of her mouth, a small line of saliva dripping down her chin. My voice strained with need, I rasp, "Take out my cock." Her fingers move instantly, fumbling with my belt. She rushes to undue my button and zipper the moment the belt clicks open. I suck in a breath when her hand slips into my boxers and wraps around my dick.

Paige pushes down my boxers and grasps the base of my cock in a firm grip, looking up at me for further direction. *Fuck me.* "Good girl," I praise and watch as her pupils dilate. "Now wrap those pretty little lips around my cock." Paige leans forward and takes me into her mouth. I tip my head back and release a long moan as the wet heat encircles my cock.

She doesn't need any more direction from me as she runs her tongue over the head and sucks. Her hand still wrapped around the base begins stroking up and down. I jump as she reaches her other hand up and cups my balls, massaging lightly.

"Fuck, baby." I groan. With my hand at the back of her head, I push her farther forward until I hear her muffled gagging around my dick. My balls tighten and I hold my breath.

It's been so long, *too long*, and her mouth is heaven.

Paige gives my balls a light tug and I can't hold back any longer. Knocking her hands away, I grip her face between mine to hold her steady as I pull back and thrust into her mouth. She gags again, the sound making me more feral. I begin to fuck her mouth with ruthless, punishing thrusts. Her hands grip my thighs, fingers digging into the fabric of my jeans. I watch her face as I take my pleasure from her. My balls slap up and hit her chin with each slam of my hips. Her lips stretch around my cock, tears running down her face, saliva dripping from her mouth.

Fucking perfect.

Picking up my speed, I grunt each word between thrusts. "This mouth was made for me." She whimpers, opening up her throat with the sound. My hips buck as I bump into the back of her throat. "Shit. Fuck. I'm gonna come." That's all the warning she gets before I shove deep and still, warm spurts of my cum shoot into her throat as I moan through my release.

Pulling out, I watch with rapt attention as Paige swallows down the cum, a small amount spilling out. I reach forward and gather it up with two fingers. Pushing them back into her mouth, she licks my fingers clean with a moan. I slip my fingers free and gently cup her chin. "You're so perfect." I murmur, leaning down to press a kiss against her lips.

Forcing myself back, I tuck away my dick and straighten my pants as Paige clambers to her feet. I throw an arm around her shoulders and direct her attention back to the man hanging before us. "Time to play, little bird." I whisper into her ear, causing a shiver to run down her body. A smile pulls at my lips as I guide her forward, turning to the table where I've set up all my favorite tools to choose from.

Stopping in front of the table, I gesture toward it and Paige tentatively leans forward. "What are these for?" She asks in a hushed voice, running her fingers along a machete.

I chuckle. "I think you know." She dips her chin as she focuses her attention on the table. Picking up a metal stake, she weighs it in her hand before setting it back down. She meticulously works her way through each of the items. I watch her, enthralled by her intense focus, curiosity flaming as I wait to see what she is going to choose.

Taking a deep breath, she slowly lets the air out of her lungs and reaches forward. I let out a laugh as she lifts the tool, nodding to herself. I'm leveled by her glare and I hold up my hands, trying to hold back my laughter. "I'm just surprised." I chuckle. Huffing, she turns and makes her way over to the man dangling from the chains attached to his wrists.

Nicholas Spurr.

I don't usually pick my victims on some faulty moral code, but when I made the decision to bring Paige along for this one, I thought it would be easier for her if there was some wrongdoing they had committed. And this man? This man deserved death.

Paige stops in front of him and tentatively reaches out, poking him in the shoulder. He doesn't move or respond to her touch. She peers over her shoulder in concern. "Did you...did you already kill him?" Her brow furrows as she looks back at the man in question.

I laugh again, causing her to narrow her eyes at me. "No, sweetheart. I didn't kill him yet. He's still under the drugs. I wasn't sure how much, uh, convincing you would need." I rub the back of my neck. "So I gave him more than I usually do. I can wake him up if you're ready?" I gesture toward the table, offering her a half smile.

She looks back at Nicholas and shakes her head, taking a step back. "I-I don't think I can do this." Her voice trembles, hand tightening around the weapon.

I walk up behind her and slide my arms around her waist. Pulling her body back against mine, I nuzzle into her neck. My lips at her ear, I murmur, "Would it make it any easier to know he's a bad man?" She sucks in a breath and nods, eyes still fixed forward. "He is. A very bad man."

Shuddering, Paige presses into me. "What did he do?" She whispers.

Flashes of the information I dug up in my research fill my mind. Gritting my teeth, I exhale heavily as I attempt to keep my emotions in check. "He sold his daughter so he could get a fix." I growl, fury boiling my blood. Paige gasps and lifts a shaky hand to her mouth, eyes wide in horror. "She was only 11 when he started this. I also discovered he has continued to do so. She's 16 now." My arms tighten as the demand for payment in blood for his actions surges through me.

Old memories try to push through as I'm reminded of another drug addict who sold someone's body for his own benefit. I close my eyes and try to fight against the images.

My mother crying after her body was brutally used by some bastard. My father shaking hands with various men, exchanging money or drugs between their clasped hands. My bruised face staring in the reflection as I yet again failed to stop it from happening. My mother's crumpled body lying at the feet of my father. My father's butchered face as I finally enacted my revenge years later.

Paige shifts in my arms, bringing me back to the room. Her eyes slide closed as she breathes through her nose. After a few deep breaths, she opens her eyes and the rage I feel inside is reflected back in those liquid caramel orbs. Turning sharply, Paige drops the crowbar she had originally chosen and snatches up the machete. Staring at me with fiery determination, she speaks, her voice low. "Wake him up."

A wicked grin spreads across my face as I reach for the smelling salts.

Chapter 22

Paige

Hatred. Burning, hot rage. My body fills with the liquid molten lava of pure fury coursing through my veins.

A child, his fucking child! This man is going to scream. He's going to beg.

A small part of me is whispering that this isn't me, that once I do this, there's no turning back. I beat that part back. I didn't feel like I had a choice before, but now? Now I am choosing this, and I'm going to make it hurt.

Mick strides over to the vile man and passes the salts under his nose. He jerks and looks around, confusion changing to fear as he sees Mick glaring down at him. "Hello Nicholas." Mick spits at him. The man, Nicholas, shrinks away from the venom in his voice.

"Whe-where am I?" Shaking his head, Mick clucks his tongue but doesn't answer the question. Growing angry at being ignored, Nicholas' voice raises with each word. "What's going on? Who are you?"

Mick sighs and rubs his jaw, looking over the man. "You're asking the wrong questions."

"W-what?" He sputters.

Another sigh. "You shouldn't be asking who I am. Your real concern is my girl over there." Mick gestures in my direction and Nicholas' eyes finally slide over to me, widening when he notices the machete in my hands. I bare my teeth at him and Mick chuckles. "Magnificent, isn't she?" He claps Nicholas' cheek then turns around and strides back to me, drawing me in for a kiss that leaves me breathless. When he pulls back, he runs a finger along my chin, desire burning in his eyes. "All yours, baby."

With that, Mick steps around me and leans back against the table, crossing his ankles. I take a couple steadying breaths, fingers flexing on the handle.

Now or never.

I go to take a step forward but my legs are shaking too much and I stumble. I quickly catch my balance but Nicholas barks a laugh. Leveling him with a glare, I'm about to tell him to go to hell when movement catches my eye.

In a few long strides, Mick is suddenly in front of him again. His hand wrapping around the man's throat, Mick leans forward and growls in his face. "Did you just laugh at my woman?" Nicholas lets out a little whimper but Mick doesn't wait for a response as he pulls back his other hand and snaps it forward.

I flinch at the sound of bone crunching and Nicholas lets out a blood curdling scream. He's begging but it falls on deaf ears as Mick pummels his face, hitting him again and again. I watch, frozen in place. It's like witnessing a wild animal. There's no thought to his attack, just action as he punches. Mick continues his throws long after Nicholas has fallen silent. It's not until the sound of the machete hitting the ground reaches his ears that he stops.

Freezing, he slowly turns toward me and I let out a cry at the sight. Blood has splattered over Mick's face, his knuckles are busted open and his chest rises and falls heavily as he pants. Behind him, I see Nicholas' face, or what's left of it. Blood pours down and drips onto the floor, his nose is caved in along with half his jaw. One eye has burst several vessels and the once white sclera is now bright red. His eyebrow is swollen and several gashes litter the skin, having broken from the impact of Mick's fist.

I stumble back a step and look back to Mick, eyes wide in horror. It's not just the gruesome sight before me that has me falling apart, it's the reality that I was only moments away from doing something just as violent to the man.

I blink as my vision blurs and find my lungs can't fill with air. Raising a hand to my chest, I hunch forward and desperately try to suck in the much needed oxygen. My body shakes violently and tears splash on the ground below me. My stomach rolls and I start gagging, causing my already blurred vision to swim as I grow more lightheaded. Spinning around, I dart to the wall and lean against it heavily, bracing myself with my hands as I vomit.

I feel gentle hands pull my braid back and wipe the sweat from my forehead as I heave. My throat burns from the stomach acid rising. Tremors rack my body as it tries to purge this sickness from me. Salty tears mix with the flavor of vomit. I wipe my mouth with the back of my hand and shuffle away, bracing against the wall and sliding to the ground.

My body has revolted against me, forcing me to attempt to remove the darkness in any way necessary. The problem is, it's not a physical evil that needs to be expelled, it's me.

My mind, my soul, has been tainted and all I can think of is that if Mick hadn't already killed Nicholas, I would pick up the weapon I dropped and do it myself.

After my exorcist worthy reaction, Mick left and came back with a rag, cleaning up my face and hand. He pressed a soft kiss to my forehead and knuckles, then stood and cleaned up the rest of the mess.

I watched with unseeing eyes as he lowered the chains and Nicholas' body crumpled to the floor. Mick proceeded to meticulously remove every tooth and burn off the pads of each of his fingers and toes. He disappeared again and returned with a large tarp, proceeding to wrap the corpse up before hauling it out of the building. When he returned, he grabbed a hose I hadn't noticed before and sprayed down the blood and vomit on the floor, pushing it to the drain in the middle of the room.

After a few more minutes spent rearranging the items on the table to their spots along the back walls, Mick slowly approaches me, palms up. I stare at him, unblinking, as he grows closer. "Paige, baby." He softly says as he kneels in front of me. I don't react, continuing to stare, my entire body numb. He stretches out both arms and cradles my face in his hands. "Are you okay, little bird?"

I take a shaky breath and give a slight shake of my head, as much as his hands allow. Dropping my gaze, I notice a blotch of red on his shirt and reach out my hand, my fingers resting lightly on the wet stain. I brush my fingertips across his chest, moving around the blood. Lifting my hand to my eyes while rubbing together my fingers, I watch the red liquid work into my skin and whimper.

Mick immediately pulls me into his arms, holding me tight against his chest. "Shh, it's okay. Shh." He soothes, rubbing my back.

When I finally speak, my voice is hollow. "I was gonna do it."

You still would.

I flinch at the truth in the words. No matter how much I want to argue with that annoying voice, I know I can't.

Mick continues circling my back, pressing a kiss to the top of my head. "I know, baby."

I shake my head and pull back, looking into his eyes. "No. I was going to kill him. I didn't even stop to think. If you hadn't..." My voice trails off as a shudder runs through me. Mick stares back at me, then nods.

His eyes are full of pride and passion as he looks at me. My stomach clenches and I swallow as he begins to speak again. Moving his hand to my throat, he slips his thumb along my jaw. "I know. I've seen it. You have the same darkness in you that I do." He keeps gently rubbing my jaw, murmuring, almost as if he's lost in thought and I'm not meant to hear his words. "We are made of the same, two pieces of the same soul." His eyes refocus, his gaze intense. "I *know* you, Paige. Let me show you who you really are." I don't get a chance to respond before he leans forward and takes my mouth. This kiss is different than any that we've shared. It is slow and full of passion. I can feel Mick pouring himself into it, begging me to see him, to recognize him as he has recognized me.

I'm frozen, unwilling to acknowledge this connection between us, scared of what it will mean if I do. I sit there, overwhelmed by the feel of him. He pulls back just enough to speak, his lips brushing mine with the words. "Please. Please let me." He presses our lips together again, sticking out his tongue to lick mine. He doesn't force them apart, instead he waits for my invitation.

I hear his words ringing in my ears and the sound fills me, stretching out to all the empty spaces of my being.

"I know you, Paige."

I open my lips, my heart, my soul.

I open and let him in.

Chapter 23

Paige

2 months later

My phone vibrates in my back pocket and I push back my smile. The man in front of me continues to ask endless questions. I'm beginning to wonder if he's ever going to order anything. My foot taps as my patience wears thin and I glance at the clock again.

Twenty minutes. I can do this for twenty more minutes.

I've been giving myself the same pep talk for the last hour as time crawls at a snail's pace. I'm anxious to leave work. I have big plans tonight and I'm buzzing in anticipation.

The customer draws my attention back as he finally orders a small black coffee. I grip the pen in my hand and plaster on a fake smile and write down his order. I'm tempted to shove the pen somewhere but decide now isn't the time. I take his money, give him his change, and make quick work of pouring his drink.

Since he was the last customer in line, I dart back to the storage area and pull out my phone to check the message.

Mick

You ready for tonight, baby?

Me

*Yes! I am nervous though *nervous face emoji**

Mick

Don't be, you'll do great

I don't reply, opting to heart react to his message instead.

It's going to be my first time doing this alone, not that I really believe Mick will let me do it by myself. If it wasn't just for his obsessive need to protect me, he'd still demand to be there because he gets off on this shit. My face heats as I remember just how worked up he got the last time. I had bruises for a week from the intensity of his passion.

Schooling my face, I head back to Brandi's office to let her know I'm taking off. I knock on the door softly and wait. "Come in." I hear her call through the door. I push into the room and give her a smile. "Oh, hey Paige. Heading out for the day?"

I give her a nod. "Yup, just served the last customer and Sophie is already all set up with the till." Brandi makes a noncommittal noise and I see a brief moment of nervousness cross her face before she hides it away.

Clearing her throat, she asks, "So, any plans for the evening?"

I try to hide my irritation. I'm grateful that she cares, really. After I've disappeared from work not once but twice, by Mick's hand, I can understand her misgivings. She doesn't know who we are to each other though, and there's no way I'm about to explain it to her. Not if I want to stay out of prison or a psych ward. So instead I shrug. "Nothing big." I lie.

"Hmm." It's obvious she doesn't believe me. I brace myself as I see her make the decision to say something further. In a hushed tone, she rushes out, "I don't like him, Paige. There's something wrong with that guy." My gaze turns icy as she speaks and she quickly throws up her hands, leaning back in her seat. "I'm just worried about you, that's all."

I let out a sigh. "I know Brandi. And thank you, truly. After what I've been through..." Brief images of being chained up flash through my mind and I suppress a shudder.

No one knows the extent of my captivity. When Mick let me go home the night of Nicholas' murder, I decided the less people knew the better, for both of us. "Anyway, I appreciate your concern. But there's really no need. Mick's a great guy and he really cares about me. Once you get past his quirks," *Like the fact that he enjoys murdering people.* "He's a big sweetheart."

Brandi snorts and gives me a small smile, seemingly having decided that she's not going to press the issue today. "Alright dear. Have a good night." Having been dismissed, I tell her the same and head out.

Let's get this party started.

"Babe, you know I worry about you." Taylor's voice carries through the speaker of my car. Another pang of guilt hits me at the sound of her concern. It's not fair to her that I have to keep lying. One time was bad enough, but now twice?

My mind swirls as I stretch my fingers around the wheel.

No point in beating yourself up, there's nothing you can do about it. Not like you can say, "Sorry love, I swear I didn't just go crazy and disappear for weeks without calling. No, I was taken again by the same man as before but this time was different. Like certifiably insane different. You know, he chained me to a wall, then released me and gave me limited freedom to exist while doing things to my body I didn't even know were possible. Oh but that's not the best part! He showed me that I might, sort of, possibly, be okay with murdering people. People who deserve it of course. So yeah, no big right? No hard feelings?"

Trying not to groan, I force myself to stay focused on my friend's voice. "I really think you should come over tonight. I just have this, like, I dunno, bad feeling?" I wince, maybe she picked up more on things than I thought.

Keeping my tone soft, I try to reassure her. "I'm okay, I promise Tay. I know I disappeared for a while but I won't do it again." I can hear her huff on the other end of the line. "Why don't we get coffee together on Sunday? I have a shift tomorrow that I can't miss but let's plan to catch up." The desperation seeps into my voice, terrified of pushing away my closest friend.

Silence fills the car as I wait for her response, my heart beating erratically in my chest. A sigh precedes her quiet resignation. "Okay. Sunday. But be careful please Paige. I can't lose you."

My eyes fill with tears and I nod, even though she can't see me. "I will Tay. I promise." I pause briefly before adding, "And I love you. So fucking much."

I can hear the unshed tears in her voice as it cracks. "I love you too bitch. Don't scare me like that again." She lets out a laugh at her poor attempt to alleviate the tension. Because I'll take any excuse to move on from my own fuck-ups, I join in her laughter. "Listen, I've got to go. Beau is going to be here any minute. But text me later to plan Sunday, yeah?" I'm relieved the sound of her pain has lessened, even if it's just barely.

"Yes dear. Sunday. It's a date." I confirm and we disconnect the call. I sit in silence for a good portion of the drive before deciding to switch on the radio.

"-confirmation that the body found has been linked to notorious serial killer, dubbed the Blood Shadow, who is still at large. We have reached out to the police department for an official statement and have been advised that the case is still ongoing and they can make no further comment. We, at News 27, will report back as soon as we have any further information."

"Thank you Gerr-"

I click off the radio as I pull up to the small park. There's not many people around, most likely due to the fact that the police discovered Nicholas' body three nights ago.

I had flown into a panic when the alert popped up on my phone. Mick spent several hours comforting me and promising that there was nothing to lead back to us. I wanted to believe him, but I've seen enough crime documentaries to know that it's being cocky that gets most people caught. After making him swear to be extra careful while the investigation was still fresh, he ran me a bath and I drank through an entire bottle of wine.

Circling the parking lot, I spot a space that's partially obscured by trees.

Perfect.

Butterflies flutter in my stomach as I turn the car off and glance around. There's a handful of other vehicles sporadically parked around the lot. My eyes roam until I zero in on the one I'm looking for. Because of the late hour, only a couple light posts provide any visual aid through the darkness. Despite the lack of proper lighting, I can tell this is the correct car. It's an old van showing clear signs of years of neglect. Several dents line the body and the once shining gray paint has faded and begun to chip off from too much exposure to the elements.

I watch intently, my eyes straining to see if there is anyone inside. A bright light flashes next to me, drawing my attention away. I look over and see my phone has lit up with a text. Snatching it up, I quickly open the chat.

Mick

You see her yet?

Me

Not yet, found the van though.

Mick

Great job baby. You're amazing. Text me if you need me.

Me

*I won't *winking emoji* *kissy face emoji**

Setting my phone back down, I return my attention to the vehicle. I'm not entirely confident but we've run through the scenarios so many times I could do them in my sleep.

Something shifted inside of me the night of Nicholas' death. I could feel it clawing its way out of a deeply suppressed part of me. I hadn't wanted to admit at the time that I was craving the violence that I witnessed Mick unleash.

After he bared himself to me and I opened to him, we didn't speak another word. We had gotten back in the car and he drove me straight to my apartment. The whole ride, I was in shock, my brain short circuiting as it replayed the night in my head. Mick gave me the space to work through it all. When he pulled up to my building, it took me several moments to register where we were.

He ushered me up to my apartment and inside, setting my purse down on the counter and handing me my cell phone. "I put my number in there so you can contact me whenever you need to." He winked. "Or want to." I smiled at him robotically and watched as he leaned forward, pressing a kiss to my forehead before turning and leaving.

Mick had immediately texted me, reiterating what he had said. It must have been obvious I wasn't able to fully comprehend much at the time.

After a much needed shower, I had opted to just crash, and crash I did. Waking up 14 hours later to several texts from Mick along with a few calls.

8:54am
Mick
Good morning baby
9:17am
Mick
*You still sleeping huh? *laughing emoji**
9:32am
Mick
You good?

2 missed calls

9:53am
Mick
Paige, answer your phone. I need to know you're okay.

4 missed calls

10:15am

Mick

Paige. Answer me.

1 missed call

10:21am

Mick

Okay, I'm coming over. If this is you hiding, know there is nowhere you can hide, little bird, that I won't find you.

11:26am

Mick

You look so beautiful sleeping. There's a bottle of water and some pills next to the bed for your head. I'll be outside.

I glanced over and, sure enough, found the water and painkillers lying on my nightstand.

That had been the moment that our relationship changed too. Instead of being captor and captive, we became partners. Two people who cared and cared for each other.

Motion pulls me back to the present. Rolling my shoulders, I focus on the task at hand.

Chapter 24

Mick

My spot on the street gives me the perfect view to see both Paige and her target.

Paige had insisted she was ready to do this on her own but I can't bring myself to leave her alone when so many things could go wrong, especially with the discovery of Nicholas' body still fresh on the public's mind. I had insisted that we were fine and nothing could lead back to us, and I meant it. But I'm still not willing to chance some do-gooder spotting her.

I see her pick her phone up and respond to my texts, smiling as I reply. After her last message, she sets down her phone and squares her shoulders, attention focused on the target vehicle.

Since taking Paige home, she has come to accept the darkness inside of her. Accompanying me on stakeouts and another visit to my kill room.

She had participated in the violence this time and I almost came in my pants like a fucking teenager. She was glorious, heaving breaths with blood sprayed over her. I had fucked her right there, in front of the man slowly bleeding to death.

After that, Paige asked if she could choose the next victim and take them. I was hesitant but unwilling to squelch her enthusiasm. So I agreed and made a mental promise to myself that I wouldn't let her out of my sight.

Making true on that promise, I am now stalking my woman while she stalks another.

I shift in my seat to reach the binoculars stashed in my glove compartment. Peering through them, I see her look around briefly before sliding out of her car and sneaking over to the van. Once next to the doors, she reaches back and pulls out something, grasping tightly. She shifts and I notice it is the vial of Propofol, my nerves steady as I watch her proceed with our plan perfectly.

Reaching her hand out, Paige grasps the handle and slides the large door open. She peers in and looks confused, glancing around at her surroundings. A tingling starts running up my spine.

Something isn't right.

As I adjust to climb out of my vehicle to go investigate, a scream pierces the air and my entire body freezes. In slow motion, I turn my head and watch as Paige is yanked into the back of the van. The door slams shut as the engine roars to life and peels out of the parking lot.

Frozen for the length of a heartbeat, I come back to my awareness and let out a roar as I start my own vehicle and slam on the gas.

No one takes what is mine.

No one.

CHAPTER 25

PAIGE

My head pounds, my eyes burn, and there's something hot and wet on my scalp. Reaching my hand up to investigate, I find my arm unable to move. I suppress a sigh as I discreetly pull against the binds on my wrists.

I'm getting real tired of people tying me up. I think bitterly, wincing as the pounding in my head increases with each tug of my arms.

I should never have insisted on doing this alone, it was cocky and dangerous. But I had wanted to prove I could, to Mick and to myself.

Great job, look where that got you.

I suck in a quiet breath and pause my futile attempts. Willing my thrashing heartbeat to calm down, I force my body still to give me more time before my captors realize I'm awake.

There was added danger to this particular victim, but that was the reason I chose her.

Vanessa Farley is a bait and switch for one of the local sex trafficking groups. Her job is to lure unsuspecting women in so her employers can capture them easily. Mick had thrown a huge fit when I told him my plan, saying it was much too dangerous. I was so confident we could do this that I eventually wore him down. At the moment, I'm wishing he would have stuck to his guns.

Grinding my teeth, I chance a peek around me. I'm in the back of a large vehicle, most likely the van I was staking out. It's dark and empty except for the two rows of bench seating on either side of the space. Cautiously, I peer down and see that my legs have been strapped to the floor, a rope running through a metal ring soldered to the floorboard. Contorting my body, I peek over my shoulder. My eyes focus on my bound wrists, finding they have been tied together and the attached rope secured to another similar looking metal ring on the bench.

I resign to the reality that there is no way I am going to get myself out of this, my only hope is that Mick was predictable and saw me get taken. Forcing my breathing to remain even, my mind retraces the events leading up to my capture. There had been no sign of Vanessa, or anyone else, when I approached the van. I was shocked to find the vehicle empty when I slid open the door. At least I *thought* it was empty, until large hands gripped my forearms and yanked me back into the dark space.

There's no way they could have known I was coming, or why, which meant there was only one real possibility behind my kidnapping. They were at that park for a reason. Rather than taking Vanessa and putting her schemes to an end, I handed myself over on a silver platter.

My fear ratchets up as the severity of my situation sets in.

I'm alone.

I don't have my phone or any way to contact anyone.

No one but Mick knew where I was going tonight.

I'm being kidnapped. Again. And somehow I think I'd prefer to be chained up in Mick's room to whatever these people have planned for me.

I push down the tears that are threatening to well up in my eyes. Closing them instead, I send out a plea I wouldn't have thought would cross my mind two months ago.

Mick, please save me.

The van jostles, startling me awake. I don't remember falling asleep but must have at some point. My head throbs and the moisture seems to have spread farther, causing me to think I hit it hard when they pulled me inside. Concerned I might have a concussion, I make a vow to stay awake.

Keeping my eyes closed, I attempt to stave off the worsening of my injury by avoiding unnecessary strain to my eyes. A sound has my ears perking up. My sluggish brain works to place it, recognizing the inflection of a voice. Multiple voices.

"We're almost there. You're going to need to go back out and get another girl tonight, in case this one doesn't make it." A gruff voice rumbles from somewhere within the confined space.

A feminine voice snides in response, "We wouldn't have to worry about that if you hadn't hit her head." The wound aches at the reminder.

Ah, so that's what happened.

I bite my cheek against the pain, straining to hear the conversation.

"She wouldn't stop screaming!" The deep voice snaps back. "It was going to draw too much attention and you know it."

A sigh sounds before the woman concedes. "I suppose, Ronaldo. Just hurry up, I was hoping to get out early tonight. Drake and I have plans."

I cringe at the fiendish tone of her voice. I'm pretty sure whatever plans she is referring to are going to be at the expense of someone else. A pang of guilt stabs through me as I wish again that I had accomplished the job.

Ronaldo snickers. "Aye aye captain."

Neither speak again until we pull up somewhere and come to a stop. The breaks press down hard and I'm thrown to the side, only stopped by the ropes tying me in place. I take several deep breaths to calm myself and brace for whatever's about to come next.

In and out. In and out.

I repeat the mantra in my head to calm the storm in my mind.

The door slides open and I see the woman I had set out the night planning to capture. Her appearance is carefully designed to appear ragged and defenseless, aiding in her ability to draw in the help of her targets. The gleam in her eyes as she scans over my body reveals there is nothing helpless about this woman. She is a predator in every sense of the word and I have fallen into her trap.

I steal my shoulders and refuse to cower before her gaze.

She may be dangerous, but so am I.

Whatever Mick awoke in me is thirsting for blood, screaming for violence, demanding to be unleashed. The side of her mouth ticks up in a sinister grin, her eyes holding my own as she purrs, "Well hello there. I see you're awake." Her head tilts to the side as she studies me. "I am impressed you aren't crying or screaming. Most girls in your position are quite out of sorts." I scowl at her which only causes her grin to widen. "Ah, you are going to be so fun to break."

Turning away from the van, Vanessa shouts something and a large man takes her place. I shrink back instinctively when he reaches in and unhooks the rope from the floor, leaving my feet still tied but free from the metal ring. Grunting, he climbs into the van and grabs hold of my shirt. Yanking me forward, he shoves my head between my legs while placing a firm hand onto the back of my scalp. I wince as the pressure in my head increases from the angle and painful grip he has on me. I can hear him fumbling with the rope on my wrists with his free hand.

Swallowing the pained noise from the jostling, I focus on my breathing again.

In and out. In and out.

The hand holding my head down disappears seconds before I'm lifted up and carried out of the van. He slings me over his shoulder as he strides toward our destination, the bouncing from his steps sending spears of agony through my head. I taste the metallic tinge of blood as my teeth sink into my cheek to keep from crying out.

We must enter a building as the dirt ground below us changes to concrete slabs. The man continues his agonizing pace until coming to a sudden halt. I hear a light rapping sound on wood and someone calls out, "Come in." My head is fuzzy from the blood pooling but something familiar about the voice tugs at my mind. The movement starts again and a small moan escapes my lips before I can stop it. Ignoring my pain, the man deposits me onto a metal chair, fastening the dangling ropes to more metal hooks secured to the ground below. He pulls the ropes tight enough that my back has to arch to alleviate the pressure, causing my breasts to be fully on display.

I glare daggers at the man until he steps aside and Vanessa fills my vision again. Striding toward me, her eyes roam again and narrow on my chest. She stops in front of me and reaches out. I bare my teeth at her, venom pouring from my eyes. Ignoring me, she grabs the zipper of my jacket and tears it down, revealing the thin black tank top I'm wearing underneath.

I'm wearing the same outfit Mick had laid out for me the first night we went to his kill room together. I had been so proud and excited dressing in it. I even opted to go without underwear again, so sure we would be celebrating a victory. Now my stomach sours as I realize there is even less protection between me and these perverted monsters.

Vanessa eyes me again and steps back, holding her hand out to the large man next to her. "Thank you, Ronaldo." She purrs when he hands over a small flick knife. She opens the blade and grasps the top of my tank, pulling the material away from my skin and slicing through until it falls to the side along my jacket. Closing the knife, her eyes light as she takes in my exposed breasts, only protected now by the lace bra. She gives herself a nod and pulls out her phone. Pressing it to her ear, she speaks too softly for my frazzled brain to comprehend. She ends the call quickly and slides the phone back into her pocket. "Stay here with her and make sure she doesn't try anything." Vanessa strides out of the room, leaving me alone with the brute.

My stomach rolls again. Ronaldo's gaze drags over my exposed skin, lingering on my breasts. The uneasiness grows as he slowly licks his lips and takes half a step forward. Before I can say or do anything, the door slams open. He jumps back, straightening his posture and masking his expression. I have a small moment of relief until my vision settles on the newcomer.

Striding into the room without a care in the world, Detective Kristoph Lary appraises my body before his eyes land on mine. He freezes in place, shock shrouding his expression, no doubt reflecting the same as mine. He blinks several times before a smile creeps onto his face. A shudder runs down my spine as he begins to speak.

"Hello Miss Greene. I'm surprised to see you here but can't say I'm unhappy." He drops his eyes to my breasts and drags them back up, one eyebrow raised. "I see what he was so enamored with." I'm about to ask who when the distant sound of gunfire fills the space. Annoyed by the interruption, Kristoph turns to Ronaldo. Glowering, he snaps, "Go check that out." When Ronaldo hesitates, Kristoph curses and shouts, "Now!"

At the command, the large man whirls on his heels and sprints out of the room.

Taking a moment to compose himself, Kristoph turns and shuts the door. My heart races as I watch him slide a metal bolt across and lock us inside the small room. "Sorry for the disruption, Miss Greene. I can assure you that I take this business quite seriously and will ensure your safety, at least until you have been procured for the right price." His eyes twinkle from some hidden joke.

I fight back the bile rising in my throat, trying to focus on how I'm going to get out of this. My mind is a twisted mess and offers no help. The only thing I'm sure of is that I need to keep him talking. I have the sickening feeling that once he's done with me, I will disappear and even Mick won't be able to find me.

Racking my brain, I grasp for something, anything, to say. A thought pushes past the tangles, a reminder of something he said earlier. "Who were you talking about?" Part of me doesn't want to know the answer but the misgiving that there's another unknown connection to this world in my life pushes for me to find out anyway.

"Hmm?" He ponders my question, glancing back at the door as the shots quiet. "Oh, that. I suppose it wouldn't hurt to tell you now. You will find out soon enough anyway." Kristoph opens his mouth to continue when something heavy rams into the door, rattling the lock. He whirls around, hopping back from the entrance. Reaching into his pocket, he pulls out a gun and takes aim at the door.

I quietly tug on the ropes, finding they won't budge. Taking in a deep breath, I fight against the panic building in my chest. I don't know what's happening out there but this is my best chance of getting free from these psychopaths.

Think Paige, what can you use? There's gotta be something...

I tug against the rope again and smile when I feel something prick the skin of my wrist.

They didn't find the syringe I had stuffed into my jacket sleeve when I felt the hands yanking me off my feet.

Keeping an eye on Kristoph, I work the needle down until it's grasped in my hand. I work it into the knot, hoping it will hold up against the rope. My previous attempts at prayer have all failed so I don't aim my silent pleas toward anyone. Instead, I call out to the new violence inside of me, willing it to overtake my fear.

The pounding on the door persists and I can see the strain on the small lock. Knowing I don't have much time, I plead again.

Please let this work.

Continuing to shove the needle into the rope, I pull as far as my bound wrists allow, repeating the process over and over. I stifle my cry of victory and frustration as the knot loosens a fraction.

Yes, yes, yes! I chant in my head.

A shout of pain stops my hands.

I know that voice.

The familiar wave of rage crashes over me, a shift happening as the need for vengeance courses through my body.

No one hurts what's mine. No one.

I attack the binds with a new fervor. The rope loosens and I yank my hands free. Leaning forward, I quickly remove the ties around my ankles. A shriek of fury erupts from my chest as the door flies open and Kristoph raises his gun, aiming at the man who was once my source of torture but has quickly become my guide to freedom. I lunge forward as the sound of a gunshot rings in the small room.

Chapter 26

Mick

I pull into the tree line bordering the industrial building they drove her to. I can hear my blood pounding through my veins as every cell demands payment for what they have done.

I knew it was a bad idea to go after that horrid excuse for a woman but I couldn't say no to Paige.

Breathing through my clenched teeth, I watch as a man climbs out of the van and tosses Paige over his shoulder. I memorize him so I can ensure he pays in blood for touching my woman.

I bide my time until I see Vanessa exit the building alone. Sensing my moment, I stalk through the trees and slip behind the vehicle. She pauses on the other side and pulls out a cell phone, typing furiously. I quickly survey the area and see there is no one else around.

Silent on my feet, I sneak up behind her. Slapping a hand over her mouth and nose, I snatch the phone from her hands. Startled by my sudden appearance, Vanessa is momentarily frozen in place. It's only a split second but plenty of time for me to incapacitate her.

With a swift kick, I buckle her knee, my hand covering the wail she releases. I wrap my other arm around her waist, trapping her arms against her body. Adjusting my stance, I lower the injured leg down so her knee rests on the ground. Using the toe of my boot, I nudge her leg out to the side and bring down my foot on her ankle. I relish in the sound of bone snapping and muffled screams.

Fighting the urge to continue my brutalization of her body, I hoist her up, her back to my chest and feet dangling. I stride to my hidden car and throw her on the ground. Now that we are out of earshot, I'm not concerned about noise. Vanessa lays sideways, half propped up on her good leg. I pull out the rope I had stuffed into my jacket pocket and make quick work of tying her up in a similar manner to how they had Paige.

Looking down at her, I feel a moment of satisfaction before the fury seeps back in. Growling, I bend down so I'm eye level with the bitch. "Where is she?" I hiss.

Vanessa blinks up at me until realization hits her. She throws back her head and laughs. I have to clench my fists to avoid punching the smile off her face. She finally stops her laughter and levels me with a look that promises pain. Little does she know, it will be hers.

Holding on to that reminder, I am able to calm down my rage.

I'll find out what I need. I will save my little bird. Then I can make this waste of space pay.

I remain still and silent, waiting.

Vanessa looks between my eyes, a brief flicker of fear passing her face. *Good.* "She is long gone by now. You'll never see that bitch again." Her voice has a slight tremble but she tries to hide it with a laugh.

Her laughter is cut off as my hand shoots forward and grabs her throat. I close the distance between our faces and spit the words at her between clenched teeth. "For your sake, you better hope you are wrong." I squeeze my fingers, cutting off her oxygen. She claws uselessly at my hand and I tighten my grip again, feeling the muscles in her neck protesting against the force. I watch as her limbs sag and her eyes rolls back in her head, only releasing her as her lips begin to turn an ashy shade.

I drop my hold and Vanessa's body slumps lifelessly to the ground. Reaching out, I press two fingers to her neck and confirm she still has a pulse. I push up and make my way to the trunk, pulling out my bag and slipping the syringe from the side pocket. Walking back to her, I inject the clear liquid, ensuring she won't wake up and attempt anything.

Moving quickly, I hoist her up and toss her into the trunk, shutting it with a soft click. Rounding the car, I open the back door and push down on one of the secret buttons lining the interior door. The seat cushion pops up and I reach inside, grabbing a couple pistols and shoving them into my jeans waistband. Reaching back in, I grab the machete Paige has taken a liking to, along with a long curved knife.

I close up my car and lock the doors before turning and sprinting into the building. Despite Vanessa's claims, I believe Paige is still inside, I have to.

Hold on baby, I'm coming.

There is a shocking lack of security for what goes on inside. I've counted four men so far, all of whom have fallen victim to my assault. Once I make it inside, I recognize the space as an old paper mill that shut down nearly a decade ago. There are several rooms that branch off the main entrance and prove difficult to navigate.

I'm on my way down another hall when I hear muffled voices from a room to my left.

Sneaking up to the door, I press my ear against the wood. The voice is deep with a slight accent that gives me pause, familiarity ringing. I strain my ears and catch two words that confirm I have the right room and the identity of the man who has dared to take what is mine.

"...Miss Greene..."

I back up and lift my foot, kicking against the wood with all the strength I possess. I curse when the door doesn't give. The bastard must have something blocking it. I back up several steps and run into the door, batting against it with my shoulder. It still doesn't give and I can feel the desperation building inside.

She's there. She's right there. But I still can't get to her.

I back up farther, bracing myself for the impact as I run and leap. My body lands against the door half a second before I am slammed into from the back. The force of the attack finally causes the door to give way and I catch a glimpse of my raven-haired goddess shrieking and flying through the air at the man pointing a gun at me.

I hear the gun go off and feel a sharp pain hit my body as I fall, face first, into the splintered wood below.

Chapter 27

Paige

I collide with the back of Kristoph, causing the gun to fly out of his hand. We fall forward and I start pummeling the back of his head with my fists. Striking again and again. I spare a quick glance up and see Mick lying on the ground, a puddle of blood pooling around his body. There's something large on his back but my eyes won't focus enough through the tears. I scream in agonized rage and return to hitting Kristoph with everything in me. His movements to get me off his back stop as I see blood matting his hair.

It's not enough.

This man just took everything from me. He took him *from me.*

A choked sob leaves me and I jump up to my feet, kicking Kristoph over so he's lying on his back. I leap back onto him and begin punching his face, clawing his eyes, tearing at his hair and clothes. I throw my knees into his ribs, elbow his chest. I inflict as much damage as my exhausted body can manage.

When the flames of my hatred begin to simmer instead of burn, I straddle his motionless body and slide both hands around his throat and squeeze with clawed fingers. I squeeze until my knuckles are white and my fingertips coat with blood. Tears fall down my face as I pour all of my agony into ending this vile man. With one last scream, I dig my fingers in deeper and yank back. My nails rip through his skin, leaving a gaping hole in his throat.

Breathing heavy, I brace myself against his lifeless corpse and hang my head, my hair falling in curtains around my face. "No. No no no no no." I sob.

Hands grip my shoulders and pull me from the dead man. I scream and flail, my arms flying out wildly. The hands give me a sharp shake causing me to thrash harder, my fingers clawing into the arms trying to surround me. I can feel breath against my ear but can't hear anything beyond the pounding of my head.

"Let me go!" I shriek.

At least, I hope I say it out loud, my mind seems to have disconnected itself from my body.

I think I hear the sound of Mick's voice and my wails become louder. "You killed him. You killed him!" Images of Mick's body lying in his own pooling blood flash before my eyes and my cries fade to sobs. All the fight leaves me and I choke for breath, my head lolling forward. The adrenaline wearing off leaves my body exhausted, blackness clouds my vision as the pounding in my head increases.

The sound of Mick's voice echoes around me as I slip from consciousness.

"I'm here, little bird."

I bolt upright, a scream ripping from my throat.

Disoriented, I look around the space. I'm laying on something soft, a bed, I think. I can feel the pull of familiarity tugging at my mind but can't focus enough to register what I'm seeing. A groan slips past my lips when I turn my head too sharply, causing a wave of nausea to hit me.

Not seeing anything near to use, I lean over the side of the bed and vomit onto the floor, wincing as the force of my body purging itself causes agonizing spikes to my head. I wipe my mouth and slowly sit up. Lifting up a hand, I press it to the back of my head, finding some kind of padding wrapped around it.

Confused, I try to remember what happened.

I was at work, then I went to the park to stake out Vanessa. I remember texting Mick and...

I gasp and my hands fly to my mouth as the memories flood in.

The kidnapping, Kristoph, Mick. Mick lying on the floor. Someone grabbing me.

I look around wildly again, ignoring the throbbing in my head.

I need to get out, I need to find him.

The adrenaline helps my eyes to focus and I take in the room around me full of dark neutral colors of gray and black with splashes of dark red.

I freeze.

It can't be.

Slowly, I tilt my head back and look at the wall behind me. There, hanging proudly, is a sight that makes me sob.

A bloody heart painting.

Filled with tentative hope, I crawl out of the bed and gingerly step on the ground, careful to avoid my earlier mess. Padding over to the door, I test the knob. It turns and I creak open the door, peering into the rest of the house. My eyes land on a sleeping form on the couch and I run.

Leaping onto him, Mick lets out a pained groan and grips my arms to hold me still. "Careful, baby." He grumbles.

Ignoring him, I lean forward, crushing my mouth to his. I kiss him with an unyielding passion, pouring all of my fear and desperation into his lips. His hands slide down to my hips as I reach mine up to his hair. I tug the blonde locks and force my tongue into his mouth, both of us moaning as our tongues collide.

He's alive.

That single thought swirls through my mind as I cling to him.

My hands fly down to his shirt and start tugging, desperate to feel his skin on mine. Mick shifts so he can pull his shirt off while I quickly strip from mine. We both sit there, eyes eating the other up as we pant breathlessly. As if pulled by an invisible string, we both lean forward at the same time. His hands reach up and grip my breasts, pinching my hard nipples. I arch into his touch and moan.

Mick lowers his head to take one of my breasts into his mouth, tweaking my other nipple between his fingers. Gasping, I move my hands back to his hair and scrape my nails against his scalp. "More." I pant, jerking his head back and gazing into his eyes. "I need more, Mick. Please." He moves his hand up to my face and softly strokes my cheek. I shift on his lap, rubbing against his erection. Mick's hand stills and his eyes darken. Flexing his hips, he presses his hard dick against my aching center.

Shifting his hand so he is now firmly gripping my jaw, he leans forward, his breath ghosting my lips. "This what you want?" He teases while flexing his hips again. "You want my cock? Want me to fuck this pussy?" He snaps his other hand out and slaps my pussy. My gasp turns into a moan as he roughly shoves two fingers inside of me. "Fuck. You're so wet. This all for me, baby?"

Mick twists his fingers and rubs against a spot inside that heightens the pleasure. I nod wildly, my vision darkening as he continues his motions, hitting that spot again and again. "All." I gasp between heavy breaths. "All. Yours." I whimper as he pulls his fingers from inside of me, the loss a physical ache.

He chuckles and grasps my hips, lifting me from his lap and lying me back against the couch. The moment my back hits the cushions, Mick slides between my legs and shoves his tongue inside of my aching pussy. I groan loudly and claw at the material of the couch. He rolls his tongue before licking up and down my lips. "Fuck." He rasps as I arch into him, begging incoherently. Mick's tongue works its way up and laps at my clit, alternating between licking and sucking.

"Mick." I beg, writhing below him and feeling the painful ache of emptiness. *I need* him. Sensing what I'm asking for, Mick pushes his fingers back inside of me, stroking in and out in time with his alternating movements on my clit. Desperate to release all the pent up emotions from the last few days, I move my hands to my breasts, kneading them and pinching my nipples. The sound of Mick groaning lets me know he sees what I'm doing and that knowledge enhances the sensations. "Oh god, don't stop." The pressure builds and builds but I can't let go. My mind is too full. I'm whimpering and squirming, seeking extra friction to push me over the edge.

Mick pulls back so he's on his knees between my legs, my arousal glistening on his face. He continues the slow movement of his fingers as he studies me. "What do you need?"

I look up at him, kneeling and completely perfect. "You. I need you." He opens his mouth and I shake my head, knowing what he's going to say. "I know, I have you but..." I bite my lip and look away. Mick reaches up with his other hand and gently nudges my chin so I look at him.

"But what, little bird?"

The nickname is too much, causing tears to slip down my face.

I thought I'd never hear that again, and yet, here he is.

Mick wipes away the tears as he patiently waits. Swallowing down my erratic emotions, I whisper, "I need to feel you, all of you. I thought I lost you, Mick. I saw you lying there and I thought..." My breath hitches, overwhelmed by despair.

Leaning forward, Mick kisses me tenderly while brushing my hair back, his fingers still pumping inside of me. "Anything. I'll give you anything. You have all of me, and I'm not going anywhere." He vows. Pulling away, he quickly sheds his pants and boxers until he's standing before me in all his naked glory. My eyes hungrily take him in as he climbs back onto the couch and lines himself with my entrance. "You have all of me." He repeats as he pushes inside in one slow motion, closing his eyes and gritting his teeth with each inch further he slides in.

Once fully seated, he moves to hover over me. Our chests barely inches from each other and his forearms braced on either side of my head. He gazes into my eyes as he pulls out and pushes back in, continuing his agonizingly slow pace. I press my breasts into him, sliding my hands around his back. He hisses as I drag my nails down, scraping his skin. His eyes don't leave mine and his pace never speeds up. I stare back at him and everything else falls away, there's only me and him.

I can feel our connection deepening. With each thrust, we give more of ourselves until there isn't a him and me, there's only an us.

The pressure builds in me again as Mick's movements rub against my clit. The constant rhythm of his hips, pressure on my clit, and friction on my aching nipples as he pours himself into me through his eyes are finally enough. I come with the force of a bomb, every cell in my body exploding. I let out a silent cry as I hold his gaze and watch him let go too.

We lie there on the couch, both of us unwilling to let the other go. Mick continues to watch me as he gently strokes my face and I feel the last part of me shift into place. I bite my lip as I relinquish myself to the new me.

I may have already given this man my body and heart, but I now realize he has also given me his. There's only one word that explains what I'm feeling, and even it isn't enough.

Love.

I love him.

Chapter 28

Mick

Paige and I spent several hours going over everything that happened. I wanted to force her to get some rest but she pointed out that we needed to talk while the memories were still fresh and I reluctantly agreed.

I had punched a hole in the wall when Paige told me Kristoph mentioned another man, furious there was someone else after her still. She calmed me down and shifted the conversation, asking how I made it out after losing all that blood. I knelt next to her and pulled her into my arms as those tears came back again, gutting me like they did every time. While running a hand through her hair, I explained that the blood hadn't been mine. Some big guy had rammed into me as I was trying to break through the door and his momentum caused me to fall forward faster so he took the bullet meant for me. I was still mad I couldn't make him pay for what he had done to Paige but glad he was dead all the same.

The few wounds we had weren't that bad compared to what could have happened. I had landed on a broken piece of wood from the door that left a decent sized cut along my ribs and I still worried about the open gash on her head but they would both heal fine and didn't require any stitches.

Paige ate a few bites of food before returning to bed to sleep. I insisted she use the bed instead of the couch and she agreed, only having a brief moment of haunting memories as she stepped inside. I had followed her in and saw the mess on the floor, arching an eyebrow as she shrugged and apologized, embarrassment covering her features. I chuckled in return, softly kissing her forehead and ushering her toward the bed as I worked to clean it up.

After finishing, I crawled under the covers and pulled her body flush against mine, letting out a heavy sigh of relief to have her in my arms. She fell asleep quickly and I lay there for a while, listening to her breathing and soft snores before sleep found me as well.

I fight to stay asleep, not wanting the dream to end.

Lips wrapped around my cock, Paige pumps her head up and down my length, sucking on the tip before pushing back down. I moan as I feel the back of her throat bump against me and the sound of her gagging fills my ears as she tries to loosen her muscles enough to accommodate my size. "Paige." I breathe and hear her hum in response, hollowing out her cheeks before resuming her movements.

It feels so good, unlike any wet dream I've had before. My eyes creak open and I freeze at the sight before me. Paige is kneeling between my legs, bent over at the waist as she works my cock. My mind takes several long beats to catch up and realize I'm not dreaming.

Fuck me, this woman is perfect.

The lingering sleepiness burns away by intense flames of desire.

I reach out and grasp the back of her head, careful to avoid the wound. Her eyes shift up to mine and I groan loudly as I take her in. Her lips stretch around my cock, cheeks pink and eyes watery as she gazes at me. Guiding her farther down my shaft, her breaths become desperate pants as her nose bumps into my pubic bone. My hand tightens its grip, keeping her pressed down. I lose myself in the feeling of her swallowing around my cock, starving for air. Even as her eyes flutter closed, Paige doesn't fight against my hold.

She's going to be the death of me.

I groan as the thought, not for the first time, crosses my mind. Easing my grasp, I allow her to pull back far enough to suck down much needed oxygen. I stroke her face with my free hand, wiping away the tears and saliva dripping from her chin. "So beautiful." I murmur, caught in the enchantment of the goddess before me.

Paige's cheeks flush at my words. Capturing her chin between my fingers, I ensure her attention is on me as I attempt to convey just how exquisite she is. "You are perfection, little bird. I didn't believe such a thing existed before I met you. I've never encountered anyone who deserves to live in this life. But you?" Her breath catches, a flicker of need crossing her eyes. My heart swells as I find there is no longer any fear emanating from her when she looks at me.

Caressing her with my fingertips, I memorize the feel of her under my touch. "You don't deserve to just live. No, you are meant to rule, baby." I bring my lips to hers, pouring my adoration into her. Breaking the kiss, I rest my forehead against hers, inhaling a deep breath as I vow, "I'll follow you to the ends of the earth. I'll kneel before you, worshiping you as you deserve. I don't believe there is an afterlife, I don't believe there are deities hidden among us, but I believe in you." Moving my mouth to hers again, my lips brush against her as I breathe, "You are my goddess, little bird. Every day with you is as close to heaven as I will ever come." Pressing my lips to hers, Paige melts into the kiss.

We cling to each other as we express with our bodies all the things words can never hope to do.

Our kisses grow heated, hands clawing at each other. Paige pulls away from me, shifting down the mattress. I watch with rapt attention as she takes my cock back into her mouth, sucking in a breath as her hand wraps around the base. Stroking the shaft, she moans while sucking the head of my cock. My hips thrust upward, seeking more friction. Her tongue runs along the thick veins as she sinks deeper, her other hand snaking up to take hold of my aching balls. My control shatters as she squeezes her fingers.

Grunting, I spear my fingers in her hair, immobilizing her head as I fuck her mouth from below. Her hands move to grip my thighs, nails digging into my skin enhancing the pleasure with the hint of pain. Losing myself in her, I drop my hips and pull her head back between each upward thrust. I keep up the merciless rhythm until I feel my orgasm creeping up, the pressure building low in my pelvis. Yanking her off, I pinch the tip of my dick to stave off my release.

Paige watches me and slowly licks her lips, eliciting another low groan from me. I tilt her head back, speaking a command that offers no room for argument. *She started this after all.* "I need to fuck you." I rasp. "On your hands and knees, baby." She quickly clambers to obey me and I bite my knuckle, urging myself to slow down so I don't come in the first thrust inside of her.

Paige looks over her shoulder at me giving her ass a little shake, mischief shining in her eyes. "Do you know what you do to me?" I ask as I shift behind her, rubbing my stiff erection against her. When she doesn't answer, I smooth my hands over her ass before giving a sharp smack. "I asked you a question." I warn, rubbing my hand to soothe the sting before slapping again in the same spot.

Paige whimpers and pushes herself back against me. "Y-yes." She pants, wriggling under my hands.

"Hmm." I hum, massaging her supple cheek. "Your skin looks so pretty all red from my hands." I smack her again, harder this time, causing her to cry out. Smoothing my palm in circles, I continue. "But you know what's more beautiful?" Paige shakes her head, pushing back against me. I lean over her and speak low into her ear. "Your blood against my blade as it slices open this gorgeous body." I lean down further and bite her neck as Paige shudders. Licking my way back up, I breathe, "You like that, baby? The thought of me cutting you open while I fuck you?" I hum again, not waiting for a response as we both already know the answer. "Of course you do. We're the same, after all, you and I. The need for blood burns inside of you just as it does me."

Pulling back, I climb off the bed, taking in the sight of her before warning, "Don't move, not a muscle." Paige watches me, remaining frozen in place as she waits. "Good girl." I praise as I stride out the door.

I make my way to the bags stashed in the corner, grabbing my knife and a few other supplies before turning back to the room. My phone lights up on the kitchen table where I left it last night. After a brief internal debate, I snatch it up and see a text from Jesse.

Jesse

You coming in today?

I rack my brain for why he would be asking and curse as I remember. *Of course that would be today.*

Me

Yeah but I'll be late, have to take care of something first.

Jesse

Okay man. Just get here as quick as you can.

Me

Yes, mom.

Jesse

rolling eyes emoji* *middle finger emoji

Jesse

Fuck off asshole. See you later.

I put my phone down and stride back into the bedroom. Excitement and disappointment fill me as I see Paige listened. I would have loved to punish her but her obeying me without question has my aching cock throbbing, precum spilling out the tip.

I close the distance, setting everything down on the bed before opening the nightstand and pulling a couple more items out. Paige watches me curiously, her eyes widening when she sees what's in my hand. "What is that?" She asks, voice barely more than a whisper.

I chuckle. "I think you know, sweetheart. And if you don't, you will soon." Paige trembles as I set the new additions onto the bed and snatch up the rope. "Arms above your head." She obediently stretches her arms. I hum my approval as I tie each wrist up and secure them to either bed post. Circling around behind her, I tap the back of her thigh. "Slide this forward but keep your ass in the air." Paige hesitates before moving her leg, keeping her body arched. I wrap another piece of rope around her leg, securing the angle before connecting the rope to her arm. I repeat the process on the other side so she is immobilized and stretched out, her pussy and ass on perfect display.

Climbing onto the bed behind her, I rub my hands over her bare pussy, moving over her cheeks, along her back and up her spine. I memorize each inch of her skin with my hands as I repeat the path in reverse. She attempts to wiggle, seeking out my fingers, but is unable to move. Letting out a frustrated huff, she arches her back again, tempting me with her gorgeous body.

My hands make their way back to her center and I let out a groan as I slip my middle finger inside of her. Holding it still, I tease her with just the tip. Paige shifts in her binds. "Please, Mick." She whines, trying to push back against me.

I relish in her desperate pleas. "You're so beautiful when you beg." I murmur, pushing my finger in a half inch more before sliding it out completely. Paige whimpers and drops her forehead against the covers. Chuckling, I grip her hips. "This is going to hurt, but I'll make it feel good too." I promise. Paige doesn't respond so I slap her pussy. "Do you understand?" Paige nods her head into the bed. Unable to resist the urge, I smack her again, her cry muffled against the blanket. "Good girl." I praise, rewarding her by sliding a finger back inside of her wet cunt.

Pumping the digit in and out of her pussy, I build her up until I feel her walls tensing. She lets out a frustrated groan when I pull out my finger but doesn't try to move. Reaching behind me, I grab hold of the cloth and duct tape. My fingers slide around her throat and I pull her head away from the bed, arching her neck until I can see her face. Confusion and desire war in her eyes, quickly turning to rage as I shove the cloth into her mouth and slap a strip of tape straight across her lips. I tear off a couple more pieces with my teeth and lay them over in an X pattern, careful to avoid covering her nose.

Satisfied with my work, I toss the duct tape aside and grab the last few items from my bag. "I'm going to cut off all of your senses except what you can feel." Paige tries to mumble around the cloth and tape, shaking her head. I press an upside down kiss on her forehead. "It's okay, I've got you. I promise this will feel just as good as it hurts." Pausing, I peer down at her. "Do you trust me?" I ask, holding my breath as I wait for her answer.

It's something I've never cared about before but I find the need for her to place her trust in me overpowers the other desires flowing through my body.

She stares at me for a long time and blinks once before slowly nodding her head. My smile stretches across my face and I open the pack of earplugs, placing one into each of her ears. Lastly, I slide the safety glasses over her eyes. I've taped cloth over the lenses to block out the view.

I take a moment to appreciate the woman before me, completely and willingly at my mercy. Her breathing becomes choppy as her apprehension grows. Sliding my hands up her back, I soothe her with my touch, peppering soft kisses along her spine. Her body trembles under me, overwhelmed by the sensation from the loss of her other senses.

Kneeling back, I tease her clit in soft circles, working her up until she is moaning and shifting on the bed. I slip a finger into her dripping pussy, still rubbing circles on her clit, as I grab the bottle of lube. Flicking it open with my free hand, I squirt a generous amount between her cheeks. Paige stills, her body shaking. I put down the bottle and move my thumb over the tight hole, rubbing circles to match the pace on her clit. I continue my patterned movement until I feel her relax under my touch. Once her body starts to tighten with her approaching orgasm, I gently push the tip of my thumb inside.

Paige inhales heavily through her nose, unintelligible words trying to make their way around her gag. "Shh, I've got you." I murmur, even though she can't hear me. Pushing my thumb in a little more, I leave it there as I pick up the speed of my fingers pumping in her pussy and my movement on her clit. Her arousal is covering my hand, showing me she is enjoying this as much as I am. My cock twitches, desperate to be inside of her. Ignoring it, I continue working Paige's body.

I feel her relax around my thumb again and slowly ease it farther in before pulling out and matching the pumps of my other fingers. Paige squirms and moans below me, mumbling and breathing heavily. I continue to work her pussy and ass until she screams her orgasm. Leaning over her again, I still my hands and press a kiss to the base of her spine as the last waves of pleasure roll through her.

Sliding my fingers out, I grab the last item and the discarded lube. Squirting more cool gel between her cheeks, I work it into her ass with two fingers as I slide the plug into her pussy, wetting it with her cum. Paige pushes back, seeking more. I chuckle and mutter to myself, "So needy." Shifting, I lean over and place a kiss on her back, running my tongue up her soft skin. She shivers and pushes against me as far as her binds will allow, fucking herself with my fingers.

Satisfied she's ready, I straighten and slip out my fingers, quickly replacing them with the tip of the plug. I slowly work it into her ass, watching closely as the muscles clench around the intrusion. Pausing as she tenses, I rub soothing circles on her back. Once the toy is completely seated inside of her, I lean back on my heels and lazily stroke my cock. "So damn gorgeous." I murmur, gripping the handle of my knife with my other hand. Sliding the tip along her skin, I relish in the small shivers that run through her from the sharp point.

Rising up to my knees, I line up my cock and push just the head inside her pussy, teasing us both. I move the blade and run it down her spine, applying enough pressure to lightly scratch her skin but not pierce through. Paige's fingers curl into her palms as she fights to remain still. I flex my hips and my cock slides in another inch, causing her body to arch as her head falls back, moaning loudly.

"Fuck." I let out on a breath.

Unable to hold back any longer, I shift the knife and slice into her back as I shove inside of her fully. Paige screams into the gag and yanks her arms against the ropes. I'm transfixed by the blood seeping from the cut, small bubbles of crimson forming before filling the line. I slide a finger through the liquid and paint her surrounding skin.

Pulling back again, I leave just the tip of my cock inside of her as I shift the blade to her other side. I slam into her again as I cut through her skin, repeating this over again until small cuts litter her back. Paige writhes below me, begging wordlessly to end her torment and allow her to take her pleasure. I toss aside the knife and grip her hip in one hand, my other tracing over the artwork of her skin. I pound into her, adjusting my angle until she flings her head back and cries out.

Slamming into her, I hit that spot over and over as I slide my hand from her hip to her clit. I pinch lightly before moving my fingers in tight circles, feeling her tense around me. With my other hand, I smack her ass. Alternating between both cheeks, I revel in the red staining her skin on the inside and out as the blood pooling beneath her skin mixes with the bloodied handprints I leave from my own tainted skin. With one more pinch of my fingers on her clit and slap to her ass, Paige cries out, her body so tight she strangles my cock inside of her. I grit my teeth to stave off my orgasm a little longer as I continue thrusting into her.

Paige collapses into the bed, head resting on the covers. I move both of my hands to her hips and bend forward, licking along her back, tracing each of the cuts with my tongue. After tasting each inch I've marked, I pull back and lift her hips higher, propping her onto her bound knees. Using my strength to support her, I thrust forward, chasing my orgasm. As I feel myself close to the edge, I lick my lips and the metallic taste of her blood on them sends me cascading into oblivion. I roar out my orgasm and still as my cock twitches inside of her.

After the last pulse of my cum stops, I carefully pull out, making quick work of removing the ear plugs and glasses. Paige doesn't move, quietly panting in her position on the bed, her head facing the wall. I remove the duct tape and pull the cloth from her lips, placing a kiss on her sweaty head. "You okay, baby?" Paige mumbles something then hums. Taking that as a yes, I gently remove the plug from her ass, causing her to moan and my spent cock to twitch. Lastly, I remove all the rope bindings and softly massage the irritated skin.

Climbing out of the bed, I cradle her body in my arms as I lift her up. She leans into me and wraps her arms loosely around my neck, pressing a kiss into my skin. I stride into the bathroom, setting her down on the bench seat in the shower corner.

Turning around, I remove the shower head and adjust the temperature. Once satisfied, I methodically clean her. Careful to not spray directly on her back, I let the water trickle down and clean the wounds. The entire time Paige doesn't say anything, just watches me and winces periodically from the sting of water on her sensitive skin. After she's clean, I quickly wash myself and turn off the water. Stepping out of the shower, I wrap a towel around my waist and return with one for her. She raises her arms and allows me to dry her off before scooping her back into my arms.

Carrying her to the sink, I set her down on the counter facing the mirror and indicate for her to cross her legs underneath her body. As she gets comfortable, I grab out the first aid kit and get to work on the cuts on her back. I kiss each one before applying antiseptic and bandaging it up. Paige continues to watch me silently in the mirror, a look in her eyes that makes me nervous. I continue working over her back until all the wounds have been cleaned and covered. Checking the gash on her head again, I'm satisfied with the healing progress.

I lift her into my arms once more and carry her out to the couch, gently setting her down. Clearing my throat, I rub the back of my neck anxiously. "I'm going to, uh, change the sheets and order some food to be delivered." Paige nods and looks away, staring off into the distance. I scuff my foot on the floor before turning and getting to work.

Nearly an hour later, we are seated at the table eating pizza. She still hasn't said a word to me and my nervous energy is growing sharp edges. When Paige picks at the pepperoni on her slice, I finally snap. "Okay, what are you thinking?" I demand.

Startled, she looks up at me before quickly averting her gaze. "It's nothing." She mutters.

I narrow my eyes and grip her chin, forcing her to face me. "Don't lie to me, little bird." Softer, I add, "Please tell me what's wrong." I hold my breath as she stares at me, debating. Finally, Paige lets out a sigh and nods. I release her face and pick up my slice of pizza, taking a bite and chewing slowly. My unease continues to grow with each passing second of silence.

She picks at her food for another moment before taking a deep breath. Blowing out the air in her lungs, Paige studies her food intently as she mumbles, "It's just. I think there's something...wrong with me." Confused, I just watch and wait for her to continue. Sighing again, Paige speaks so quickly I almost don't catch what she says. "I shouldn't have liked that, you know. *Normal* people don't enjoy...Does it, does it mean I'm broken if I wanted it to..." She trails off, staring down at her hands.

I continue to wait, holding my breath. Paige looks up at me through her lashes and speaks two words that turn my world upside down.

In a hushed tone, Paige whispers, "Hurt more."

"Are you sure you're going to be okay?" I ask for the tenth time since we decided to split ways. It made the most sense as I'm needed at work and she has to get ready for her own shift. I still don't like it, especially after everything that happened yesterday.

Paige rolls her eyes at me. "I'll be fine. I've already missed too much work as it is. I'm lucky Brandi hasn't fired me yet." She gives me a look that reminds me I'm the reason for her increased absences as of late.

Unashamed, I shrug. Maybe I didn't go about it the best way but it still ended with her in my arms. To get that, I'd do anything.

Paige stretches up on her tiptoes and kisses me before giving me a shove. I'm startled enough I fall back half a step before regaining my balance. I glare down at her and she just smiles up at me innocently. "Time to go." She shoos me out of her apartment and into the hall.

Before she can shut the door, I reach through and yank her into my arms, taking her lips with mine. I kiss her until she's left breathless. When I pull back, Paige reaches up a hand to her door to steady herself and I bite back my laughter. "See you later." I wink at her as I turn and exit the apartment building.

Sliding into my car, I pull out my phone and shoot off a quick text to let Jesse know I'm heading in. My fingers hover over her name before I decide to put away my phone. I don't know a lot about relationships, but this feels like a moment to give her space.

During my drive to work, I replay the conversation in my head, still shocked. I knew Paige would enjoy it, but I had gotten worried I'd gone too far, not that it's stopped me in the past but something about her has changed me. I find I want to give her pleasure more than taking my own and it worries me the power this little black haired woman has over me.

My head isn't any clearer by the time I pull up to Mickstruction. Regardless, I can't be focused on Paige right now. There's a lot on the line with this meeting and the fact that Jesse needs me there tells me all I need to know. We need this to go well.

Focusing on the task at hand, I step out of my car and head inside.

Showtime.

Chapter 29

Paige

The second I see Mick's car pull away, I drop my head in my hands and groan.

I can't believe I said that. Why *did I say that? Things were going so well between us and then I had to get all up in my head.*

After Mick forced the truth out of me, he became weirdly quiet, not speaking the entire drive back to my apartment. Now we're spending the day apart with no plans to meet up afterward.

He wouldn't dump me for that, right?

No, of course not, he seemed really into it. Maybe he likes it less when the girl likes it?

The thought of another woman with him makes me want to punch something.

Great, juuuust great now I'm the jealous, crazy girlfriend.

Wait, am *I the girlfriend?*

Reality slaps me in the face as I realize we've never had "the conversation."

I mean, sure we've murdered people together, definitely slept together, fuck we've bled for each other. But, does that mean we're a thing?

Smacking my forehead with my palms, I curse myself.

This is stupid, of course he likes me like that. Doesn't he?

Instinctively, I reach for my phone to call Taylor but pause.

How do I explain the situation to her so she understands but that doesn't implicate me in a murder?

Okay, murders.

Fuck!

Giving up on the idea, I begin getting ready for work instead.

I'm finishing up the last of my makeup when I hear a knock on my door. Confused, I pull up the app for my security camera and try to see who's out there. The feed catches up and shows a man with a baseball cap pulled over his face. I try to see if I recognize anything about him as an uneasy feeling forms in the pit of my stomach. Pushing the button to talk, I ask, "What do you want?"

"It's me, Paige. Can we talk?"

I let out an exasperated sigh.

I don't have the time or energy to deal with this right now.

"Can we do this later, Seth? I'm running late for work."

It's mostly not a lie, I just want some time alone and I do *need to leave for work soon.*

Biting my lip, I push off the guilt trying to creep up on me.

"I could give you a lift?" Seth offers, dangling his keys for the camera but still keeping his face averted. It seems odd but I really don't feel like driving.

And at least I'll have an excuse to exit the conversation once we get there.

Running my hand through my hair, I glance at the clock. I force back the groan as I concede. "Okay. Just give me a few minutes and we'll head out."

Seth nods and stuffs his keys back into his pocket. "Cool, I'll meet you outside." He quickly turns around and strides off, not waiting for a response. I roll my eyes and mutter "men" as I finish getting ready.

About ten minutes later, I'm walking out of the apartment building and look around. I spot Seth leaning against a vehicle that looks oddly familiar, cap still pulled low. Deciding I don't care enough to ask, I walk up to him.

Hearing my approach, Seth looks up at me. "Still as punctual as ever." He drawls sarcastically.

I place a hand on my hip and glare up at him. "I didn't ask you for a ride. If you've got an issue or somewhere else to be, go ahead." I turn to storm toward my car and halt as Seth's hand wraps around my wrist.

Looking back, I see him run a hand down his face. "Fuck, I'm sorry Paige. It's fine. Let's just go, yeah?" With him this close, I take the opportunity to study his face. There are dark circles under his eyes and the beginning of what looks like a bruise forming around his left one. I narrow my own as I look and he quickly averts his gaze, opening the door for me to climb in. "Ready?" He grumbles, barely containing the irritation in his voice.

Something is making alarm bells ring in my head but I can't figure out what it is. I glance at the car and back at Seth, his fingers tighten around the doorframe as his muscles bunch up. I might be paranoid but my hours of true crime consumption are giving me the urge to be extra cautious. "Oh fuck." I smack my head with my palm.

Seth looks at me, confused and suspicious. "What?"

"I forgot my shop keys in my apartment, I need them to lock up tonight. You mind staying here and I'll run up and grab them? Only take a couple minutes, promise." I smile up at him and his face softens, easing some of the tension.

"Sure, just be quick. You're late, remember?" He teases, the corner of his mouth turning up in a smile that doesn't reach his eyes.

I nod and turn to the apartment, trying to keep my pace to a non-suspicious *"I forgot something and I'm running late"* rather than *"I think something's wrong and I need to tell my serial killer maybe-boyfriend who I'm with in case I go missing"*. Judging by the fact I'm not tackled on my way inside, I think I've pulled it off.

I scramble up to my apartment and hurry inside, shutting the door behind me in case Seth decides to come investigate. Once inside, I whip out my phone and pull up Mick's number. I press call with shaky hands and wait. It rings several times before going to voicemail.

Shit. Okay, a text is still better than nothing.

Typing quickly, I shoot off a series of text messages, keeping an eye on the time. When I think I've pushed my luck as far as I can, I silence my phone and go to put it in my pocket. Pausing, I stare down at the small device, flashes of the last times I needed it but didn't flash through my mind.

After a quick internal debate, I hide the phone in my boot. Sliding my shop keys out of my bag, I grasp them tightly in my hand. I turn and fling open the door, about to rush downstairs when I run into a firm body.

Seth reaches out and steadies me. I look up and smile, waving my keys in my hand. "Got them, ready to go?" I ask, trying to keep my tone light.

He nods and gestures for me to head downstairs first. The uneasiness returns in full force as I turn my back on him and start toward the stairs. We make it out of the apartment building and into his car with no incidents. I start feeling a little embarrassed about my behavior as we take off.

Perfect, add paranoid to the list of my apparent red flags. No wonder I've been single for so long.

Attempting to distract myself from my internal deprecation, I study Seth's profile as he drives. His cheeks are taut and the stubble he had last time I saw him has grown to a small beard. His eyes are bloodshot and there's more than just the first bruise I had noticed earlier. As I move my gaze down, I notice he has cuts and bruises along most of his exposed skin.

Gingerly, I reach out and brush an especially nasty one on his forearm. "Seth?" I ask softly. He doesn't respond, only glances at me and looks away again. I try again, concern outweighing the survival instinct in me screaming for me to shut up. "Seth, what happened to you?"

He clenches his jaw, I can see the muscle working as he fights with something inside. Finally, he sighs and tightens his grip on the wheel. Still not looking at me, he simply says, "You."

Flinching, I remove my hand and lean back against the car door. "What? I didn't do this!" I cry, my heart thundering in my chest. That familiar tug pulls at me again, something trying to work its way into my head.

"Yes, you did!" He snaps. "You and that stupid asshole."

My eyes widen.

He can't mean...How would he know about Mick? Last time they saw each other, Seth was all but fangirling over making a new "friend".

I blink several times, trying to get my emotions under control. A memory pushes its way from my subconscious, a voice replaying in my head.

"I see what he was so enamored with...I suppose it wouldn't hurt to tell you now. You will find out soon enough..."

My racing heart stutters to a halt, my lungs seizing right along with it. *No. It can't be.* Even as I try to deny it, I'm reminded of how buddy-buddy Seth and Kristoph were that day in the shop. That Kristoph knew someone else who wanted me. That something about it was funny to him.

My gaze shifts back to Seth and it's like I've never seen him before. Glaring at him, I lean farther away, hand clasping the door handle. "Pull over Seth." I try to keep my voice steady as apprehension fills me. "I mean it, you need to pull over and let me out. Right now." He doesn't respond, flexing his fingers repeatedly over the wheel. Growing panic and anger rise within me.

I need to get out of this car.

Finally giving in to the fear, I screech, "Pull the fucking car over!" He still says nothing, just calmly reaches over and hits the lock button for the doors and windows. I shriek, yanking on the handle and shoving my body against the door. It's useless but I continue to beat on the inside of the car, desperately trying to escape while screaming curses at Seth.

He doesn't say a word as he turns the opposite direction of my destination.

God fucking damnit. I'm being kidnapped again!

Fuck. My. Life.

Chapter 30

Mick

Jesse and I laugh and wave our goodbyes as we step out of the conference room. Our laughter dies immediately and we are silent on the way to my office. Once inside, I groan and massage my temple.

"I know man. That was terrible." Jesse offers, shoving his hands in his pockets.

I nod, sighing as I run a hand over my jaw. "At least we got the account." I drop my hand and pull out my phone. Jesse says something else but I don't hear him as panic floods my system.

1 missed call

8 unread text messages

"Hey, you okay?" I startle at the feeling of a hand on my shoulder. Looking up I see Jesse staring at me, concern on his face.

Shrugging, I look back at my phone. "Dunno, I think there might be something wrong." I mumble as I pull up the text chat. My panic morphs to anger as I read and I'm running out the door the second I finish the last text.

I hope I'm not too late.

Paige

Hey, I'm sure it's nothing and sorry to bother you but Seth showed up at my apartment.

Paige

He's just acting super weird and I've got a bad feeling, ya know?

Paige

Don't worry though, I'm sure I'm just overreacting.

Paige

*Rather be safe than sorry, right? *laughing face emoji**

Paige

Anyway, he's insisting on driving me to work. I snuck off to text you just in case anything, I dunno, weird happens.

Paige

I gotta go though, he's expecting me back.

Paige

*Oh and before I forget, I got the info for his car. Cause I'm awesome *sunglasses emoji* *winking emoji**

Paige

Silver Chrysler 300, license plate CFP573

My tires screech as I pull up to Paige's apartment. I see her car in the parking lot and the darkness pulls me further down. Jumping out, I run into the building and pick the lock on her door, quickly disabling the alarm system once inside. I knew that she wouldn't be here but I need to try and find out any information on where they could have gone.

Frantically, I tear apart her place but don't find anything useful. Running my fingers through my hair, I pace the small space, trying to think of what to do. After a few deep breaths to get myself under control, I pull out my phone and go through the texts again.

I should have known.

The minute Paige said Kristoph had mentioned another man, I should have thought of Seth. The fact that I didn't put the two together until I saw the text with Kristoph's car information is eating me up. After I discovered Kristoph knew her, I gathered all the information I could about the corrupt detective. My plan had been to take care of him and Seth but my attention had been pulled elsewhere.

It will be my fault if anything happens to her. I can't let anything happen to her.

Pinching the bridge of my nose, I try to come up with a plan.

She said he wanted to give her a ride to work. Maybe this is all just a misunderstanding. Unlikely, but still possible.

I run out of the apartment building to my car and speed off to the coffee shop. On the drive over, another idea hits me, giving me a sense of calm.

I have someone I can ask.

A deadly smile forms on my face.

Oh yes, someone who is overdue a visit anyway.

The shop is relatively empty when I walk up. I slip inside and look around, hoping to catch a glimpse of raven hair. Instead of finding my woman, I come face-to-face with an angry middle aged one. The same woman who had promised danger with her eyes when she had watched me walk out with Paige several months ago.

I rack my brain for a name, knowing Paige has mentioned her before.

I think it starts with a t. Or a d? Diane? No. Tami? No, that's not it. Although that sounds close...

I resist the urge to pump my fist in the air as it hits me.

"Hi, Brandi, right?" I offer her a smile and try to appear calm. She maintains her fuming gaze but gives me a small nod. "Great." I rush on, fighting back the desperation trying to overpower me. "Listen, have you heard from Paige? She was supposed to text me when she got here but I haven't heard from her." It's close enough to the truth to convey my concern without raising her suspicions. The last thing we need is more corrupt members of our boys in blue to show up and muddle my search.

Brandi's shoulders release some of their tension as the worry lines in her forehead deepen. "No, she didn't show up for her shift. I assumed she was with-" She gestures to me, not hiding the look of disdain.

I shake my head, letting my smile drop and a little of my own worry to come through. "She's not with me." I admit, guilt and anger eating away at me. "Hey, here's my number." I pull out one of my Mickstruction business cards and jot down my cell number on the back before setting it on the counter in front of her. "Call me if she shows up or you hear from her, okay?"

Brandi stares at the card like she's afraid it will bite if she gets too close. Cautiously, she reaches out and picks it up, inspecting the number closely before flipping it over. Her eyes widen as she reads who I am. Judging from the look on her face, she recognizes the name. Not that I'm surprised. When she looks at me again it's like she's seeing a completely different person than a moment ago. Trying to keep down my impatience and desire to shake an answer out of her so I can leave, I wait for Brandi to reply.

Seeming to realize she hasn't acknowledged what I said, Brandi glances at the clock and back at me. Speaking in a hushed tone to keep the few customers in the lobby with us from hearing, she asks, "Is Paige okay? Do I need to be worried about her?"

I shake my head, fighting against my own fear. "I'm sure she's fine, probably just lost track of time." I lie.

Brandi looks like she wants to argue but decides against it. "Okay, I'll let you know if I hear anything." She agrees, tucking the card into her apron.

Offering her a sad smile, I muster as much gratitude as I can. "Thank you. Really." I force out, spinning on my heel and striding out the door. Cracking my knuckles, I walk to my car.

Time to get some answers.

Vanessa screams as the cold water hits her. I opted to strap her to the metal chair when I had brought her back here after Paige's kidnapping. She was going to be a gift for said woman, but plans have changed and now I am going to get her to tell me exactly what's going on.

She shoots daggers at me with her eyes but doesn't speak. The only sound in the space is from her chattering teeth. That will change soon enough.

"Hello Vanessa." I drawl, pulling another chair in front of her. Spinning it around, I straddle the seat with my arms resting on the back. She sneers at me but doesn't respond. I cluck my tongue. "That won't do. Did they not teach you any manners? It's only polite to say hello back when you're having a conversation. And we *are* having a conversation." My gaze darkens as I lean forward. "Or we could do this the hard way. I can promise you, you'll not like that." I wink and lean back, a sly smile on my face.

Contemplating my words, her eyes dart around the room. I wait. No matter how she reacts, this is not going to end pretty for the woman responsible for the pain inflicted on my girl. My smirk transforms into a full grin as Vanessa returns her gaze to mine, squares her shoulders, and spits the words at me. "Fuck. You."

I clap my hands together, making her jump. "Oh, I was hoping we would get to do it this way." I push off the chair and move to the far wall, snatching up the small metal nutcracker tool. It's an unassuming little thing and takes a little effort to use properly but the results are worth it.

Vanessa eyes me warily as I approach.

Stopping in front of her, I run my hand along the tool. "This was a nice find. I picked it up at an antique store, gave it a little TLC, and good as new!" Opening it, I brush my finger over the sharpened metal teeth. "See, the nice thing about vintage is there aren't all the pesky safety precautions. With the right amount of pressure, this guy can cause some serious damage." I pull my finger out and snap it shut, causing Vanessa to flinch. Slowly, I bend to a squat in front of her and grab hold of one of her hands. She tries to pull away but is unable to with her arms and legs all tied securely to the chair. Tightening my hold, I prop up one of her fingers and secure the teeth around the appendage. I glance up at her. "Ready?"

She shakes her head. "Plea-" Her words are cut off with a scream as I roughly snap the tool closed. The sharpened teeth dig into her skin as the pressure crushes the bones. I remove the mutilated finger and move to the next. Pausing just long enough for her to notice and the anticipation to build before crushing that finger as well.

I stand up, releasing her hand. The two brutalized fingers hang limp from her hand, blood pooling around the jagged cuts. Vanessa whimpers and sobs as her fingers reflexively flex, trying to regain the lost sensation but only serving to further her agony.

"Now, let's talk."

Chapter 31

Paige

It's been hours and Seth still hasn't stopped. My demands grew silent after the first hour and now I sit quietly, my mind working to think of a way out of this situation. The bigger concern is, I still don't know what the actual situation is exactly.

It's obvious Seth has been attacked and he blames me. I'm not entirely sure why or how but the only logical conclusion I can come up with is that this is somehow connected to what happened to Kristoph.

If that's the case, how involved was he?

The possibility that he was part of snatching women from the streets while we were together makes me sick. And furious.

I spot a sign for a rest area up ahead. "Hey, I need to pee. Can we stop there?" I request, gesturing at the sign.

Seth glances at me, checks his watch, and inclines his head. "Yeah. We have to be quick though." I look at him and am met with a deadly expression on his face, causing me to gulp. "Don't try anything." He warns in a low tone, holding my gaze. All I can do is nod in response, the words sticking in my throat.

I'm in so much trouble.

We pull off the highway and park next to the bathroom building. Seth climbs out of his side and rounds the car, not unlocking my door until he is standing next to it. Before I can move, he reaches in and grabs my elbow, yanking me to my feet. I glare at him and try to pull my arm free but he tightens his grip and marches us toward the door. "Ouch, Seth, you're hurting me." He doesn't reply, continuing to drag me toward the women's restroom. My eyes widen in horror as I realize he is planning on escorting me into the building itself. "Seth." I snap, digging my heels into the ground.

He huffs a breath and whirls on me. "What?" Straightening my posture, I meet his irritated gaze head on, refusing to be intimidated.

This man is playing bad but I've survived worse. I've gone toe-to-toe with true evil and I now call him mine. And when he realizes I'm missing, Seth will have unleashed a true monster on the world.

Leveling him with a glare of my own, I growl, "You are not going in there with me." I hold up my free hand when he tries to argue. "No." I say firmly. Gesturing toward the building, I continue, "Look, there's only one exit and the windows are too high and too small for me to try to squeeze through. You can stay right out by the door but I am *not* letting you watch or hear me piss." I lock my jaw and glare at him, daring him to fight me on this.

Studying the building, Seth looks like he still wants to argue. He shifts his gaze to my angry one and sighs. "Fine. But I'll be right here." Letting me go, he waves an arm toward the entrance.

I push past him and hurry inside. A quick inspection shows me I'm alone. Hurrying my steps, I slip into a stall, sliding the lock. I pull my phone out and open Mick's contact, pressing the call button.

He answers on the first ring. "Paige? Where are you?"

I close my eyes and push away the tears, knowing I have to be quick. "Mick, I don't have long. I convinced Seth to let me use the restroom and he's waiting for me outside." Mick growls but I rush on. "I think he was working with Kristoph. I'm not sure where we're going but he was pretty beaten up when he came and got me. I think whoever they worked for isn't happy about what we did." The line goes silent and I check to make sure the connection is still there. Bringing the phone back to my ear, I whisper, "Mick, I'm scared." I try not to cry but a hiccuped sob slips past my defenses.

He speaks then, his tone comforting but edged with danger, making a shiver run down my spine. "I know, baby. But don't worry, I'm coming for you. Just be patient. And smart."

"Okay." I mumble, chewing on my thumb.

Another beat of silence passes before Mick's voice comes through the receiver. "And Paige?"

I close my eyes and allow the deep rumble to wash over me. "Yes?" My fingers tighten around the phone as I wait, already missing the sound of his voice.

"Remember, there is nowhere you can go that I won't find you, little bird." He disconnects the call and I clasp the phone to my chest.

He's going to find me.

The certainty and conviction when he promised that gives me a small glimmer of hope.

"And I always keep my promises."

Mick's words repeat in my head, ones that terrified me at the time they were spoken but now bring nothing but comfort.

I slip my phone back into my shoe and quickly use the restroom. Washing my hands, I peer at my reflection in the mirror.

Remember who you are, Paige. You're not a weak damsel in distress. You're a killer too and Seth has no idea who he's messed with.

Climbing back into the car, I glance back at my purse and contemplate if I can reach it before Seth crosses to the other side. I suppress my frustrated sigh as I hear the driver's door pop open. I'll just have to bide my time.

Shortly after it had become clear that Seth was taking me somewhere, he had pulled off to the side of the road and snatched my bag away from me. He had then gotten out of the car and pulled me out, threatening to knock me out if I tried anything. Fighting against my desire to knock *him* out, I stood there while he patted me down. Thankfully, he either was too distracted or too dumb to check my shoes, so I still had access to my cell phone. I lost everything else but knew if I got the opportunity, I could snatch back my purse and grab the small syringe I kept stashed in there for emergencies. Another precaution I had rolled my eyes at Mick for at the time when he insisted I keep it.

Shooting a rueful glance back, I am overwhelmed with gratitude for my overprotective and overprepared man. I quickly turn my gaze out the window as Seth clambers into his seat. Having no intention of allowing him to notice my desire for the bag and losing the opportunity I have to escape, I focus on the darkness surrounding us.

My mind wanders as I contemplate what our destination might be. We've been on the road for at least three, maybe four, hours and appear to be heading northwest. I know we aren't going to Bloomsburg as we are headed in the opposite direction. Plus, I can't imagine Seth would want to explain any of this to Brie.

"Why aren't you with Brie?" The question slips out before I can stop it. The thought of her sending my mind reeling. So many things about this situation don't make sense, for some unfathomable reason, this one seems to be bothering me the most.

I chance a glance in his direction and catch the surprise flit across his face before he's able to mask the emotion. *Odd.* Observing him, I get the feeling this might be my way around the stone wall he's erected. Bolstered by the possibility, I press on. "Seth, why aren't you with Brie?" He narrows his eyes and flexes his fingers around the wheel but doesn't say anything. "I saw, you know." My voice comes out quiet as I look back at the road, reliving the memory. "That's why I left. I came home early and-" I slowly turn back toward him, tears pricking my eyes, swallowing as the feelings of hurt and betrayal hit me again. "I saw you two together." I confess, my chest aching.

Seth releases a harsh breath. "Fuck Paige. I'm sorry. I'm so fucking sorry." My heart contracts at his words. "It wasn't supposed to be like that. Her and I. It was meant to just be work. Then you disappeared and wouldn't answer my calls. When Brie told me what happened, I wanted to strangle her. But I couldn't, I had no choice." He glances at me, pleading with his eyes. "You have to believe me, baby girl. You were it for me. Still are."

My expression is incredulous.

How could he think there would be anything left between us?

"Stop lying to me." I hiss, anger breaking through my shock.

Seth has the gall to look offended. "I'm not."

"Oh yeah?" I scoff. "Then how do you explain the engagement?"

He looks at me again, confused. "We're not engaged anymore, you called it off." His voice is seeped in pain and a small amount of hope that makes my stomach roll.

"Not our engagement, jackass. You and Brie." I cross my arms and glare at him. I can't explain why this still bothers me so much. I have no interest in the cheating scumbag and the only desire I have toward him now is for his blood to spill by my hands.

Seth looks even more confused. "We're not engaged." I snort in disbelief, refusing to be gaslit. "I swear to you Paige, I am not engaged to Brie."

"Then why the fuck did she post that you are?" I retort, mentally smacking my forehead as I admit to stalking their socials. Triumph and amusement cover his face briefly before confusion and anger take over. He doesn't say anything, just shakes his head. "What? You don't believe me? Check yourself then!" My voice raises to match my humiliation.

None of this should matter to me. I should be focusing on how to get free, not debating my ex's current relationship status with him.

Seth indicates his turn and pulls off to the side of the highway, throwing on his emergency blinkers. He whips out his phone the moment the vehicle is in park and begins aggressively swiping. I glance back at my purse again as his attention remains on the small screen. Tentatively, I stretch an arm back, keeping my eyes on him. I can feel the material graze my fingers and hold my breath as they slip into the large pocket. Seth mutters something under his breath and I still, my heart pounding. He continues his search and I cautiously move my fingers around until I feel the small tube. I grasp it in my hand and subtly shift to pull my arm back up front. Slipping the syringe into my jacket pocket, I readjust my position again.

Seth lets out a loud curse and I jump.

Deep breaths, he didn't see you.

I look back over at him and find his attention solely on the phone held inches from his face. His gaze is murderous. "That fucking bitch. She set me up." Cursing again, he begins typing furiously before chucking his phone into the cup holder and dropping his face into his hands. "This is what I get for not checking." He mumbles against his palms.

He stays like that, head buried in his hands, and I contemplate if now would be the best time to act. I decide against it as I'm not sure where we are and I won't have long after injecting the drug before its effects wear off. And, if I'm being honest with myself, I want to know why he's having this reaction. It goes against everything I thought I knew.

Par for the course. I think bitterly.

After several minutes of tense silence, Seth lifts his head and stares at me, the intensity of his gaze making me squirm in my seat. He lets out a long breath and his shoulders slump. "I'm sorry Paige." I don't respond to his apology, frozen in place. Reaching a hand out, he brushes a lock of hair behind my ear. I cringe at his touch causing his eyes to darken as a scowl overtakes his face. His hand moves to take hold of my hair, pulling my head back.

Hissing at the sting, I glare at him. "Take your fucking hands off me Seth." I snarl.

He only tightens his grip in response. "It wasn't supposed to be like this." He snaps. "We could have been happy together, baby girl. But you *women*," Seth spits out the word in disgust. "Have to ruin everything. Can't just be happy and do as you're told." He yanks my head back farther with a sharp tug. I bite my cheek to keep from crying out, a painful throb emanating from my still healing wound.

Gritting my teeth against the pain, I spit at him, "Fuck you."

Seth glowers at me but I refuse to back down, promising retaliation. The standoff only serves to anger him more. "Is that what you want?

Because I'll gladly fuck you and remind this pussy who I am." He snarls, eyes wild.

My eyes widen and I fight against his hold. Panic overwhelms my brain as I am unable to move.

There is no way I'm going to let this asshole touch me. There's only one psychopath allowed to do that and Seth is certainly not him.

"Let me go!" I scream in frustration, clawing at his hand and arm. He laughs, pulling my face closer. I shudder at the desire burning in his eyes, fighting the need to throw up as my stomach rolls.

How did I ever want this man?

"You fighting it only makes me want you more." He sneers, leaning in to lick up the side of my face. I try to recoil but his grip is too strong.

"Stop it Seth." I snap, furious that my voice trembles, betraying my fear.

Remember who you are Paige.

Seth ignores me. Reaching over with his other hand, he slides the zipper of my jacket down. Pushing the material aside, he roughly grasps the neck of my oversized shirt, pulling it down below my chest. My vision swims as his fingers push down my exposed bra and encircle my breast. "God, I missed these tits." He murmurs, massaging my breast before lowering his head and latching onto my nipple with his mouth.

Angry tears roll down my face.

This can't be happening. This isn't happening. I'm not going to just sit here and let this happen.

With Seth's attention focused on my chest, I dart my eyes around the cab, looking for anything I can use as a weapon. My pulse speeds up as I zero in on my only option.

Sitting under the console is a pen, one of the fancy monogrammed ones with a metal tip that people use to flaunt their wealth. Silently, I stretch my hand toward the small writing utensil. Grasping blindly, my fingers wrap around the pen.

My next movements are a blur.

I let out an angry shriek moments before my arm comes down on Seth's neck. Yanking out the makeshift weapon, I stab into his bloodied skin over and over. I don't know how many times I attack my ex-turned-assailant. The bloodlust I have become familiar with, thanks to Mick, has taken over and is demanding payment.

My arm finally sags, exhaustion overtaking my limbs. I blink away the watery tears clouding my vision and peer down at the form hunched over me. Crimson liquid spills from a multitude of wounds in his neck, staining my disheveled shirt. His eyes are closed, mouth parted in shock. With shaking fingers, I press onto his neck. A faint pulse meets me.

Taking a deep breath, I fix my clothes as I assess the situation, trying to determine what to do next. Except my mind won't work, it's stuck in a constant loop of fear and bloodlust. I start growing desperate, unable to form a coherent thought.

A face pops into my vision and the calm hits me as a wave, washing over and soothing my frayed nerves.

Mick. Mick will know what to do.

I shove Seth's limp body off of me and pull out my phone. Taking a deep breath, I dial the number.

Chapter 32

Mick

The cool night air hits me as I exit the building. The metallic scent of fresh blood does nothing to calm the rage boiling inside. Stopping, I tilt my head back and scream at the sky, my body shakes as I howl my pain again and again.

"You're too late. If Seth has her, you'll never see her again." Vanessa chokes around the blood filling her mouth. I stare into her eyes, willing the words to be yet another lie out of the disgusting woman's mouth. All I see is her empty acceptance of what's going to happen to her, a dejected form of honesty.

"Fuck!" I yell, my throat burning against the assault to my vocal cords. Wringing my hands, I pace across the gravel. My fingers twitch, aching to wrap around the motherfucker's throat. Of all the people, Paige had to know this piece of shit. A flash of the man walking past me as I smiled and wished him luck crosses my mind.

If only I had known. Had done something...

My shaking fingers work through my hair, tugging hard against my scalp. I welcome the stinging pain, a small price for my failure to protect her.

Another rough cry erupts from my chest as I whirl around and slam my fist into the building. The weathered brick isn't fazed by my attacks as I punch repeatedly, my knuckles splitting and staining the wall.

A sound pulls me out of my destructive meltdown. I feel the buzz in my pocket and whip out my phone, answering without looking. "What?" I snap.

"Wow. I was calling to see if you were good but I think I have my answer."

Clenching my fist, I ignore his snide comment. "What do you want Jesse? I'm not in the mood for a chat." The line goes silent. When he finally does reply, all traces of humor have left his voice, leaving behind an unmasked tone of concern.

"I'm worried about you man. The way you took off earlier..." Jesse sucks in a breath and I brace myself, apprehensive of what he's going to say next. "Look, I've known you for a long time." He pauses, clearing his throat. "You've been acting strange these past few months. I don't know what's going on and I've tried to just give you space to work through whatever the fuck it is. But Mick. You gotta talk to me." My defenses shoot up, there's no way I'm discussing Paige with him. I'm about to tell him to piss off when he starts again, his voice lowered. "I'm really worried about you. Please, let me help."

I don't say anything for a while, not trusting what would come out of my mouth. The cool night air breezes, blowing cool wafts around me. I can feel my control slipping as the chilly wind cools some of the burning emotions consuming me. Without making the conscious decision, I find myself whispering into the line, desperately reaching out to my oldest friend.

In a voice I can't be certain the phone picks up, I brokenly whisper, "She's gone."

The moment the words leave my lips reality crushes me. Words echoing in my head and clawing at my heart.

You're too late. She's gone. You'll never see her again.

I sink to the ground and lean back against the wall. Pain that I haven't felt since I was a small child consuming me.

I've failed again. The only other woman I've ever loved and I've lost her too. Just like...

My thoughts cut off abruptly as it hits me.

Paige has not only become my obsession, my desire. She has stolen my heart.

A strangled sound leaves me.

I love her.

"Mick? Hello? What's going on?" The sound of my friend shouting through the phone pulls me out of my anguished thoughts.

"I'm here." I mutter.

Jesse lets out a relieved sigh at the sound of my voice. "Good. Did you say *she's* gone?" I don't reply and he presses, his tone cautious. "Who's gone Mick?"

The most important person to exist.

At my continued silence, Jesse keeps talking. "Do you mean Veronica?" I let out a low growl.

Not that fucking woman.

"Okay, not V. Then who are you talking about dude? You haven't mentioned anyone else to me. Fuck, I didn't even know there *was* a she."

Taking a deep breath, I cut off his rambling. "Her name's Paige. And she's everything. But she's gone and I don't know how to get her back." My heart cracks as the words leave my mouth.

Jesse exhales heavily. "Shit man." In a soft voice, he offers, "Why don't you come over and we can try to figure this out together?"

Desperation overtakes me and I cling to the small hope my friend offers. "Okay."

"Okay." He repeats cautiously.

After confirming where to meet up, I end the call and stare down at the phone.

If I just knew you were okay, little bird. Just let me know you're okay.

The silence suffocates me until I get up, trudging to my car and making my way down the long road.

Jesse whips open the door before I'm up the first step. He doesn't say anything, crossing his arms and leaning against the doorway. I take in the space around me, reminded again how much we differ.

Jesse Rolland takes great pleasure in the finer things in life and really enjoys flaunting his wealth. After me, he makes the highest salary at our company, so he has plenty to show off. Where I prefer to keep my living low key, he has splurged in every sense of the word.

His home is a large three level mid-century style house. Most of the walls are glass, providing plenty of light but no privacy. The garage and parking area are on a sunken level alongside the basement with steps leading up to the main entrance. Above the door, the second story is visible from the ground level. The colors are also in contrast to my preferred dark undertones. Jesse elected more earthy tones to decorate his space. Natural wood, muted gray and dusty blue make up the primary colors. Brick pillars spattered almost randomly around the building, breaking up the otherwise sharp angles of the design.

If I were to need to describe the style of my friend's house, the most accurate thing I could say would be pretentious confusion.

It's a good thing he's in construction and not design.

My lips twitch as the thought almost brings a smile to my face. However, the small burst of amusement is not quite enough to push past the dark hopelessness surrounding me.

Jesse claps my shoulder as I walk past him into the house. Shutting the door, he starts off down the hall. We make our way to his kitchen in silence. I slide into one of the seats surrounding the large island that takes up a large chunk of the room while Jesse opens the fridge and pulls out two beers. Popping the cap off of each, he hands me one and takes a large swig of his own. I tilt my head in thanks and sip at mine, fiddling with the bottle.

After a few minutes of stilted silence, Jesse clears his throat. "So, uh, can you fill me in on some more details? You said she, this Paige woman," I bristle at his casual mention of her and he holds up his hands in defense. "You said she's gone. What do you mean by that? Did she leave?"

I had taken the drive here to contemplate how to describe our situation. While I'm not ashamed of the things I do, the things I've done, I'm also aware that there are consequences within our society for my actions. Due to this, providing an accurate description proves difficult.

Taking a few more seconds to compose my thoughts, I gulp down more beer. Jesse watches me patiently, leaning back against the counter opposite from my seat. Ripping the bandaid off, I blurt out the words before I can change my mind.

"Paige is my...girlfriend." Jesse doesn't respond to my hesitation over the word, simply raising an eyebrow and indicating for me to continue.

"Earlier today during our meeting, she called and texted me. She said an old friend of hers was there to take her to work but she didn't feel right about it. Something about him seeming off." I twirl the bottle in my hands to keep them busy. Jesse wouldn't appreciate me destroying his things. With my emotions the way they are, there's a very real possibility I will.

Taking a breath to calm the raging chaos inside, I exhale slowly as I continue. "Her last text was the info for his car and I recognized it as someone else's. Someone who is a real fucked up guy. So I knew something bad was going to happen if I couldn't get to her." The skin on my hand has paled from the grip I have on the glass. Shame hits me again in full force at the mention of Seth using Kristoph's car.

Such a fucking idiot. I should have known.

"That's why you ran out." Jesse mutters, interrupting my mental berating.

I nod, "Yeah. I went straight to her apartment and she was gone, her car still there. Which wasn't a huge surprise but not good. I checked her work and she never showed up or called. I-" Putting down the bottle, I drop my head into my hands. "I haven't heard from her since." I admit, my chest aching, feeling the physical pain of her absence. I have become so dependent on her presence that her being gone has left a gaping hole. One I won't be able to fill without her.

Silence fills the room, suffocating and imposing. My admittance of failure dredging up memories I had long since suppressed.

"Fucking worthless whore." He screams into her face. She cowers back but there is nowhere for her to escape. "Useless. That's what you are!" He lifts his hand and brings it down hard across her face. She cries out in pain, clutching the reddened cheek.

"P-please." She begs. It never works, he never listens.

He scoffs, spitting in her face. "You have one job. Do it. I hope I don't need to remind you what will happen if you don't."

I ball my fists at my side, wishing that I was big enough to stop him. To do something to save her.

My mother looks at me with tears in her eyes. Trembling, she returns her attention to my father. "Okay, I'm sorry." She murmurs, casting her eyes down. Hand still clutched to the injured cheek, her shoulders slump as she resigns to the demands of the bastard.

My father glares at her, his eyes cloudy from whatever drug he shot up before storming into the room. "Get back in there then." He snaps, gesturing through the open door to a room down the hall. No doubt where one of the "clients" is waiting.

I force myself to stay in place, knowing from experience if I try to intervene I'll just make things worse. My mother shuffles out of the room but my attention remains on the man. I'll kill you for this one day. *I vow. One day, we will be free from this worthless shit.*

Coming out of the memory, my body shudders. I lift my head and look at Jesse, my desperation seeping through each word as I speak. "I have to find her, Jesse. I have to get her back."

He nods, pulling his phone out. "You said she sent you the car information?"

"Yes." I picture the old, crappy vehicle. I never understood the desire to drive something that screams corrupt cop but I suppose Kristoph believed he really was untouchable. My lips twitch and heart swells with pride as I remember the bloodied state of his corpse after Paige was done with him.

"Good. I can send it over to my buddy on the force and he can-" Jesse cuts off mid sentence, startled as I slam my hands down on the countertop.

"No!" I shout. My muscles tighten as I envision what would happen if they found her linked to the disappearance of their beloved detective. Jesse stares at me incredulously, mouth agape. In a quieter tone, I grit out, "Just...no cops. Okay? I need you to promise." Jesse tries to argue but I cut him off again. "Promise me." He watches me for a moment in shock. I'm sure I sound insane but there's no way I'm involving any more law enforcement.

Finally, Jesse reluctantly agrees, shrugging his shoulders. "Alright. I promise. It's going to make this a hell of a lot harder but if it's what you want?" He leaves the question hanging in the air. I meet his gaze unwaveringly, causing him to sigh. "Okay, right. There's another option, it's gonna be tricky though cause we need to ge-"

My phone rings and I whip it out, tuning out Jesse's words as the name flashes over the screen. I answer the call immediately. "Paige? Where are you?" I demand, wincing at my forceful tone. Every cell inside of me is screaming to go to her, to track her down and drag her back.

I may even chain her up again so she doesn't disappear on me anymore.

Shaking my head, I return my attention to the woman who owns me, the one for whom I would do anything. I listen to her, relishing the sound of her voice.

She's alive. She's okay.

Paige whispers, "Mick, I'm scared." Causing my blackened heart to shatter.

She shouldn't be scared, I'm meant to protect her. I will *protect her.*

I attempt to keep my voice soothing, battling against the murderous rage pulsing through me. "I know, baby. But don't worry, I'm coming for you. Just be patient." I hesitate then add, "And smart."

Paige is silent for a moment before agreeing. I'm finally free of the debilitating fear that has consumed me since I read her texts.

My raven-haired beauty is alive. I will get her back, no matter where that fucker tries to take her. She is mine, and I will claim her once again.

"And Paige?"

"Yes?" She replies, her voice sounding distant.

Knowing she doesn't have much time, I push all of my resolve and emotion into my next promise. "Remember, there is nowhere you can go that I won't find you, little bird." I end the call before she can reply, ready to get started on tracking her down. A smile stretches across my face knowing what I'm going to do to the prick who dared to take what is mine.

Jesse chuckles. "Damn." I look over at him as he shakes his head. "You've got it bad, huh?"

"You have no idea." I respond, shoving back the seat and rising to my feet. "What was your plan?"

"Oh, yeah." Jesse clears his throat and rubs the back of his neck. "I was going to suggest Paige downloads a tracking app on her phone."

I groan, knowing it's a great idea, and one that I can't do anything about now. "Shit. Okay, any other ideas?"

Jesse and I debate other options. He insists on ordering a pizza, claiming this could take a while and our brains will work better on a full stomach. I ignore him as he places the call, replaying the conversation with Paige in my brain over and over.

"Mick, I'm scared."

Loops inside my mind, an agonizing accompaniment to my thundering heartbeats. I drop my head in my hands and tug against the strands of hair falling forward.

I'll find you, little bird. Just hang on.

Forty minutes later, I hear the doorbell and curse.

Of course they would show up when Jesse went to take a piss.

Grumbling, I make my way toward the front door. I open the door and a lanky teenager tells me the total while juggling the large box in his hands. Pulling out some cash, I practically throw it at him. I have no idea how much money I just gave but by the brief glimpse of shock on his face, I'm betting he just received a significant tip.

Turning, I slam the door shut with my foot and head back toward the kitchen. I only make it a few steps before my phone starts to ring. Shuffling the box to one hand, I reach into my pocket and pull out my phone. "Hello?" No answer comes. Striding toward the island, I place down the food before speaking again. "Hello?" I repeat as I pull a slice out. My hand pauses midway to my mouth as a small sniffle comes through the line. I watch a piece of pepperoni slowly slip off my pizza slice and splat onto the counter.

Another sniffle and I hear Paige whimper. "Mick?" She whispers.

Her voice is so soft I almost don't hear her as she says my name. My hand tightens around the phone, pressing hard against my ear. "Paige? What's wrong?" Still unable to move, I can feel my blood pressure rising as the need to harm whoever has caused her to cry overpowers my senses.

"Seth. He...he-" Paige lets out a small cry and my vision clouds.

"He what?" I demand through gritted teeth.

If he hurt her, I'm going to murder him. Slowly.

"I need you Mick." She says instead of answering my question. "Please."

I glance at Jesse who just made his way back into the room and is now watching me intently. Inhaling, I push back my emotions. "I'll come get you, baby. Do you know where you are?"

Her answer is immediate. "No."

"Okay. I need you to do something for me then. I'm going to put you on speaker and have Jesse, my friend, walk you through what you need to do." I give him a nod and flip the call to speaker.

Jesse straightens and comes closer. "Hi Paige." He says softly, eyeing me. "Do you have any data on your phone?"

Shuffling sounds through the line before she responds, her voice farther away. "Yes."

"Great. We're gonna have you download an app onto your phone called FindMe. Once it's downloaded, it'll give you a randomly generated code that you'll give us so we can connect and see your location. Okay?"

"Got it." Paige's voice has lost the emotional distress from earlier but the monotone concerns me just as much. I wring my hands, thoughts of what could be causing the hot and cold in her flash through my mind. None of them are good.

I shuffle my feet as the seconds tick on, each bringing us closer to reuniting. I bite back a groan as the image of claiming her in front of Seth's dangling corpse fills my mind. Jesse says something and I snap back to the present, needing to focus so we can get to her.

"-29n1jwi1go. Jesus, that's a long code." Paige grumbles, causing Jesse to chuckle. I glare at him, warning not to get any ideas. He rolls his eyes and taps away on my phone.

Snapping his fingers, he points at the small dot blinking on the screen. "Got it!" A name is listed above the dot. My heart swells and a small smile breaks through as I read the username she chose.

Little Bird

Leaning closer, I inspect the map, my brow furrowing. They are at least a three hour drive from here and appear to be heading to nowhere. A sinking feeling forms in my gut. "Paige." I snap, anxiety sharpening my voice.

"Hmm?" She replies in the same monotonous tone as before.

I pinch my fingers over the flashing dot and zoom out the screen, dragging it in both directions. No matter where I move away from the dot, there's nothing but empty woods spanning miles. "Are you alone?"

Paige inhales sharply, "No. Seth is...here?"

I look up and meet Jesse's eyes, confusion clouding my mind. "If he's there, why were you able to call me?"

"I, um," She hesitates, clearly wanting to avoid the topic. I wait in silence for her to answer, needing to know. "I stabbed him. *A lot.*" She whispers the last two words and Jesse's eyes widen.

Fuck.

"Why did you stab him, baby?" I ask carefully, holding Jesse's astonished gaze. His forehead creases as he contemplates the words.

I can hear Paige shifting in her seat and another sniffle. My fingers curl and I press them into the countertop, enraged by her pain. "He tried to...he did...I couldn't..." She starts and stops her thoughts repeatedly.

Growing impatient and increasingly worried, I demand, "Paige. Tell me what he did."

Paige brokenly whispers, confirming my fears, "He assaulted me. Tried to rape me." A quiet sob follows the revelation.

In a blink, I heave the stool into the wall. Roaring, I chuck anything my fingers can reach. The room quickly fills with shattered glass, broken dishes, and upended furniture. No longer caring I have an audience, I shout curses and vows. Promises to drain the life from Seth, ending his pathetic existence. I'm a caged animal, demanding to flee to avenge my mate.

My soiled little bird. He will pay for this.

I hear a soft gasp come over the speakers and pause my rampage, chest heaving.

"No." She whimpers. I stalk back to my phone, snatching it up. Switching off speaker, I press it against my ear. "Fuck. Stop!" I hear her cry out, the sound quickly cutting off.

"Paige?" She doesn't respond, the silence thick.

A shuffling noise breaks the quiet before a low chuckle. "Hey asshole." If I wasn't already planning to peel every inch of skin from his body, the cocky prick would have just added himself to my kill list. I remain silent, unable to speak past the hellacious rage. Seth sighs dramatically. "Alright. I'm not sure what your plan was, but you're too late. She's mine, always has been." Grinding my teeth, a low growl rumbles from my chest. "You'll never find us, so I suggest you just leave it alone." He ends the call, having issued his warning.

I slowly lower the phone down, flattening my palm over it on the counter. My only hope is Jesse knows what he's talking about. If not, I'll be too far gone to the darkness. If I can't get her back, I'll destroy everyone and everything in my way.

Even my oldest friend.

Chapter 33

Paige

I wake with a start, my head pounding. A strong sense of deja vu hits me as I'm reminded of my first night at Mick's. I test my arms and find them, thankfully, free. A chill runs through me as my fingers brush against cotton fabric. My hands explore my body and horror fills me as I find my clothes have been replaced by a short dress. My bra and underwear have been removed, leaving my nipples to pebble under the thin fabric in the cold room. Focusing on my breathing, I force myself to stay calm despite the sickening reason behind the change.

Turning my attention to the space, I strain my eyes to take in my surroundings. The room is cast in darkness, the only light pouring through the edges of a door. The small light shows a flight of stairs leading up to the exit but is unable to penetrate the black beyond the steps. Another chill runs through me. Shivering, I wrap my arms around my legs and tuck my face into my knees.

I was so close, I should have just pushed him out of the car and took off in any direction.

I grip my hair tightly and press my closed eyes into my knees.

This is it. I'm not sure what I did to deserve it, but my life is yet again at the mercy of someone else. Only this time, I don't know if I have the strength to fight anymore.

I expect to feel tears well up but find myself empty, devoid of emotion.

I thought I was strong.

I thought I had taken back my power.

I was wrong.

The wood creaks as the rusted hinges work to open. I don't move, head still tucked into my curved body. Heavy steps descend the stairs, each one creaking in protest to the weight. Once the footfalls reach the hard floor, I hear the sound of metal scraping along the concrete. Something clatters on the floor and I hear a heavy sigh echo around the room.

"Are you going to just mope there?"

I don't move or respond, past the point of caring.

Seth exhales again shortly before fingers grip my hair and yank my head back. Keeping my eyes closed, I refuse to give him anything I still have control over. "Look at me." He demands, his hot breath wafting across my face. Squeezing my lids tighter, I hug my knees closer to my chest. A hand slaps my cheek at the same time Seth releases my hair. My head whips to the side, skin stinging from the blow but I refuse to react.

Angered by my disobedience, he grips my hair again and drags me to my feet by the strands. I let out a small cry as I try to steady my wobbly legs. Before I can get my balance, Seth punches my stomach, the air whooshing out of me. If he wasn't holding my hair so tightly, I would double over from the impact. Taking my jaw in his free hand, he squeezes hard enough to bruise. "I said look at me you ungrateful bitch." He snarls, fingers tightening in my hair as he releases my face. The relief only lasts a second as another harsh blow hits my cheek. "It's either your eyes or your mouth." He warns, venom dripping from his words.

I open my eyes and scowl at him. His neck has several bandages wrapped around it and water drips from his damp hair onto a fresh shirt, the other one most likely ruined. A brief moment of satisfaction breaks through my cold emotions, knowing I'm the reason behind the damage. The warmth seeps out again as I watch him run his hungry eyes over my body.

I'm not sure how I never noticed the predatory glint in his eyes before. There's no fondness in his expression, nothing like I've come to know with Mick. Even when he had tied me up and removed my freedom, there was still a look of adoration shining through when Mick looked at me. Seth, on the other hand, looks at me as if I'm a bag of meat, waiting to be prepared, devoured and discarded. A chill runs down my spine, knowing I am fully at his mercy to do just that.

Seth's eyes slide up and meet mine. "See? Now was that so fucking hard?" He shakes me, emphasizing his words. "You will learn to listen when I say something." I don't reply, meeting his gaze without a hint of emotion. He licks his lips while running a hand across his jaw. "It'll only be a matter of time before you realize we belong together. We *will* be together, once you remember who you are." Seth releases me and steps back, gesturing to the floor. "There's some food and water. You'll have to eat with your hands after your last little stunt." He gingerly runs his fingers over the bandaging covering his neck. "I suggest you eat and sleep. You're going to need it." He turns and marches up the steps, slamming the door shut behind him.

I hear the sound of locks sliding into place, confirming my suspicion that I'm trapped down here. Crumpling to the ground, I stretch my hand out and fumble around until I feel a plastic tray. Sliding it toward myself, I choke down the food and gulp the water. Within a few minutes, my eyelids grow heavy and I'm unable to stay upright. Resting on the cool concrete, I succumb to the darkness.

Time becomes meaningless within my world. Seth repeatedly visits me with food and water. Each time I consume the provisions, I fall asleep within minutes and wake up in confusion, my body aching. A small part of me is aware that the soreness isn't just from sleeping on a hard surface but I refuse to think on it.

Barely clinging to my sanity, I let my mind wander. I imagine Mick bursting through the door to rescue me. I'm beyond the capability of escaping myself, my soul has been battered one too many times. So, instead, I envision my dark knight riding in.

The door opens and I curse myself for the heartbreak I feel as I see a mop of unkempt black hair rather than the blonde curls I'm desperate to see again.

Seth plods down the stairs and dumps another tray on the ground. I wait for him to leave but he walks into the darkness and returns with a chair instead. Apprehension filling me, I keep my eyes fixed on his movements as he lowers himself into the chair. Crossing an ankle over his knee, Seth runs his fingers through his hair. "When are you going to move on from this?" He grouches, gesturing toward me.

I sit in silence. There's nothing I want to say to him and he'll keep talking anyway. I had forgotten how much Seth liked the sound of his own voice. I truly can't remember what I ever liked about him. His personality is foul and his entitlement disgusting. Watching him with an impassive expression, I wait.

Sighing dramatically, he strokes his chin. "Don't you want to go back to how things were? We used to be so happy together." I cringe at the reminder. I was a different girl then, meek and submissive. I never talked back, always attempted to smooth the waters rather than stir up a fight. Of course Seth would want that back.

One thing has become clear during my time with him inside this dark room. Seth gets off on subservient behavior, his need to control driving him to destroy any individuality in me. The difference in Seth's version of dominance and Mick's brings forth tears that I thought had dried out. Where Seth desires to crush me, Mick wants to empower me. For every bit Mick broke, he built me back up. I was wholly myself with him, freed from the chains wrapped around my soul. Something stirs inside me deep down. I feel a shift from the cold hopelessness that has consumed me since Seth snatched my phone from my hand. A fire melting the ice encasing my heart, flames licking up my being and rekindling my determination.

Unaware of the changes happening inside of me, Seth continues on. "It really is a shame you jumped to conclusions without giving me a chance." I hear the frustration bleed into his voice. "If you had just fucking waited, I would have told you. But no, you're too fucking emotional and just took off." Shame attempts to douse out the fire raging in me but is quickly snuffed out.

Seth may have been able to convince me it was my fault once upon a time, but that time has long since passed. I know who I am now, I know what I'm worth.

"Always so goddamn emotional, you women are." He grumbles. "You see, fucking Brie was insurance." I wince, the image of their bodies moving together flashing into my mind. "It wasn't my idea but I couldn't say no. Like I said, it was just work. Meant nothing." Seth stops talking and I find myself desperate to know, needing closure if nothing else.

"Why?" I whisper, my voice distorted from lack of use. Seth's eyes light up as he finally gets a reaction out of me.

Leaning forward, he braces his arms on his knees. "Why?" He repeats. "Because she stumbled onto something she shouldn't have." He pauses, clasping his hands together. "I suppose much like you did. Except she didn't have a murdering shadow following her around." My eyes widen, wondering how much Seth actually knows. He chuckles humorlessly. "Yeah, I know all about your boy toy and his little hero act. He was sloppy and will get his own soon enough, I'll make sure of that." I shudder at the excitement shining in his eyes. Focusing back on me, his glee dies off. "Anyway, Brie walked in on one of my *business* conversations with Kristoph." My stomach recoils. Verbal confirmation of my fear he had been doing this the entire time we were together makes me feel sick. Caught up in his story, Seth rattles on. "You see, after that we had to make sure Brie wouldn't say anything, so I was sent to get some collateral. You were never meant to know, Paige. And then the bitch blasts on the Internet that her and I are not only together but *engaged*?" Seth glowers, dropping his hands and leaning back. "Not to worry, though. She's been taken care of for her part in this."

My head swims as the oxygen in the room escapes. Breathlessly, I whisper, "What did you do to her?" I'm still hurt by my former friend, but concern outweighs the pain.

It sounds like...

A sinister grin spreads across his face. "Oh *I* didn't do anything." He allows the heaviness of the implication to hang in the air before continuing. "We'll just say she won't be getting between us. Ever again." He snickers.

My vision clouds as I stare at the merciless face before me. Guilt punching into me as I'm reminded of all the times I wished harm and death on the two of them.

Seth's right about one thing, I should have waited for an explanation, just not his.

My heart hurts as I realize Brie knew what she was doing. On at least some level she must have known what it would mean for her. A part of me wonders if she did it for me, so I could move on and not suffer the same fate she had by stumbling on something I shouldn't.

A new resolve fills me, bolstering my regained confidence.

I am going to make it out of this fucking basement. I'm going to escape and then I'm going to destroy the man who caused all the needless pain. For me and for Brie.

"You're going to regret this Seth." I promise, my voice even and assured.

He scoffs, pushing to his feet. "Oh yeah? You really think so? Because from what I can tell, the only one with regrets is you." Seth stalks up the stairs and latches the door, plunging me into darkness again.

I carefully grab the bottle of water and granola bar from the tray. Bracing my hand on the wall, I slide around the room, seeking out a safe spot. Relief fills me when I locate a shelf with something resting on top. My exploring fingers roam over the object. It feels like a small vase, large enough for what I need. Shoving down the crumpled bar and pouring the water into the neck, I resume my search. My hand grasps the trash tightly, knowing I'll need it.

I fumble around in the dark, my free hand roaming over anything I can reach. Laughter bubbles up as my fingers curl around something small enough to fit in my palm but sharp enough I can feel it slice into my skin.

Ignoring the pain radiating from my cut palm, I make my way back toward the space below the stairs. I place the trash down on the tray, curl my fingers around the small treasure, and lay down. Closing my eyes, I even out my breath and mimic sleep, waiting for Seth to return.

You're right, Seth. You won't have any regrets. You can't have them if you're no longer breathing.

It feels like an eternity that I lay there, keeping my breaths even. The nervous anticipation humming through my veins increases when I hear a familiar creak. My fingers tighten as I force my eyes to stay shut.

Seth makes his way down the stairs, stopping over me. He breathes heavily as I hear the clinking of metal followed by a zipping sound. I push back the panic as my fears are confirmed. Remaining motionless, I can hear Seth fumbling with his jeans before kneeling next to me. His fingers go to the hem of the soiled dress, shoving the material up. My heart beats wildly as he grips my hips and readjusts my body, giving him access to my sex.

Oblivious to the fact I'm not drugged, he grips his cock and lines it up with my entrance. My fingers move carefully, slipping the sharp edge of the object in my hand so it's facing inward. Seth moves his head over mine and leans down, pressing his lips against mine as he shoves inside.

I cry out at the intrusion, driving the object into his cheek at the same time. Seth roars and flings himself back, landing on his heels. I catch a glimpse of metal, the makeshift weapon piercing through his mouth.

Not wasting a second, I scramble upright and fly up the stairs on my bare feet. I can hear Seth's cries behind me as I race toward freedom. Reaching the doorway, I sprint through and fling the door shut a moment before a heavy body crashes against it.

With trembling fingers, I slide the first lock into place followed by the second. Seth pounds against the door, screaming curses at me. I slump against the wood and collapse to the ground, tears leaking soundlessly down my face. I don't move, unable to muster the energy.

I escaped. I'm safe.

For now.

Chapter 34

Mick

"Useless piece of shit." I snarl, jabbing my finger against the small screen.

It's been weeks since I spoke with Paige. Weeks.

The location app continues to blink, showing the last location that Paige's phone was active. Seth had chosen a smart spot to hide away, completely surrounded by woodland for hundreds of miles in any direction. I have spent every moment scouring the forest and continually come up empty. Jesse had tried to help me search but backed off shortly after I threatened to break his nose, opting to search separate areas after that.

I know it's not his fault, but there is no more logical thought inside of me. I've given into the monster in my desperation to reunite with my missing woman. It's that same creature fueling my search, refusing to stop for longer than a couple hours at a time.

I'm going to find her. There's no other option.

Jesse's face fills the screen. I answer, starting my car again and driving toward another offshoot from the main road.

"Hey man, any luck?"

My teeth grind as I exhale through my nose. "No." I bite out.

"Fuck." I can hear voices in the background as Jesse sighs. "I'll head back up after this meeting and help look. Send me the spots you checked already, I'll let you know where I'll search once I get there."

I grunt in response and end the call.

Returning my attention to the hunt, I stare down at the small dot.

I'm coming, little bird. I'll find you.

Her screams echo down the hall, the closed door doing nothing to stifle the sound. I cover my ears with my hands, tucked away inside the small cabinet nestled along the hallway wall. The cabinet doors are cracked just enough for me to peer out without compromising my position. She screams again and I force my body to stay put.

She told you to hide. *I remind myself.*

We could tell it was going to be another bad night when Louie showed up. Dad was always angrier after using Louie's supply. Mom had ushered me away from the two men and sternly instructed me to hide and not come out, no matter what I heard. I blinked back tears, trying to stay tough for her. Mom had wrapped me up in a tight hug, squeezing me like a lifeline and placing a kiss on my head.

"I love you Mick." She whispered in my ear. "Now promise me," She pulled back and held my gaze. "You won't come out, no matter what."

I sniffled and squared my shoulders. "I promise."

Mom smiled, her eyes cast in sadness. "That's my good boy. I love you so much."

"I love you too." I whispered before tucking into the spot.

The screams continue throughout the night. I succumb to sleep with the track of my mother's misery at the hand of my father, feeling pieces of me shattering as I am yet again unable to do anything to stop him. To save her.

A persistent dinging noise rouses me from my sleep. I glance at the dash, noting I've only been asleep for about an hour. Groaning, I scrub my face with my hands and fight the exhaustion threatening to overtake me. The continuous lack of sleep and stress is beginning to take a real toll on my body.

Another ding sounds and I reach blindly toward the noise. My hand grips the phone and I shake off the last tendrils of sleep clinging to me. Expecting to find another useless message from Jesse reminding me of my continued failure, I resist the urge to just shut the damn thing off. Bringing the screen into view, I stare at the notification.

The words jumble as I try to understand their meaning.

Is this really?

Closing my eyes, I take a deep breath and let it out slowly. When I open them again, I carefully read the alert, willing it to be true and not a mirage of my sleep-deprived brain.

New location alert

Little Bird is active, click this message to view the new location

A hysterical laugh builds as I lean heavily against the steering wheel. Paige's phone is on again and now I know where she is. My laughter dies out as the knowledge hits me.

I know where she is.

Sitting upright, I click on the message.

The app pulls up and a new dot blinks several miles away. I quickly inspect the map, gaining my bearings and plotting the best route. Once I have a plan, I climb out of the car and round to the trunk. Pulling out anything I might need, I move the tools to the passenger seat before climbing back behind the wheel.

The tires squeal as I accelerate down the road, thoughts focused solely on the woman waiting for me.

Chapter 35

Paige

"Shit, shit, shit." I mutter, waving the phone around. "Come on you piece of junk." The message bubble appears and I hold my breath.

Please.

The red x pops up below the message, indicating the delivery failure. I scream in frustration and chuck the phone onto the couch. Pacing, I chew on my nail and try to think of what else to do.

I had been so relieved when I found where Seth had stashed my things. Finding my phone nestled inside my purse was the first time since this all started that I thought things might go my way. That hope has been decimated as the service proves to be too spotty to actually communicate with anyone. I've also yet to find the keys to Seth's car and my skill set doesn't include hot wiring.

Note to self, add that to the list of survival musts to learn. Right after I figure out how to read maps. Someone should really have a checklist for this stuff. Maybe I'll make one, if I ever get out of here.

Pausing my movement, I look up at the ceiling, blowing out a breath.

I can't give up now, I've just got to figure something out.

I glance over at the door leading to the basement.

It's been a few hours since I escaped and locked Seth down there instead. The silence from the other side concerns me, causing my skin to prickle. Deciding I'd rather be prepared, I make my way toward the small kitchen, rummaging around until I find a large knife. I study the blade, wishing I still had the syringe to use instead. I don't want Seth's end to be quick and know if I need to use this as a weapon, it will have to be if I want to get out alive.

A noise outside the cabin startles me. Pulse thumping, I creep toward the door, tucking myself out of view. I glance at the basement door again.

There's no way he got out somehow. Right?

Feeling less sure at each passing second, I tighten my grip on the knife handle. A soft scraping sounds at the door and I tense. The door creaks open and a large shadow crosses the threshold at the same time I scream and lunge.

The figure stumbles backward, lifting an arm to protect their face moments before I'm able slice across their cheek. A familiar grunt echoes in the room and I freeze. "Goddamnit." He curses, wrapping his fingers around the bleeding wound. His eyes shift from the cut to me and my breath catches in my throat. "Paige?" He whispers.

As if the sound of my name on his lips breaks my body from a spell, I find my feet moving as I leap at him.

Mick catches me and crushes my body against him, his injury forgotten. Wrapping my legs around him, I bury my face in his neck and sob. Every emotion I had shut off during my captivity pours out through my tears. Mick comforts me while roaming his hands all over my body as if he can't believe I'm really here.

I understand the feeling.

Pulling back, I clasp his face in my hands and gaze at him, memorizing every feature. His eyes are bloodshot with dark circles underneath, the curls normally styled are a tangled mess, a scruffy beard has begun to form from an extended length of time not shaving.

I tighten my hold and close the distance between us, capturing his mouth with mine. The kiss is forceful and messy, a clash of teeth and lips as we try to assure ourselves that this is real, that we've found each other again. Pulling back just far enough to suck in a breath, I whisper against his lips, "You came."

Mick smooths his hand down my hair while murmuring, "Of course I did. I will always come for you, baby." He presses another kiss to my lips. This one is tender and full of promise, leaving me just as breathless as the last. I cling to him, momentarily lost in his presence.

A distant clang brings me back to reality and I grudgingly climb down his body. Mick keeps his arms wrapped around me as he glances around the space. It's a small cabin filled with wooden furniture to match the wood walls. Several forest themed paintings line the room. A coffee table, sofa and area rug furnish the space. The focal point being a large fireplace tucked into the far corner. Adjoining the living area is a simple kitchen housing a stove, fridge, sink and two-person dining table. In a different setting, it would be quite cozy.

Seeming satisfied with his inspection, Mick looks down at me. I can't hide the shiver that runs through me at the deadly glint in his eyes. "Where is he?" I don't need to ask who as I gesture toward the locked door. He follows my direction and quirks an eyebrow. Looking back at me, his expression fills with adoration and amazement. Tears prick at the back of my eyes again as I have visual evidence of how he sees me.

"You are amazing." He kisses me again, crushing my body to his as his tongue works its way into my mouth.

I moan into the kiss, curling my fingers into his shirt.

He's here. I'm free.

The thoughts unleash the moisture in my eyes. Mick pulls back and kisses the tears falling down my face, whispering comforting words between each one. Collecting myself, I pull away and wipe my face as I head toward the basement. I can hear him following me. Stopping at the door, I look back as I declare, "He has to die, Mick."

Reaching out, he squeezes my shoulder. "I can promise that much." He pauses and a devilish smirk covers his face. "I have special plans for him." Mick winks at me and I feel heat flood my core. I squirm, trying to relieve some of the pressure. His eyes darken as he takes in my movements, tongue flicking out and slowly licking his lips. I bite mine, my eyes traveling to the bulge in his jeans. Mick pushes into my back, his arms circling me and pulling my body flush with his, whispering in my ear, "Naughty little bird. Does the thought of me torturing that piece of shit turn you on?" I shake my head. Mick tsks, taking my earlobe between his teeth and biting. I gasp as he releases it and breathes, "Liar."

I'm trembling in his arms as he moves his head, kissing down my jaw and neck. Biting down on my lip again, I try to stifle the moan when Mick's hand slips down to my legs, fingers playing with the hem of the ratty dress. Running his nose back up the path of his lips, he stops next to my ear. "If I were to check," His fingers push up the fabric on my thighs, I suck in a breath as he continues. "Would I find out just how much of a liar you are?" The tips of his fingers brush against my pussy, teasing me. "Hmm, Paige? Am I going to find you wet?" I can't speak, my thoughts are jumbled. I'm aching for him to touch me, needing to replace the feeling of Seth being there. Mick slides a finger through my folds. "Fuck," He groans. "You're soaked."

I lean into his touch, begging for more of him. "Please." He chuckles as he pushes a fingertip in, just enough to tease me but not what I need. "Please Mick. I need..." I push against his finger but he doesn't allow it to go any deeper.

"What do you need, baby?" He murmurs, kissing my neck. I shudder, clinging to his arm wrapped around me. My nails dig in and I feel warmth spread on my hand. Looking down, I notice the wound on his arm has opened more, blood smearing on my skin where we connect. Mick flexes his fingers and I feel him push in another inch before retreating again, leaving only the tip inside. "Tell me what you need." He repeats before biting down on my shoulder.

I whimper as he licks the bite to soothe the sting, placing a soft kiss over the mark. My answer is barely a whisper, my need and pain overwhelming my senses. "I need you to replace him. Please Mick, I need to feel you."

Mick freezes. I try to turn my head to look at him but his hold on me prevents the movement. In a low voice, he finally speaks. "What did you say?" He rasps.

I shrink at the tone, fear spreading through me. "I need you." I repeat, knowing it's the wrong thing to say the second it leaves my lips.

Mick moves in a blur. Yanking his hand out from my legs, he grips my arms and flings me over his shoulder. Stomping toward the kitchen, he sets me on the counter and steps between my legs. I stare at him with wide eyes as he frames my face with his hands. "Paige." The look in his eyes as he says my name sends a shiver down my spine. Pain, guilt, and fury shine within the blue orbs. His jaw twitches as he clenches his teeth. "What happened?" He demands, fingers tightening and gaze boring into me.

My eyes cast down as shame floods me. I have nothing to feel ashamed for, but the feeling haunts me regardless.

Mick waits, I can feel his eyes still on me. Blowing out a breath, I glance at him and quickly away again as I speak. "I had stopped him in the car, when I called you." I pause, taking another breath. "I had the drug in my pocket, I was going to use it on him once I had a plan of where to go, but he woke up before I could. He found it and must have used it on me cause the next thing I knew I woke up in a dark basement." My gaze shifts to the door again, reminding myself it's locked and I'm safe on the other side. "He would bring me food and I would pass out right after eating. It took me a while to realize he was still drugging me." Mick's fingers dig into my skin but he doesn't say anything. In a quieter voice, I continue, "I always woke up in pain and sore. Each time, another part of me broke, until there was nothing but shattered pieces." A tear slips free. "I had my suspicions that he was doing something to me but couldn't be sure. Until..." I stop, not sure how to say it.

Mick smooths his thumbs along my jaw. "Until?" He prompts softly.

I look back at him and the words spill out as my chest cracks open. "Until I found a way to trick him into thinking I had taken the drugs. I dumped the food and found a piece of broken metal. Waited for him to come, hoping he wouldn't. But he did." A choked sob interrupts my words. I push on, needing to get this out. "He came down and moved me so he could fuck my body while I was unconscious. It definitely wasn't the first time either." Anger replaces the shame, burning hot at the memory. "I stabbed him in his fucking face and ran. He's been trapped down there since." I gesture toward the basement as I finish, looking at Mick, heart thumping as I wait for his response. He doesn't say anything, his face shuttered.

Unable to bear the silence, I tentatively reach out, placing a hand flat on his chest. He looks down at my hand as I whisper, "Mick?" A tremor runs through his body and he exhales harshly, dropping his hands from my face. Without a word, he turns on his heel and storms out of the room.

I remain on the counter frozen in place, my mind at war with itself. Equally powerful thoughts shout at me.

He left me, I just told him the worst thing to happen to me and he left.

My head shakes in disbelief.

He wouldn't leave. He came for me. He wouldn't leave me.

I press my hands over my mouth to trap the heartbreak inside.

What if he doesn't want me anymore? What if he thinks I'm disgusting now?

Before I'm able to succumb to hysteria, Mick walks back into the kitchen carrying a large duffel bag. Seeing my state, he drops the bag and rushes to me, capturing me back in his arms. "I'm so sorry baby. He will pay for this." He murmurs, rubbing my back.

I shake my head against his chest, mumbling, "I thought you left me."

"No." Mick's voice is forceful as he leans back and tilts my chin up to look at him. "I will *never* leave you. Do you hear me? Never." My lip trembles, the intensity of his declaration overwhelming my fragile emotions. Mick runs a finger over my lip before bending down and pressing a soft kiss. "You're mine, little bird." He pulls away, trailing his fingers down my arm. "Now, let's grab the bastard and show him that he messed with the wrong monsters." I shiver at his words, the familiar tug of violence pulling me from the ledge of despair.

Mick's face breaks out in a grin as I nod.

Time to show Seth who I really am.

Chapter 36

Mick

Even in her current state, Paige is the most beautiful creature I've encountered. Though she has tear stains along her face, there is a power emanating from her. Seth may have violated her, but he didn't break her.

No, my raven-haired goddess will descend on her attacker as a vengeful angel.

I adjust my cock in anticipation of watching her exact her revenge.

It had been my intention to sneak in and incapacitate him, assuming he had locked her away somewhere. The surprise of finding Paige free and Seth locked up was even more of a reminder that my girl is extraordinary.

Following behind her closely, we approach the locked door. I push down the desire to tuck her away somewhere safe and take care of the prick myself. She deserves the chance to exercise her pain on his flesh. Paige pauses, hand trembling where it rests on the lock. I reach around her body and place my own hand over hers. "I'm right behind you." I assure her, my other hand brushing down her stomach. She nods, stealing her shoulders. I remove my hand moments before she throws open the lock, quickly followed by the second.

As the door creaks open, I'm hit by a rancid smell. It wafts up from the dark space and causes me to clench my teeth, furious that she was forced to reside down there all this time. The hypocrisy of my reaction is not lost on me, but I am the only one allowed to subject her to such punishments.

Paige takes a tentative step down onto the first stair, one hand wrapped tightly around the railing, the other clutching the knife in front of her. My arm throbs, a reminder of how badly I want this woman who drew my blood without a second thought. We reach the bottom steps and I strain my eyes, looking for any movement in the blackened room.

I sense his presence before seeing him. Darting my arm out, I yank Paige back moments before a fist slices through the air. "Fucking cunt," Seth sneers, revving back to attack again. I hold my hand up, catching his fist in my palm. Seth looks at me with wide eyes, finally registering that they aren't alone.

I smile at him, my own eyes wild with rage. Tightening my hold, I bend his arm, forcing his body to twist. With his back now toward us, arm bent far enough to overextend the joints, I look to Paige for instruction. I want to allow her some of the control she lost. She stares at the prick writhing in my grip, expression blank. "Baby?" I prod, willing her back from wherever her mind has gone. "Little bird." I call out when I get no response.

She turns her head toward me and meets my gaze. I watch as the blank look dissipates, replaced by a hunger I'm all too familiar. "Bring him upstairs." Paige commands, turning and climbing up the steps, her ass swaying with each movement of her hips. I bite back a groan as I'm reminded of how long it's been since I've plunged balls deep into her.

Soon.

I push Seth up the stairs, twisting his arm farther as he tries to hinder the progress. "You heard the woman." I chuckle, excitement coursing through my veins. We step out of the basement and I direct him toward an empty chair next to the dining table. Shoving him down, I glance toward my bag, calculating the distance. "Little bird, bring me the rope from my bag."

Stepping behind him, I pull out a switchblade from my pocket. Flicking it open, I press the sharp metal against his throat, immobilizing him in the chair. Paige rummages through the supplies and brings the rope over. The moment she's in arms reach, I swoop her into a kiss, leaving her breathless as I pull away. Taking the rope from her hands, I tie Seth to the chair, stepping back to admire my handiwork as he struggles against the binds.

Satisfied he isn't going anywhere, I snatch Paige into my arms again, pressing my lips to hers. She moans as I force my tongue inside, exploring every inch of her divine mouth. My hands slide down, wrapping around to grip her ass, tugging her body flush with mine. A soft gasp escapes her as she feels my hard cock rub against her abdomen. I roll my hips, showing her just how much I want her. How much I *need* her.

I'm lost in desire, momentarily forgetting the prick tied up behind us. Paige whimpers and tries pulling away. Tightening my grip, I refuse her attempts. She snakes her hands up my chest and pushes firmly. This time I allow the space, cocking my head at her, only to find her eyes are not on me. They are on the man currently living on borrowed time, her face pained as she stares. My shoulders tense as I turn slowly to face the source of the pain.

Seth glares at Paige, still futilely yanking against the rope. "Fucking whore!" He shouts.

She flinches and I'm on him in a second. Pulling my fist back, I slam it into his face. Seth's head snaps back from the impact. "The fuck did you just say?" I seethe, gripping his hair and forcing him to look at me. His eyes widen as he meets mine. I tug his hair, causing a pained noise to leave him. Moving to land another blow, a small hand grips my wrist, halting my progress.

I glance back and see my Paige. Not the hurting girl from moments before, the Paige before me is a goddess of death, one I have missed so dearly.

Running her hand up my arm, she pulls me back. "Let me." She asserts, confidence radiating from her. I back away and lean against the back of the sofa, arms crossed. I'm more than happy to allow her this but the bloodlust thrumming inside causes me to clench my hands into fists to restrain myself.

Paige moves in front of Seth and grips his jaw, her fingers curled into talons. Leaning closer, she digs her nails into his skin as he tries to shake himself from her hold. "You kept saying to remember who I am." A sinister smile forms on her face, her pupils dilating as her focus fixes on the small beads of blood pooling around her fingers. "I suppose I should thank you for the constant reminders, as I had forgotten. I'd allowed myself to become the scared, pathetic Paige you knew. But you see, *detective,*" She spits the title at him, crinkling her nose. "You shouldn't have pushed. Because I've remembered now. I remember everything. And now you'll get to truly know who I am." She shoves his face back and steps away.

My gaze stays fixed on her as she saunters toward the supply bag. Reaching inside, she withdraws the machete I brought just for her. While

I enjoy the creative approach to my kills, my girl prefers her weapon of choice.

Spinning around, she runs the flat of the blade across her palm as she stalks back toward Seth. He recoils, swinging his head, trying to find an escape route. "P-Paige." He stammers, tugging against the rope. "You don't have to do this."

Her chuckle goes straight to my dick. "You're right. I don't have to." She stops her movement, running her finger along the edge of the machete, a small line of blood trickling from the cut. Seth watches her with cautious eyes as she slowly brings her finger to her mouth. Pressing it to her lips, she sucks on the cut. She smiles while lowering her hand, blood coating her teeth. I can't hold back the groan from the sight. Paige's eyes flicker to me, heating as they meet mine before looking back at Seth. Her voice husky as she speaks again. "I *want* to."

Best. Foreplay. Ever.

"Fuck." I mutter as she strides forward and grabs hold of his left hand.

Seth flings his body around, trying to free himself. Paige lifts the machete into the air. "Wait! Ple-" His pleas are cut off as she brings down the blade, slicing through his wrist. She huffs as the blade lodges part way through the appendage, her brows furrowing as she yanks on the handle. Seth wails as she struggles to free the weapon.

Intending to help, I push off the couch. Paige scowls at me. Freezing, I lift my hands, shrugging before returning to my resting position. She focuses again on dislodging the machete, letting out a triumphant squeal once the blade rips free from Seth's wrist. His eyes are glazed from shock as she hacks away until his hand drops. A soft thud sounds as it hits the floor.

Paige wipes the sweat from her forehead, smearing blood across her skin. I grip the edge of the couch to remain still at the sight. Reaching out with her unoccupied hand, she grips Seth's hair and yanks his head back.

His hooded eyes attempt to focus as his body fights the loss. "That's for touching me." She hisses. His eyes roll back, losing consciousness.

Paige's shoulders tense, jaw locked. Releasing his head, she slaps him across the face, repeating the motion until he groans. The moment his eyes flutter open, she fists his hair again. "We're not done yet." Paige snarls, shifting her hand still holding the bloodied machete, the tip now resting on his crotch. Seth shakes his head against her grip, silently pleading. He's still yet to learn, my little bird has no mercy to give.

Seth whimpers as she leans into the handle, digging the blade into the fabric of his jeans. "This?" She applies more pressure. "This is for raping me." Paige throws her weight against the handle, pushing the machete through his dick and imbedding it into the chair below.

Seth's face contorts in agony, mouth open in a silent scream as the pain overwhelms his body. Paige releases his hair and takes a step back, watching as his head lolls forward, having passed out again.

Unable to restrain myself any longer, I rush forward. Spearing my fingers in her hair, I capture Paige's mouth. "Jesus fuck." I groan into her. "That was so goddamn hot." Pulling away from her mouth, I lick the blood on her face, the metallic taste making my already stiff dick ache. I kiss down her jaw and sink my teeth into her pulse point. She whimpers, clinging to my arms. Kissing the bite, I run my lips up to her ear and growl, "I need to fuck you." Tightening her grip, she tilts her pelvis toward me.

I slip one hand out of her hair, sliding it down her body and between her legs. My fingers graze her pussy, eliciting a feral moan as I feel the slick heat. "This pussy is dripping." I groan, shoving two fingers inside, making her cry out. Pumping them inside her, I pull her hair, arching her slender neck. She hisses at the sting to her scalp but doesn't fight my hold.

"You are fucking magnificent. I knew the moment I saw you that you were going to be my new obsession." I run my nose along her throat, humming, "My raven-haired goddess of death." Paige gasps softly. Pulling back, I meet her eyes, tears glistening in her caramel orbs as she tries to blink them away.

I'm captivated by her beauty, her softness still there amidst the hard edge of her reality. Unable to stop myself, I lean forward, placing soft kisses over the tear tracks still on her face. "Let me worship you as you deserve." I murmur between kisses, slipping my fingers from her. She makes a sound of protest at the loss that shifts into surprise as I sink to my knees.

Holding her gaze, I run my hands up her thighs, gathering the material of her dress and pushing it up. My attention pulls lower, drawn to her bare pussy as it glistens from her arousal. I lick my lips, transfixed by the sight. Leaning forward, I dip my tongue into her, groaning at the sweet tang. "Fuck, I'd forgotten how good you taste." Paige grips my shoulders as I dive back in, running my tongue through her slit. Capturing her clit between my teeth I bite down, causing her to cry out from the sensation. I lap at her sensitive bud, her cries turning to moans as the pain and pleasure combine.

"Mick," Paige begs, rocking her hips on my face. Knowing she needs more, I push two fingers back inside her, curling them to rub her inner walls. "Oh god. Yes. Yes!" I continue finger fucking her while lapping at her clit like a starved man.

That's what I am. I'm famished for this woman. I will never get enough.

Paige's fingers dig into me, the sharp bite causing my dick to strain against my pants. I add a third finger and the added pressure is enough to send her over the edge. Screaming out her release, her body jerks. I continue working her through the orgasm, only removing my fingers and mouth when the sensations become too much for her.

Paige watches me with glassy eyes as I rise from the ground. Bringing my fingers to my mouth, I lick each one, groaning at her flavor exploding on my tastebuds. "God, I love the taste of your cum. I could live on it alone." Her mouth gapes at me and I grin wickedly back at her.

Seth lets out an agonized noise behind me, causing Paige's attention to shift. Growling, I step into her, gripping her chin and forcing her attention back on me. She opens her mouth in protest and I tighten my grip, shaking my head. "I've waited too long for you. The whole damn world could be watching and I'd still claim your body as mine before I destroyed them all for it." She lets out a surprised breath but can't hide the heat that burns in her eyes at my promise. Leaning into her, I whisper in her ear. "I'm going to fuck you in front of him and then I'm going to carve out his eyes before I slit his throat."

Paige gasps, trembling against me. Smirking, I lean back and command, "Take out my cock." Her fingers shake but she immediately obeys. The moment my cock is freed, I grip her hips and spin her around, bending her over the couch. Reaching around, I grip the neckline of her dress and tear it apart, freeing her breasts. I knead one of her tits as I push the hem up past her hips, lining up with her pussy. Paige pushes back against me, as desperate for this as I am. I slap her ass, gripping the soft flesh to hold her still. "Naughty little bird." I chuckle, teasing her with the head of my cock. "So needy. Do you want my cock?" Paige whimpers in response, earning another harsh slap. "Answer me."

"Y-yes. I want your cock." She pants, her body rigid as she tries to hold still.

I run my palm over her cheek, soothing the sting of the smacks. "Mmm. As you wish." Thrusting forward, I impale her in one swift movement. My head drops back at the feeling of her pussy strangling my dick. "Fuck baby." I groan, stilling to regain some semblance of composure.

If I'm not careful, the hold she has on me is going to make me come like a fucking virgin teenager at his first taste of pussy.

Her walls clench around me and the last of my control snaps. Releasing her breast, I grip her hips and pull back before slamming back into her. My thrusts are punishing, all the pent up anger, worry, and need spilling from me into her as I pound into her pussy again and again.

Paige cries out as her own pleasure builds. "Oh fuck. Fuck! Please, Mick." Her desperate pleas accentuated with each thrust of my hips. I move my hand back up, pinching her nipple between my fingers.

She's so close, I need to feel her coming on me. I need it more than the air I breathe.

"That's it baby." I praise, twisting my fingers on her hard nub. "Come for me. Let me feel you." Bending over her body, I murmur, "Let's show Seth what it really means to please a woman." She gasps at the reminder of her ex just a few feet from us. Before she can further react, I slip my other hand from her hip, shifting slightly to pull her back from the couch enough to reach between her legs. My fingers seek out her clit, rubbing tight circles on the sensitive bud before pinching it lightly.

Paige screams as she comes, burying her face into the cushion. "Fuck." I grunt as she spasms around me, continuing my attention on her clit through her orgasm.

As soon as her trembles lessen, I slide my hand to her throat, pulling her body back against me, my other hand flattening on her stomach. "So fucking perfect." I breathe into her ear. Turning, I adjust our position so we are facing Seth, Paige's exposed flesh on display. She squirms in my hold and I tighten my grip on her throat. Seth watches us wearily, attempting to not look at her tits or where my cock slides in and out of her. I smirk at him, lazily thrusting my hips. "You see," I taunt, "She was never yours. Were you, baby?" I squeeze my hand on her throat, demanding an answer.

Paige shudders in my arms, shaking her head. "No."

"Hmm. And whose are you?"

"Yours." Her voice is barely more than a whisper but I know he can hear her. His pale face whitens further, caught between screaming and throwing up. I relish the sight and as my gaze travels to the crimson liquid pooling around him, all teasing leaves me.

Fueled by desire and bloodlust, I thrust upward, pulling Paige back against me with each movement. The motion allows me to sink further into her, moaning as I bottom out, my hips flush with her skin. My breathing grows ragged as I get closer to climax. Paige's hips buck, her body aching for more. "Play with yourself." I rasp. "Give me one more."

She snakes her hand down, slipping it between her legs and swirling around her clit, chasing her own pleasure. "Oh god. I'm going to-" Paige throws her head back against me, eyes scrunched closed.

"Fuck, you're so tight. That's it." I groan, her fingers picking up speed at the praise. "Come. Now." I command, my voice tight as I stave off my own orgasm. The words are enough to push her over and I follow immediately after, roaring out my release, our breathing ragged as we're rocked by the intensity of our shared climax.

I press a soft kiss to her shoulder as I pull out. Yanking my shirt off, I pull it over her head, covering her exposed breasts. I may have wanted Seth to watch me pleasure my woman, but he'll never get to enjoy her perfect body again.

Paige smiles softly up at me, content in her post-orgasmic bliss. I can hear Seth muttering behind me, a stark reminder that this has gone on long enough. Pressing a kiss to her forehead, I murmur, "Now, I have a promise to keep." She blinks at me before realization dawns on her, her eyes shifting to Seth, nodding once before moving to perch on the couch.

I can hear my blood rushing through my ears as the impending death of this bastard approaches.

I thought I knew bloodthirstiness before, thought I understood what it meant to want to end another's life. I was wrong. This desire? It surpasses just the need for an outlet. This time it's personal. He messed with what's mine. He hurt my girl. Now it's time to pay the reaper. And this reaper is out for blood.

I run my hand over Paige's hair before slowly turning around, my eyes landing on Seth. He sneers at me, apparently the anger from my display is enough to override his fear.

Fine by me.

I take a step forward and chuckle as he can't control the flinch from the movement.

"Stay away from me." He hisses.

I cock my head at him, frustratingly impressed by the gumption. Even as his pallor increases from continued blood loss, he chooses to spit in the face of death. Wordlessly, I pivot and head toward the cupboards, rummaging around until I locate a large metal spoon. Making my way back toward him, I slip the small flip knife from my jeans as I pull them back up before returning my attention to Seth.

His face drains of all remaining color as he takes in the items in my hands. "You see," I muse, making my way toward him. "I made a promise. And when I give my word, I keep it." Stopping directly in front of him, I smile. "Would you like to know what I promised?"

I don't wait for a response. Darting my hand out, I grip his hair at the base of his head and yank back. With a steady hand, I line up the spoon with his right eye, the metal inches from the socket. Seth whimpers involuntarily, unable to close his eyes to avoid seeing what's about to happen. I close the distance and hum at the sound of his choked screams as I dig out his eyeball.

The sight of it hanging down his cheek, only connected by thin tissue and muscles, calms some of the need for pain raging through me. But it's still not enough. I repeat the process with his other eye, stepping back to capture a mental picture of the horror on his face as he tries not to move.

Every small movement increases the pain as his now mostly detached eyes hang down his face. Seth's eyelids attempt to blink, fighting to ease the sting but only causing the exposed nerve to brush against the lids. Each unintentional flutter sends a tremor through his body.

Peeling my gaze from the convulsing man, I look back toward Paige. Her face is set in a grimace, exhaustion lining her features. Sensing my attention on her, Paige meets my eyes. Neither of us speak, the only sounds in the small space are Seth's cries and gasps for air. I lift the hand holding the knife, raising an eyebrow. She glances at my hand, growing pensive. After several long moments, she sucks in a shaky breath and nods.

Turning back toward Seth, I savor his agony for a few seconds longer. "You're in luck that I need to get my woman home." I drawl, flicking open the knife. "If given the opportunity, I would torture you for every single minute you took her away from me." He blubbers as the cool blade presses against his neck. "I would boil you alive so I could carve every inch of skin from your body. I would make sure you lived long enough to feel every agonizing second. And even then, it wouldn't be enough." I grip his hair again and pull back, the blade scraping loudly down his throat. I lean close to whisper in his ear. "If there is a hell, I will meet you there. So if I were you, I would pray there's not. Because you've met the Blood Shadow as a human, just imagine me as a demon." Seth gasps at my confession, no doubt very aware of my infamy.

I allow him time to fully grasp all I've said, all the promises I've made.

Once a shudder runs through his weakened body and he opens his mouth to say something, I swiftly slice the knife across his throat. Blood spurts forward, flowing down his body. Unable to attempt staving off the flow, Seth's head falls forward.

Something in my chest loosens as I watch the life bleed from him. And, for the first time, I find myself wishing for an afterlife.

I have some promises to keep after all.

Chapter 37

Paige

He's dead.

I can't wrench my eyes from Seth's body. I don't know how long we've sat here watching the blood seep into the wooden floor below him.

None of it feels real.

The whirlwind of my life since Mick crashed into it feels like a fever dream.

A sudden need for physical proof that I'm awake overpowers me. I'm up and moving before making a conscious decision to do so. Mick turns to me at the sound of my footsteps, arms enveloping my body. I wrap my own around him, digging my nails into his skin.

"Shhh baby. It's okay, I've got you." Mick kisses my head, rubbing my back with his hands. The combination of his hard body against mine and low voice sounding in my ears pulls me from my panic.

I relax into his hold, my body threatening to give in to the exhaustion. Leaning back, I blink up at him with heavy eyes. Mick gazes back at me, eyes softened by emotion. Unhooking one arm, he gently strokes my cheek. My eyes flutter closed, a smile ghosting my lips as he murmurs,

"Let's go home."

The weeks following my return prove to be the most difficult adjustment following a kidnapping.

I was disappointed but not surprised when Brandi had not kept my job waiting for me. There's only so many times you can disappear into thin air and a boss will look the other way. It didn't help matters that I had to lie about what really happened.

For obvious reasons, I couldn't disclose that I was kidnapped or who I had been with during my absence. Mick and I decided it would be best to alter the narrative.

The official story for my disappearance is I was overwhelmed from trying to adjust back to my life so soon after my previous captivity. The lie was bitter as I had to tell a distraught Taylor that I left to regain some control and process everything that had happened. It put a rift in our friendship that I'm still working to mend.

The only person outside of Mick and I that is aware of what really happened is Mick's friend Jesse. I'm grateful for his help in finding me, but concerned that he could turn us in at any time. He doesn't know the full extent of what transpired but if the police were to open an investigation, our cover story would be flimsy at best.

Mick promised he would take care of it if needed before we ever got to that point. The sorrow in his eyes as he promised was enough to keep me from bringing it up again. We both knew what it would mean for him to "take care of it."

It's now been a little over a month and my worries have yet to prove to be more than that. I continue to hold out hope it remains that way.

The door flings open, pulling me from my reverie.

Mick strides through the doorway, his shirt clinging to his sweat soaked chest. I lick my lips as my eyes drift over him. A part of me still can't believe this man is real. He's so beautiful it hurts at times to look at him. Right now, he's dripping in sex and sin.

Never breaking stride, Mick crushes his body to mine. Our lips seek out the others in a feverish kiss. I stretch onto my toes, clinging to his shirt. He slips his hands under my ass and lifts me up, my legs immediately wrapping around his waist. My heated core presses against the hard line of his cock. We both groan into each other, my hips rocking against him. Spinning, Mick stumbles toward the wall until my back is pressed firmly against it. The added pressure gives me more leverage to pick up the speed of my gyrations.

Mick breaks the kiss, trailing his lips down my neck. Bracing one arm under me, he reaches up with the other to grip my top and tug down the material. His mouth captures one of my exposed breasts, sucking my hardened nipple between his teeth. "Mick," I moan, my head falling back against the wall. He bites down in response causing me to arch into him. "Oh god. Please." My breathless pleas slip from my lips.

Mick chuckles, adjusting his stance to reach between us and unbuckle his pants. Once his jeans are unzipped, I help push them down with his boxers, freeing his cock. My hand wraps around the shaft causing him to groan. His fingers roughly push up my skirt, shoving my panties to the side. I move my hand to line his cock up with my entrance, our eyes meeting. We hold each other's heated gaze as he slowly pushes inside of me. I brace my hands on his shoulders, entirely consumed by him.

Our need for one other hasn't lessened, the intensity of our obsession overtaking physical desire alone. Each thrust of his hips is a love note. My moans mingle in the air with his grunts, the sound of our heavy breathing and skin slapping together building to a crescendo. Mick comes with his face buried in my neck, my name on his lips. I topple over with him into a toe-curling orgasm.

We cling to each other, catching our breath. My eyes are closed as I rest my head back. Mick lightly grips my chin, pulling my face toward him. I open my eyes, quivering under his gaze. His fingers stroke my skin as he stares at me like I'm the most important thing in the world.

"I love you." Mick says softly, my heart breaking open as he continues. "The words aren't enough. No words ever will be. But I need you to know, little bird."

I blink back the moisture filling my eyes. "Say it again." I whisper.

Mick's eyes light up. "I love you." He murmurs, leaning forward and pressing a kiss to my cheek. "I love you." Another kiss on my other cheek. "I love you." Kissing my forehead. "I love you." He whispers in my ear before biting the lobe.

I shiver and place my hands on either side of his face as he pulls back. Pouring every ounce of emotion I can into the words, I profess, "I love you too."

Epilogue

Paige

6 years later

Our screams startle the few other patrons in the restaurant.

"Oh my god!" I cry, gripping Taylor's hand. She beams at me as I admire the ring nestled on her finger. "It's gorgeous." I drop her hand and tug my best friend into a tight hug. She giggles while embracing me back.

It's been a long road but we were able to get past my disappearance and lies. There will always be a divide now because I can't share with her Mick's extracurricular activities but nothing will keep our friendship apart.

Part of me still feels guilt over that part of my life, but Mick has promised to only hunt those who truly deserve it. Sometimes I join him when it's an especially nasty one, but for the most part the Blood Shadow still operates on his own. At my urging, he stopped staging the bodies and now destroys all evidence.

I've already had to live through thinking I would never see him again and I have no desire to do that again.

My mind drifts to thoughts of Mick and I getting married. I suppress a shudder. While I am ecstatic for Taylor, the thought of marriage for me only brings up reminders of Seth. Mick and I have made it clear how we feel about one another. He has not brought up a desire to move to the next phase in a relationship, for which I am thankful.

Taylor laughs again as we pull apart. I can't help the grin at her infectious joy. "I'm so happy for you Tay."

"Thanks, babe. I just still can't believe it!" She exclaims as we take our seats again. "I'm getting married! Who would have thought?" Taylor's chuckles fade, a horrified expression overtaking her face. "Oh my god, Paige. I'm so sorry. I didn't think..." I wave her off.

Seth had been declared a missing person shortly after my return and as the years passed, the news about his disappearance waned. He was officially declared dead a few months back so the reminder is still fresh in everyone's mind.

"Don't even Taylor." I warn jokingly, raising an eyebrow. "This is not about my stupid ex. You are getting married and I am ecstatic for you." She eyes me warily, clearly wanting to accept my assurance but also concerned. I reach forward and grip her hands in mine. "I'm fine. I have a great life and a hot as hell man." I wink and the remaining tension in her shoulders releases.

"Of course. How is Mick?"

Releasing her hands, I pick up the menu as I reply. "He's amazing. But-" I sigh, looking back up. "He's been gone at this business convention for a week and I really fucking miss him, you know?"

Taylor pats my hand sympathetically even as her eyes shine with happiness. "He's good for you." I'm startled by the declaration. Taylor continues in my silence. "I've never seen you so happy as you are with him. You deserve that. Happiness, I mean." She gives me a soft smile.

My own lights up my face. "You do too. Now, can we get back to your wedding? Because I need all the details, future Mrs. Wyland."

And all the details I get. Taylor and I spend the next several hours going over every moment of the proposal and all her plans for the big event.

My phone pings as we are saying our goodbyes. I pull it out while making my way to my car. My pulse races as I read and reread the message. Jumping into the car, I slam it into drive and take off.

Mick

Naughty little bird. Better hurry home or your punishment will only be worse.

Shit. Fuck. I knew *that was a bad idea.*

The entire drive home was filled with mental berations. I had thought it would be worth it but the closer I get to the house the less sure I am.

I pull up the drive to our secluded home.

One major perk of being with the owner of a construction company is building a dream home nestled in our own private space. The house is a simple cottage style. A chimney peaks out of the staccato roof. The outer walls are built with clay-like brick, giving the appearance of a fairytale cottage. The long driveway leads through the woods up to the garage to the left of the house. A cobbled walkway connecting the garage and the house. Even after seeing it every day, the home usually brings me peace.

Not today though.

I gulp and wipe my sweaty hands on my leggings.

No point in putting it off.

Taking a steadying breath, I trudge toward the house. As I near the entrance, the door flies open. My breath catches at the sight of Mick standing in the doorway. He emanates danger, his hand wrapped around something I can't quite make out from the distance. My footsteps stall as a shiver runs through me.

Mick's eyes heat as he senses my fear. "Inside." He commands, turning on his heel and stalking into the house.

I scramble after him, pausing to close the door. When I turn around, Mick steps up into my space. I gasp and press my back against the door. He grabs my throat in his free hand, placing a thumb under my chin to prevent me from looking closer at the object in his other. "Are you proud of yourself?" He sneers, tightening his hold. I gasp for air but don't dare move, caught in his trap. "What do you think would have happened if someone else saw, hmm?"

My face flushes. I hadn't even considered that.

As I told Taylor over lunch, Mick has been gone for a week. One long, excruciating week. Yesterday I finally gave in to my needs and played with myself. Something I hadn't needed to do since Mick and I moved in together. It felt weird on my own, so I had the brilliant idea to make a video for him. I put on a bit of a show, hoping to get a fun reaction. I hadn't expected this.

Or did you?

I shake my head at the thought. Even as I deny it, heat floods me as the anticipation of my punishment grows.

Mick leans forward to growl in my ear. "I think you know what I'd have to do. I think you get off at the thought of me killing someone for seeing you come. Just like I think you wanted to be punished for doing it." I try to shake my head again at his accusations. Mick tsks and I hear a sharp click. "You should know better than to lie to me, little bird."

My eyes widen as the feel of cold metal presses between my breasts. His hold on me prevents my ability to see what he's doing but I can feel the light touch as the blade glides over my skin. "I guess I need to teach you a lesson then, baby." In a swift motion, he slices through my shirt and bralette. The material flutters to the side, exposing my breasts. I shiver, my nipples hardening from the chilly air.

Mick's gaze is riveted on my chest as he runs the knife around my breasts. The sensations heightened from my inability to move or see what he's doing. The knife pulls away from my skin leaving an aching emptiness in its wake.

I gasp as the cold metal is pressed against my nipple. He leans forward and blows on my other nipple. The cool of the blade on one mixed with the hot breath on the other makes me moan, my hips begin to move, desperate to further the connection.

Mick chuckles, taking a step back and releasing me. I collapse back against the door. He runs his gaze over me, desire burning in his darkened eyes. "Get to the bedroom and strip." His low voice makes my pussy clench in response.

Scrambling to my feet, I brush past him as I rush toward the bedroom. I can feel his heated gaze following me. The moment I slip inside the room, I shed the tattered top before shimming out of my leggings and underwear. Once naked, I look around, uncertain where to wait. Before I can make a choice, Mick's footsteps sound behind me.

I freeze, body humming with adrenaline.

Hands slide down my body, cupping my breasts first before traveling lower. Roaming over my skin, his hands move back to my ass. Without warning, Mick slaps both hands against my cheeks. I yelp, earning another sharp smack. His hands and warmth leave me suddenly as he takes a step back. "On the bed." He barks. I quickly clamber onto the bed and turn to face him. "Lean back against the headboard, legs spread." I hesitate and he narrows his eyes at me. It's a clear enough warning. Getting into position, I twist my hands together.

Mick hums his approval. "Touch yourself." My breath catches in my throat. He takes a step closer to the bed, running a hand down his face. "You're going to make yourself come while I watch, little bird. I couldn't enjoy your last performance without the possibility of getting blood on my hands. So I'm going to enjoy it now."

I nod mutely, my body already screaming for release. Running one hand up, I massage my breast, imagining it's his rough palm. My other hand slips between my open legs, teasing my lips, arousal soaking my fingers as they dip inside. Pinching my nipple, I moan. My fingers trail up to circle my clit briefly before pushing back inside my pussy.

Mick watches with rapt attention as I work myself up, alternating breasts with one hand and finger fucking myself with the other, my palm pressed down on my clit. My eyes move down to the bulge in his pants. My own desire amping up as I realize I did that to him. He catches me staring and smirks. "You want my cock, baby?"

I groan, nodding enthusiastically. "Please." I beg, working my fingers faster.

Mick tugs off his shirt, shucking his pants and boxers. I bite my lip as I take in his naked body. He spits on his hand before gripping his dick, lazily stroking up and down. "Look what you do to me." He grunts, working his hand. "I need you to come so I can fuck you."

The strain in his voice sends a jolt through me. I pinch my nipple harder and increase my movements. Staring at his hand sliding up and down his shaft, I imagine he's inside me. Memories and remembered sensations flood me as my body tightens. "Fuck." I rasp, back arching. Mick lets out a low groan and the sound detonates my orgasm. My feet plant on the bed and back bows as pleasure crashes through me.

I collapse against the mattress as the last flutters dissipate. Mick climbs onto the bed between my legs, reaching over to place the knife still in his hand on the bedside table. I reach out and grip his wrist, stopping the movement. He peers down at me, body frozen. I lick my lips as I stare back. Mustering up my courage, I speak. "Take what you need." My eyes flicker back to the knife. "I know you need it, so take it from me." I arch my back into him, encouraging with my body as much as my words.

For several long moments, Mick remains frozen in place. Warring desires fighting in his eyes. Finally, he shifts back, moving the blade to my chest. Resting it above my left breast, he pauses, giving me the chance to change my mind. I smile at him and nod. It's all the encouragement he needs.

I suck in a breath through my teeth as the blade slices into my skin. He stares at the red line as blood bubbles up from the shallow cut. Slowly leaning forward, he licks across it, moaning as the flavor hits his tongue. My hand slips into his hair, gripping the strands tightly in my grasp. Mick runs his tongue across the cut again before pulling away.

Dropping my hand, my breath catches as he peers down at me. The earlier danger has faded, replaced by the adoration I have come to know. The look he gets when he wants to worship my body. I tremble under his gaze, body begging for everything his eyes promise.

"Fuck little bird. How did I get so lucky to trap a goddess?" He grips my hips, the cool blade pressing between his palm and my skin as he lines himself up. "I'm never letting you go, you know that right?" He slams into me before I can answer. My hands fly up, bracing against the headboard as Mick thrusts forward, each punishing thrust pulling a deep moan from me. I can already feel another orgasm building. His breathing is ragged as he ravages my body, fingers digging into me hard enough to bruise. "You are mine." He pants. "Say it."

"Your-" I struggle to say, breathless from his continued onslaught. "I'm yours." I'm rewarded immediately as Mick releases my hip with one hand, the blade dropping to the mattress. His hand slips between us, seeking out my clit. I cry out, the sensations almost too much. His fingers work tight circles as he continues to pound into me.

My mouth opens on a silent scream as my orgasm rips through my body. My eyes squeeze closed and bursting stars litter the blackness, small explosions of static light as wave after wave of pleasure flood me.

"Fuck." Mick groans, picking up the knife again. "You are so fucking beautiful when you come." Another jolt shocks me at his words moments before the blade slices through the skin on my stomach.

I gasp, resisting the urge to press against the wound. Mick lets out a noise of pure ecstasy as he runs his hand through the blood pooling on my skin. I watch as he lifts his bloodied hand and smears it across his chest. Leaning over me, he licks along the cut on my chest, the pressure of his body pressed against my stomach making me whimper. His thrusts become impossibly harder, his hand on my hip gripping tightly and his other spears into my hair, pushing my body down to meet his upward thrusts.

The heightened pain mixed with his cock impaling me with pleasure has a surprising climax overtake me on the heels of my last one. I scream out as my body jerks. Mick's movements stutter as he follows me. His head tucking into my neck, he groans as he shoots hot spurts of cum deep inside of me.

After a few moments of ragged breathing, Mick climbs off of me and disappears into the bathroom. Returning with his arms full, he proceeds to carefully clean my wounds. Once the cuts are cleaned and dressed, I climb out of bed to go relieve myself.

When I return, Mick is nestled in the blankets. He pulls back one side and pats the bed. My smile spreads across my face as I climb up and snuggle against him. We talk about his trip, I tell him about everything I've been up to while he's been gone, and we make plans for tomorrow. Everything about this moment is perfect. I'm overwhelmed by the love I have for this man.

Mick nudges me, "What's that look for?"

I cover my mouth to hide my giggle. He arches an eyebrow and I can't help the laughter that erupts from me. Doubling over, I grip my stomach, already forgetting about the large gash.

"Ouch." I hiss, immediately sitting up.

Mick runs a hand through my hair, concerned by my pain but a hint of desire shines in his eyes at the reminder of the cause.

Sighing, I flop back. "Taylor's getting married." I pause and cautiously peek at him as I rush out, "And you're my plus one."

"Wedddding day." The event coordinator, Alicia, sings.

I suppress an eye roll as I focus on my makeup. I love Taylor. So much. But I fucking hate this wedding. It's nothing to do with her or Beau, it's that blasted coordinator.

When Taylor asked me to be her maid of honor, of course I agreed. I didn't realize at the time that would mean I would be at Alicia's beck and call. If I hadn't known it would devastate my friend, I would have begged

Mick to take care of Alicia months ago. The thought still plays in the back of my mind as I apply a second coat of mascara.

"Oh Paige you look just lovely." She chirps behind me.

I give her a tight lipped smile.

Just a few more hours, then you never have to deal with her again.

Shaking away the murderous desires this woman brings up, I look toward Taylor instead. My heart swells as I watch her being pampered. If anyone deserves a fairytale wedding, it's my Tay. Feeling my gaze, she looks over and smiles. I grin back, shooting her a thumbs up. She rolls her eyes then closes them again. Turning back to the mirror, I swipe lipstick across my lips.

A few more hours, you can do this.

My eyes haven't stopped watering all night. The small packet of tissues doing nothing to keep up with the nonstop tears.

Hands slip around my waist and pull me back into a warm body. Mick nuzzles my neck, lifting one hand holding a fresh pack of tissues. "This is why I love you." I murmur, snatching the pack and ripping into it.

Mick chuckles, tightening his arms. "Not the only reason I hope." He teases. I roll my eyes, grateful he can't see my face. I usually enjoy his punishments but my fragile emotions can't handle much more at the moment.

Taylor and Beau's ceremony was beautiful and sweet, just like them. I stumbled my way through my speech and leaped on the opportunity to step away for a moment while everyone sat down to eat.

I want to be happy for my friend, I *am* happy for her. But as the day goes on, I'm hit again and again that I can't separate the occasion from

Seth. Every time he pops into my head, I'm back in that basement. I feel broken. And I can't tell anyone why, at least not the real reason.

Sensing my mood, Mick pulls back and spins me around. He cradles my face in one of his hands, running his thumb across my cheek. "What's wrong little bird?" The gentleness of his tone sends another wave of pain through me. I hiccup a sob, my hand pressing against my mouth to stifle the sound. Mick immediately pulls me against him, hugging me tightly. I sink into his arms, soaking up his strength. "Talk to me baby. What's wrong?"

I take a shaky breath, my hand fiddling with the sleeve of his jacket. "I think I'm...broken." I squeeze my eyes shut at the whispered admission.

Mick stills, the sound of his heart beating erratically thrums in my ear. Carefully, he pulls me back to look into my eyes. "Why?" I can see the rage building in him as he forces out the question.

My heart warms a little as I watch him. My protector, always ready to take on any threat, even emotional ones.

"I just...everything about this." I wave my hand, gesturing to the banquet hall. "It all reminds me of Seth. Cause, you know, we were...engaged." Mick nods slowly, jaw ticking. If anyone disliked reminders of that fact more than me, it was Mick. "I don't think I'll ever be able to do it." I mumble, my eyes dropping to the floor, shoulders slumping.

"Do what?" His voice is tight as he works to maintain control over his emotions.

I trace the patterned tile with my eyes, gesturing around again. "This. I don't think I'll be able to ever get married." My voice drops to a whisper as I speak.

Mick nudges my chin with his hand. I cautiously look up. Instead of meeting the angry or disappointed eyes I expected, I only see love in them.

Cupping my face in his hands, he holds my gaze as he professes, “I don’t need a piece of paper from a society that I don’t fit in to prove my love for you. You are my queen, my goddess, my everything. You have all my devotion and will always hold my blackened soul in your hands. You are mine and I am yours, little bird. Always and forever.”

My heart swells. All my worry and shame washing away as Mick's words flow through me. I crush my lips to his, pouring our love into one other through the connection.

Pulling away, I smile up at him. “Always and forever.” I promise.

Thank You!

Wow! What a rollercoaster, right?

Did anyone else tear up from Mick's declaration?

I sincerely hope you loved reading Bleed for Me as much as I loved writing it!

If you'd be willing to leave a review, I would appreciate you more than I can express. As an indie author, reviews help get my book in front of new readers - even if the review is a star rating with no words, every single one helps!

Thank you for choosing to read Mick & Paige's story,

I hope to see you between the pages again in the future.

Need More Kitty Rose?

Want more? Check out My Little Girl – out on KU, ebook, and paperback! My Little Girl is book 1 in the interconnected standalone series – FindingLight. This is a dark hitman, agegap romance. Please check trigger warnings as this book delves into some very heavy mental health topics in addition to dark romance themes. Check out an excerpt from the book below!

Keep an eye out for Inked Souls, coming mid-late 2024! Inked Souls is a heart-wrenching story full of real world issues, including grief and finding love again after loss. And, of course, can't forget the murder – what would a Kitty Rose story be without some bloodshed?

If you're interested in following along for updates, check out Kitty Rose's socials:

Instagram: @authorkittyrose
Facebook: Author Kitty Rose

TikTok: @authorkittyrose
My group: Kitty's Lost Souls

***

Avamarie

Unknown number
He's dead. Here's your proof.

I stare at my phone, heart pounding.

This is some new scamming trick, it's gotta be. If they try to send a link, I'm deleting it.

I jerk forward, my phone slipping from my fingers as I flail to regain my balance. A hand snakes out and grips my wrist before I can topple over.

"Shit, I'm so sorry!"

Righting myself on my feet, I glance at the person who just plowed into me.

Pushing her glasses up her nose, the girl fidgets with the hem of her shirt. "Are you okay? I'm sorry again! I was so distracted by my book I didn't even notice you." She waves her hand clutching a worn book apologetically.

My mind finally catches up and I offer her a smile. "I'm fine. Don't worry, no harm no foul." I shrug and chuckle.

The girl smiles back, tucking a strand of her ashy blonde hair behind her ear. Shifting on her feet, she looks up the path. "Well, thanks for not being mad. Um, bye!" I don't have time to respond before she's off running.

Chuckling to myself, I bend over to pick up my phone. Inspecting it, I'm grateful to find there's no damage.

My screen lights up with a notification.

One new message

Taking a deep breath to steady my nerves, I hover my finger over the alert.

It's just a scam, remember. Nothing more.

Biting my lip, I press down and wait for the screen to load. The chat pops up and there's an image under the last message. My fingers shake as I stare down at the tiny photo.

Okay, not a scam. It can't be what I think it is though, right?

Clicking on the image, my lungs freeze and I can't remember how to breathe. I clutch the phone in my hands as my knees buckle and I slide to the ground.

Why did someone send me this? Who *sent me this? And what do they want?*

My mind races and I can't rip my eyes away.

The photo looks like it belongs in a horror movie. A decapitated body lies on the ground, blood pooling around the corpse. Next to the body is a photo of today's newspaper with a driver's license sitting next to it. My guess would be the deceased's ID. As horrific as all that is, the thing that makes my stomach turn isn't the blood. It isn't the body. It's the severed head resting between the corpses legs, safety pins lining the mouth with a string running through them and pulling the lifeless lips up into a smile.

Heaving breaths, I close out of the photo. I'm not sure what comes over me as my fingers move to type. I've hit the send button before my malfunctioning brain catches up to my actions.

Staring at the small screen, I squeak and close the text chat.

Fuck, fuck, fuck. What did I just do?

Clambering to my feet, I rush back to my apartment, glancing over my shoulder the whole way.

Me

Wrong number

***

Killian

CLDd

Wrong number

I look back at the encrypted email for the job.

I checked the number multiple times before sending confirmation of completion. My jaw grinds as I compare the number on my computer screen with the one on my phone.

Fucking Andrew. Are you fucking kidding me right now?

Groaning, I massage the bridge of my nose.

The numbers match, which only makes me feel marginally better that the fuck up wasn't mine. It doesn't matter at the end of the day whose mistake caused the problem. When the curtains fall, I'll be the one holding the bloody knife.

Fuck!

Exiting the chat I move to my contacts and select **CLDd**. Sighing, I delete the contact name.

Each job, I add the number to my phone with the initials of the target. Once I have collected the information I need to fulfill the task, I add a D, showing they're one step closer to being dead. After I send confirmation, I add the final d, completing the circle.

I don't delete the contact until payment clears my account, in case I need to track down anyone trying to stiff me.

This particular case, the contact was CLDd translating to Carl Lewis - Dead. As I am now needing to obtain the *correct* number, the name is inaccurate.

Focusing my mind, I decide in order to save my sanity, I will treat this like any other job.

I type in the new name: **WN.**

Smirking to myself, I close the phone.

Time to get to work.

Acknowledgements

Thank you to all of you lovely readers who have given my book a chance! I appreciate every single one of you.

Thank you to my amazing beta, ARC, and street teams! I appreciate you more than words can express.

Thank you so so so much to my phenomenal PA El Burnes. I don't know what I would do without you.

A special shoutout to Ireland for dealing with my craziness as I work through story ideas and freak out that no one is going to want to read my words. I'm so incredibly grateful for you!

To my band of fellow authors I've had the pleasure of meeting along the way, I love you all. The constant encouragement, laughter, and knowledge you bring to my life help me keep going. I'm so thankful for you <3

And finally, a huge thank you to my wonderful husband! His gentle nudging to pursue my dream and to just write is what led to today. I love you so much and am so excited to live my dream with you every day.

About the Author

Hey hi hello! It's me - Kitty Rose!

I'm beyond words if you've made it this far and are reading this right now. Okay, maybe not beyond words as I don't know when to stop talking, but you get the point ;)

A little about me:

I have *always* wanted to be an author, even when I went through the stereotypical "I want to be a veterinarian because I love animals soooooooooo much" phase, I still wanted to write! I started writing books in the 5th grade but they always remained unfinished until now. Bleed for Me is the first story I have completed and what a wonderful story to start with! I'm now addicted and have *loads* of others banging in my mind, demanding to let their stories be told.

When I'm not writing, I'm reading. Or spending time with my hubby and our two cats. We enjoy a good comedy, WWE match, or horror flick to pass the time. We're both *obsessed* with Halloween and if we could make every holiday Halloween instead we absolutely would.

You can find me all over social media! Right now I am set up for Insta, Facebook & TikTok. I'd love if you came and connected with me. Better yet, join my reader group (Kitty Lost Souls) so we can get to know each other better!

I'm so excited to start this journey and find where it takes me.

All I know is that 10-year-old me would be so proud, and they're who I'm rooting for.

Made in United States
Troutdale, OR
12/06/2024

26024678R00196